USA TODAY BESTSELLING AUTHOR

LILA ROSE

Coyote Copyright © 2020 by Lila Rose
Editor: Hot Tree Editing
Photographer: Wander Book Club
Cover Designer: Covers by Juan
Interior Designer: RMJ Editing & Manuscript Service

All rights reserved. No part of this eBook or book may be used or reproduced in any written, electronic, recording, or photocopying without the permission from the author as allowed under the terms and conditions under which it was purchased or as strictly permitted by applicable copyright law. Any unauthorized distribution, circulation or use of this text may be a direct infringement of the author's rights, and those responsible may be liable in law accordingly. Thank you for respecting the work of this author.

Coyote is a work of fiction. All names, characters, events and places found in this book are either from the author's imagination or used fictitiously. Any similarity to actual events, locations, organizations, or persons live or dead is entirely coincidental and not intended by the author.

First Edition 2019
ISBN: 978-0-6487998-4-9

CHAPTER ONE

CHANNA

$\mathcal{N}$o way.

No fudging way.

He was here. Right over there and *inside* the shop.

"Denise, I'll be out back if you need me," I whispered with a panicked edge to my tone before I bolted through the swinging doors behind me. Leaning over, I rested my hands on my thighs and took gulps of air.

"Channa, are you all right?" Stanley asked. He dropped the bowl on the workbench and started for me. I quickly straightened and waved him off.

"I'm fine.… I… think I swallowed a fly." And a lie. I hated lying, but I couldn't exactly tell Stanley, who was my cake-icing machine and sixty years old, that I ran like a wuss when I saw *him*. It would just be confusing, and then I would have to delve into my past, into a moment of time I wanted to forget.

Stanley screwed up his nose. "Blasted warm days stink arse. It's hotter than hell in here. My balls are sweating so bad and my icing doesn't want to work."

I moved over to the bench and pressed my hands onto the cool stainless steel. "Come on, Stanley, I know you can work your magic. I might have turned off the ovens a little late this morning, but the air con is on and it'll start freezing this place over soon."

I could have done without hearing about his balls, but I'd put up with it because Stanley was a master at making and applying icing to all my baked goods. He was a god, and I wouldn't know what to do without him. I had skills to bake, which I loved doing, but the delicate decorating just wasn't for me. I messed them up each time I tried. It was how I'd known I would have to hire someone and was lucky Stanley had approached me about the work when I'd advertised.

He huffed and said, "I'm going into the coolroom." He picked up his bowl and walked to the floor-to-ceiling coolroom at the back of the work area. He opened the door, stepped in, and I caught his shoulders sag in relief before he shut the door behind himself.

Turning back towards the front of the shop, I tippy-toed back towards the doors, thankful Stanley wasn't there to see my childish actions, and pushed them apart enough to peek out.

A squeak slipped through my lips, and I let the

doors fall closed quickly. Taking a step back, I rested my hand over my swift-beating heart.

He was right there.

At the counter.

He was smiling at something Denise was saying. That smile could steal someone's breath. It had stolen mine every single time back in high school. Only I hadn't seen it since then, for eight long years, and the power of having it directed my way had grown. His light eyes could trap another's gaze. His dark hair looked like it needed someone to run their fingers through it. His body.... All right, I had to stop there. Yes, he was handsome, but right then I didn't need my hormones seeking out someone for a roll between the sheets. Especially not him.

I only hoped he would take whatever he was ordering and go. There wasn't anything in the world that would have me out there in the bakery when Cody Marcus was inside.

I jolted when Denise popped her head through the doors. "Need help, please."

Son of a bitch.

Okay, there was nothing except that.

I couldn't let Denise deal with the lunch rush on her own. I had hoped the lunch customers would be late for the first time since opening, but luck wasn't shining down on me. Unless it actually was and Cody had exited the building already.

Taking a deep breath, I crossed my fingers and pushed through the door. I didn't look around, afraid I would lose my courage and hide again. Instead, I kept my focus on the line in front of the register and lost myself in serving people with a smile.

I loved my bakery. It had been my mum's and my dream to own and run it. What helped was that Mum had been a baker in her early twenties before she met Dad and had taught me everything I now knew.

We managed a year together owning Bakery Bliss, but then I lost her too soon to a blood clot, so I made sure to maintain the dream we'd always talked about. Things were good; the bakery was a hit in town. It also helped that we'd opened in an area where there weren't many other food businesses and had the customers from the factories around us.

"Channa, baby, when are you going to agree to run away with me?" Amos asked after I gave him his usual— a sausage roll, pie, and donut. He was a man in his forties with a pot belly, beard, and wild greying hair. He loved to tease, but I knew he was harmless. He'd been a regular since we opened three years ago.

With a laugh, I shook my head. "I've told you a million times, Amos, I'd drive you crazy within a couple of days."

"And I still don't believe you."

"I can't risk it though. So grab your coffee from Denise and skedaddle."

"One day, Channa, one day." He winked and headed down to the end of the counter, where Denise was busy making coffees.

It took another half hour before the lunch rush died

to a slower pace and I could relax a little without running all over the place to fill orders.

A chair scraped over the floor, which had me glancing that way. I wished I hadn't because it was Cody rising from his chair.

My blood froze and stopped pumping through my body. At least that was what it felt like.

I fisted my hands at my sides, annoyed by my reaction. It wasn't like he would remember me. Not like I did him. After all, it had been *one* incident. One small occasion.

Then why can't I get it out of my head?

Why do I remember him like it was yesterday?

Why does he have to be so darn good-looking?

He tapped the table with his knuckles, saying something to the man he was sitting with, which made the other guy laugh. Cody grinned and my breath caught. I coughed and he happened to look my way.

With a noise in the back of my throat, I ducked down behind the counter to land on all fours.

"Shit," I hissed. *Now I look like a jack-in-the-box fool.* Unless I didn't get up off the floor. It looked like he was leaving, so I could stay down here and wait him out.

"Channa?" Denise said with humour in her tone.

I lifted my hand and pressed a finger to my lips to shush her. She rolled her eyes and called out her order.

The doors to the back opened. "Channa, what are you doing on the ground?" Stanley called.

Dear God, please take me to heaven now.

"I, ah, lost something."

He snorted. "Well, get up. You look like a fool."

Gee, thanks for pointing out the obvious.

As I stood, Stanley slipped around me to place a tray of cupcakes on the counter, and I quickly darted out through the doors.

"Girl, get back out here," Stanley yelled. "I ain't serving, since the last time I did you yelled at me."

Closing my eyes, I ground my teeth together and drew in a deep breath through my nose. Turning, I stepped back into the front, saying, "That's because the last time you served someone, you snapped at them to hurry up."

He groaned, as if remembering that time. "They were taking forever." He walked out the back again, mumbling under his breath.

I stepped back up to the counter and smiled at the customer. "Sorry about that. What can I get you?" I asked, but I didn't hear what they said because Cody Marcus was at the door looking back at me. His friend said something, and Cody glanced at him to reply before shifting his gaze back to me for a second and then leaving.

As soon as he was out the door, I relaxed and got back to work, pushing the sight of him from my mind. I also hoped it would stay well away from my mind and that he never showed here again because I wasn't sure I could handle it.

Maybe he didn't remember *that* time, but I did, and it was one of the most embarrassing moments of my life. The memory of it flashed through my mind.

"*Channa, I don't trust him,*" *Darla said, grazing her bottom lip with her top teeth in worry. We were sitting on the school oval at lunch talking quietly so our other friends didn't hear, because I hadn't shared with them that Ron Delian, the boy who was three years above me in year ten, who I had a crush on, had asked me to meet him in the gym after school. How he knew I was into him, I didn't have a clue. Although, he could have seen me watching him a few million times. Even the girls around him had started to glare at me. Now I knew it was just jealousy because he'd asked me and not them.*

Darla and I had become friends the first day of high school, and even though that was only months ago, I knew we'd be lifelong friends. She was a popular girl with a large group of friends, and yet she took me—a nobody—under her wing. I came from a family who didn't have much, and in the last year, it had gotten worse since Dad lost his job. All he did now was drink and yell at Mum and me. But then the yelling changed to him using his fists on Mum. I tried to stop him each time it happened. Even when Mum begged me not to, I tried. And every time he turned his fists on me.

I never thought I would fear going home, but I did. Still, I always returned because Mum was there, and we supported each other. We had plans to leave him and would do it soon. Only we had to wait a little longer until we had enough money.

"Why? He wouldn't lie, right? What reason does he have to lie?" I asked, shaking myself from those bad thoughts to better ones. Much better ones. However, Darla was now putting doubt in my head when all I wanted to feel was

happy. I wanted to maybe kiss a boy before Mum and I left. But I didn't tell Darla any of this. I didn't bother her with my problems from home.

Darla shrugged. "I just don't trust him. How about I come with you?"

Smiling, I rolled my eyes. "I'll be fine. It might look weird if I show up there with a friend."

She nibbled on her lip again, still concerned. I wrapped my arms around her, ignoring the pain in my back where Dad had punched me the night before.

"Thank you for worrying. You're the best, you know that, but I want to do this, please."

She sighed. "Fine."

My stomach filled with dancing butterflies as I made my way down the hallway towards the gym. Other students moved quickly out of the school, wanting to get as far away as they could to start their weekend.

I really should have gone to the toilet before going, but I'd been too excited to see what Ron wanted. Wanted to know if he was going to kiss me or even ask me out. One could hope, and I did, because I was sure life would pick up if this one wish would come true. If the boy I'd been crushing on, after seeing him on my first day of school, would want me to be his girlfriend.

He wouldn't have asked me to meet him otherwise, right?

He wouldn't have stopped me in the hall in front of others and brushed my hair behind my ear while talking to me. God, my belly swirled at the thought of that moment. It had been the best moment I'd had in such a long time. Though, I was sure the one I was about to have would pass it by miles.

At the doors, I glanced back to see the hallway had cleared, which was good. I didn't want anyone following me and interrupting us. Taking a breath, I dimmed my smile a little so I didn't look like an idiot.

Slowly, I pushed the door open. I scrunched up my face in confusion because the gym was dark.

A hand grabbed my wrist. I let out a scream as I was dragged into the room, and the door closed behind me, engulfing me in blackness.

"Ron?" I called, since his hand had fallen away. No answer. "Ron?" I said louder, reaching my hands out to feel around. I didn't know where I was in the room, but I had to find a wall and switch on a light. Turning the way I'd come, I searched the darkness and took small steps back towards the door—well, where I thought the door was. Had he covered the outline of the door where the light should have shone through?

"This isn't funny, Ron. Turn on the light," I demanded.

"Ron," someone echoed—a girl's voice. I stilled.

"Ron," a different voice called, then laughed. His name sounded from every direction around me. My heart jumped up into my throat, my belly twisting in fear.

"Stop it," I yelled, covering my ears, but I still heard their taunting.

Next, a hand landed on my back, exactly in the spot where Dad had hit me, and pushed me forcefully forward. I stumbled, gasping. Tears pooled in my eyes as pain spread over my back. I managed to stay on my feet somehow, until another shove came at my side. My body swayed. My arms windmilled wildly to try and stay on my feet, but it was too late. I slammed into the floor, losing my breath, knocking my chin, and hurting my wrist and hip.

My bladder chose that moment to let go. Wetness pooled between my legs just as the lights got switched on. I wiped at my eyes as I looked up. I could feel wetness on my chin.

Five girls stood around me, laughing. They backed up when Ron moved in with some of his friends. All smiling or chuckling.

I didn't move my eyes from Ron, who was smirking down at me, even when a door banged open and someone shouted, "Look, she pissed herself."

More laughter. More hurtful words.

"What the fuck is goin' on?" was yelled. People were shoved aside, and then Cody Marcus, the older brother to one of the girls in my year, stood looking down at me.

Within a second, he took me in and then faced the group. "Who did this?"

"Come on, man, we were just messin' around," someone said.

"Who fuckin' did this?" he demanded, his tone low and harsh.

"Cody, don't worry about it. We're just teaching her a lesson," one of the girls said.

"Yeah? What lesson is that?" Cody asked, crossing his arms over his chest.

"It's nothing," Ron barked.

"What damn lesson?" Cody demanded.

I needed to get out of there, needed to leave and end this humiliation.

Tears formed, and I bit down on my bottom lip to keep

the sob inside. I'd wet my pants like a toddler. Everyone saw. Everyone. And it would be all over school by Monday.

I grabbed at my tee, at my chest, misery covering me, filling me.

"That she's nothing but shit and she'll never have a chance with Ron," another girl said.

They all piped up saying more. How I was pathetic, a loser, fat, ugly…. It went on until Cody roared, "Enough." As I slowly sat, I ignored the pain, the shivering, and caught Cody shake his head before he said, "You thought it'd be okay to use her interest in you to get her alone and make her think she had a chance with you? To trap her, trick her, and then fuck with her?"

No one had said it, but Cody was smart; he understood what went down even without all the information. I was surprised Ron and his friends just didn't tell Cody to get lost, but then again, Cody was in year twelve. Everyone looked up to him, and everyone also knew who his parents were. His dad, more importantly. Talon Marcus. President of the Hawks MC, one of the local motorcycle gangs.

Ron rolled his eyes. "She doesn't have a right to—"

"Stop," Cody ordered. Ron did. Cody chuckled. "I think it's time I teach you a goddamn lesson." He moved so fast Ron didn't stand a chance. The first hit had the girls screaming and running. With the second hit, another of Ron's mates tried to intervene and he caught a fist to the face. Ron tried to fight back, and Cody knocked his hands away as if they were nothing. A guy I didn't know crept up behind Cody.

"Watch out," I called, then slammed my mouth shut. At

least Cody heard me, turned, and sank a fist into the guy's gut.

I realised it was the perfect time for me to escape. My legs shook as I got to my feet. I sniffed and took a breath through the pain. I couldn't look at my jeans; I didn't want to see how wet they were. Instead, I got out of there before the fighting ended. Before Cody annihilated them all. I made sure to stop by my locker to grab my jacket and tied it around my waist. Guilt stabbed at me for leaving Cody, who'd come in and saved me, but I couldn't face him. I couldn't face anyone. I took out a piece of paper and wrote quickly, Thank you for your help. I'm sorry you got dragged into it. *On my way out of school, I slipped it into Cody's locker.*

When Mum saw me that afternoon and I broke down telling her everything that had happened, she promised I wouldn't have to go back and face anyone at school because I'd already been through enough in my life. The following weekend, when Dad had been passed out, we took what we could from the house, along with his pay from his wallet, and left. We moved into a small house just out of Ballarat, since we didn't have enough money to go further. I didn't go back to school until we changed our last name from Fry to Edwards.

Besides Mum informing the previous school, the only other person who knew I wasn't going back was Darla. However, I couldn't tell her where we were because we couldn't risk Dad finding us. I'd asked Mum one night why we couldn't have just gone to the police. Sorrow washed over her face, and she said, "I wished we could have, honey, but your father has many friends within the force, and I couldn't risk any charges being swept under and us being stuck in the situation. It's better this way."

We stayed there for five years. Both Mum and I got a job and saved everything we could because we had our dream. We both loved baking and wanted it to be in our future.

It was after I'd completed high school when we'd moved back into town. We had always loved the town and knew a business wouldn't survive in the area we'd escaped to. And since we hadn't seen or heard anything from my dad, Percy Fry, we wouldn't be hassled and could live many more years without sight of that man. There was also the chance he wouldn't recognise me if we saw each other down the street. Then again, if he did, I doubted he'd care because not once had he bothered to come looking for us. Thank God.

Darla had kept an eye on him for us, and she was the one who told us he went about his days as if we'd never existed. Which was good for us and helped ease our anxiety to live a happy life. Not only that, but I made sure I would be able to protect myself just in case another man in my life ever thought he could hurt me.

Now, after seeing Cody, it brought up that dreadful day. The humiliation and hurt. God, I wasn't sure why I was worried. I wasn't even sure if he got my note or would know who I was.

I sighed as I refilled the coffee cups. I was being

dramatic and allowing my worry to take control. I didn't need to.

In all these years, I hadn't seen him around, and he'd never been in the shop before. I highly doubted he would come back either. Honestly, I didn't think he even lived in town anymore. So many others I knew from those days had moved away, moved to the city for work, like Darla had, only she went further to overseas a couple of years ago. It was sad to see her go, but her boyfriend had a business opportunity he couldn't pass up. She now worked as a dental assistant somewhere in Ohio.

"Are you getting out of here anytime soon?" Denise asked. Like Stanley, she'd been with me from the start. I would be lost without her. She was only a few years older than me, but we became close within the first week. If it weren't for Denise and Stanley, when I lost Mum, I would have given up. I'd been beyond a wreck losing her. For a while, I didn't want to continue, wanted to give up, but I knew Mum would have smacked me upside the head and told me to "Suck it up, buttercup." Eventually, I did. It was hard, but I kept going for Mum. And even after she passed, she made sure she took care of me. I'd been surprised when I found out she had life insurance and I was the sole beneficiary to seven hundred thousand dollars. A lot of it went into the business, paying off our debts, and buying the house we'd rented together, which was conveniently just down the road from the bakery.

"I'm going." I smiled. "See you tomorrow." Denise

closed for me since the afternoons were quieter than the mornings and lunches. I also had to get up at 3:00 a.m. to cook the cakes, slices, cookies, bread, and rolls.

"You got it, and maybe then you can explain why you were hiding."

I stilled. "Um, I wasn't?"

She snorted. "Yeah, right."

Well shit. If Denise knew I'd been hiding, would Cody? Shaking my head, I walked out the back to get my things before leaving and pushing that thought from my mind. It didn't matter because I wouldn't be seeing him again.

CHAPTER TWO

CHANNA

Groaning, I reached over and slapped a hand down on my alarm clock. The only thing I hated about owning a bakery was the early mornings. Yet I wouldn't give it up for anything. After I rubbed a hand over my face, I flicked back the covers and shivered. The room was extra cold this morning since we were in autumn but headed into winter. It wouldn't be worth turning on the heater, though, because I would be out the door soon enough. I always showered the previous night, knowing I wouldn't have the energy to in the mornings. I didn't fully wake until I was at the bakery and cooking.

Dragging my feet, I went into the bathroom, splashed water on my face, and brushed my teeth. That would keep me going until I got to work. I quickly got dressed in jeans and a nice tee before making my way down the hall and into the living room.

As always, my eyes went straight to the beds in front of the window. Smiling, I called, "Morning, babies." Their tails started slapping on the floor before they even lifted their heads and then both of them raced my way for some love and attention. "Hey, Coco. Hey, Harley," I cooed, running my hands over them.

My two German shepherds were another reason I kept going after Mum passed on. They were only three years old—still young and sometimes stubborn—but they had my back when needed. When they were pups, though, I regretted my choice in breed because they were reckless. Into everything, didn't listen, and chewed whatever they could. It wasn't until we took them for dog training that they became the best monsters in the world, because now they actually listened to me.

Harley dropped to the floor and rolled onto his back while Coco sat staring up at me adorably. Laughing, I dipped lower, and while rubbing Coco's head, I patted Harley's belly; he hated early mornings like I did.

"Come on, you two. I'll get some treats." I'd made sure to have a dog door built in after we'd bought the place. The backyard was nice and big for them both, and I'd set up little play areas to help them keep entertained while I was at work. Of course, every day I had to come home and clean the yard up, but I didn't care. As long as they had fun.

After walking into the kitchen, I took out the jar of treats and undid the lid. Both monsters sat with their tails wagging beside me. They both stopped in unison, their heads twisting towards the front door, and then I heard it: the rumble of a bike.

Snorting, I shook my head. Whenever a loud bike rode by, it always caught their attention. It was a bit early and cold to be out on a bike, but I'd heard about guys who rode in any weather.

The dogs ignored the treats I held out to them and got to their feet. My brows dipped, and after a second, shot high when a screech and smash sounded out the front. More squealing of tyres and then voices. With my heart hammering, I raced to the front window and peeked through the blinds.

A bike was on its side, a man on the ground, and other men stood over him yelling, but I couldn't hear what through the ringing in my ears as adrenaline pumped through me. Coco and Harley barked at my side, not helping the situation.

"Heel," I snapped. They did, sitting on the floor, letting whimpers drop from their mouths.

I looked back out through the blinds and my blood turned to ice. One of the men standing had a gun pointed at the one on the ground while the others laid fists and kicks into him.

Didn't the crash wake my neighbours?

Couldn't they run out and stop it?

Drawing in a deep breath, I took hold of Harley's collar, knowing he would be more trouble. I opened the front door and ordered, "Stay." I slipped through, leaving the door open, and closed the screen one instead. "I've called the cops," I yelled and then cursed under my breath, realizing I really shouldn't have done that. But then it could have been too late.

The men who were laying into the one on the ground backed off. The one hurt on the ground looked up at me.

"Leave him alone," I called out, deciding it was too late to turn back now.

"Mind your business, bitch, and go inside," the one holding the gun, which was now at his side, snarled. Coco and Harley growled behind me.

Even though my body shook and fear twisted inside me, I stood my ground. "No. Go before the cops get here." *Please buy my story, please.*

"Sure, bitch, we'll leave." He nodded towards the man on the ground, and two of the four minions moved to pick him up.

"Stop! Leave him."

"Be very fucking careful, bitch," the gunman demanded. They hauled the man, who groaned, to his feet. I couldn't let them take him. I couldn't let this happen right in front of me. They were going to kill him.

I shifted, and the gun got trained on me. My dogs went crazy growling and snarling. "Leave him," I said, ignoring the shake in my voice. They didn't listen. They laughed and started for the four-wheel drive parked behind the downed bike.

Shit, shit, shit, I chanted in my head. I didn't want to risk them. Terror clutched my chest as I reached back slowly and opened the wire door.

Tears filled my eyes as I said the only word I needed, "Attack."

My beautiful beasts leapt from inside the house and raced down the steps, flying over the fence. My gut clenched as a shot was fired, then another, and I wanted to throw up, but I followed after them. They had my back and I had theirs. Harley dove at the man with the gun; his jaw latched onto the man's arm and clamped down. Coco went for one of the men holding the injured one, snapping at his ankle. He cursed and shifted his leg back and forth, but my girl held on. The man dealing with Harley howled in pain and tried to hit him off with his free hand.

I acted. I did it for my boy and girl. I did it for me because I couldn't stand to see my babies being hurt. With fury icing through me, I punched him in the face. It stunned him enough the gun dropped to the ground, but before I could pick it up, I heard Coco cry out in pain. Immediately I spat, "Move and he'll bite through your arm. Hold him, Harley." I caught the guy's wince when Harley tightened his hold.

I spun, taking in the scene within seconds. They'd dropped the injured guy, and the other one was trying to help the man Coco had, laying his foot into my girl.

Seeing red, I flew at him with a flying sidekick. He dropped to the ground, and I moved on to the one Coco still had in her jaws. Hit after hit, I punched into his face, his chest. The guy staggered back, blood spraying from his nose, his lip splitting. It was clear none of them expected I would know how to defend myself and my dogs.

"Coco, back," I ordered. She listened straight away, and I knocked the man on his arse with a roundhouse kick to the side of the face. Panting, I moved back over to the gun and picked it up.

"Call it off," the man Harley still held begged.

"Will you leave?"

"Yes, fuck."

"Harley, Coco, come," I clipped, holding the gun at my side. If it came down to it, I would use it…. At least, I would try to. I didn't know how to use a gun, but I felt like I needed to.

They all moved to the car, holding a part of their bodies. Before the gunman got into the vehicle, he glanced back at me standing with my two dogs at my side. I didn't like the look but hoped I'd proved I could handle myself because I didn't want to see him again. Any of them.

As soon as he was in the car, it took off, fishtailing down the road, and it was only then I let myself relax a little. Tension pressed back into me when my babies started to growl. I glanced down at them and then to where their eyes were pinned.

The injured man had gained consciousness and had somehow pulled himself over to the footpath opposite my house and leaned up against the fence there.

His chin tipped up. "Glad I woke enough to see you kick their arses."

"Coco, Harley, quit it," I said calmly, and they did. Harley's tail started wagging when he knew I wasn't completely worried. What helped was that I knew the guy would be in too much pain to do anything to me. Usually this neighbourhood was quiet, peaceful, and all in one morning it went to hell, for me at least, because of him.

Still wary, I kept an eye on him while I crouched to run my hands over Coco. She seemed okay. She didn't flinch or nip at me when I pressed in places.

"Why'd you help?"

Straightening, I shrugged. "I didn't want your death on my conscience when I could help."

He snorted. "Can I ask one more favour?"

"Do you want me to call an ambulance?"

He shook his head, cringing. "Nah, but I do need you to call someone."

"Who?"

"Brother."

Brother? I could do that. I would be safe since I did help him out, so his brother wasn't going to be pissed at me.

"All right." I nodded, then bit my bottom lip. Did I leave him out here while I went to grab my phone or take him in case those douches dropped back with friends? That thought twisted my insides. What would I do with Coco and Harley while I was at work? Also, thinking of work, I cursed the darkened sky because I was late; everything was going to be delayed, and Stanley was going to be a pain in the arse about it. Sighing, I said, "You should come in while we call."

I hoped he'd refuse, but he could have been thinking along the lines I'd been because he nodded. With a few groans and grunts, he managed to get to his feet but swayed. Cursing under my breath, I made my way over to him and slid an arm around his waist.

"Lean on me," I said.

He did, which told me how much pain he was actually in. Slowly, we walked towards the house with my babies following.

Once inside, I helped the man sit on the couch and went into the kitchen where my mobile was. "What number am I calling and what name do I give them?" Under the light, I saw just who sat on the couch and gulped. He was a big man, really wide and tall with long hair in a bun and tattooed hands. I expected they ran up his arms under his long-sleeved, dirty Henley. He had a neatly trimmed beard and moustache on his bruised and cut face. A face that, even with the scrapes, was good-looking.

"The brother's a member of the Hawks MC." Screw me in the arse. He had a brother in a biker club. He must have seen my widened gaze because he quickly added, "You don't need to fear me or him, honey. Promise." He then rattled off a number, and added, "Name's Texas."

Nodding, I pressed in the numbers and told the dogs to guard, which Texas smirked at before he rested his head back against the couch. I went into the kitchen and held my wrist since my hands had started shaking. The adrenaline had started to wear off.

"Who's this?" was demanded darkly into the phone.

Since Texas didn't give me the name of his brother, I said over the phone, "I have Texas in my house after he was in a crash and was jumped. He didn't want an ambulance and asked me to call you."

"Where do you live?" he asked shortly. I told him the details, and the last thing he said before hanging up was "We'll be there soon."

We?

Who was we?

I didn't agree on more people than just his brother. Oh shit. Did Texas actually mean a blood brother or one of his brother biker friends? I could have kicked myself in the cooch for not asking more questions. My pulse raced, but I had to remind myself no harm would come to me because I had stepped in and helped their brother.

When I stepped back into the living room, Texas opened his eyes and they landed on me.

"He said *they're* on the way." I paused and flicked my gaze to my babies, who were sitting in front of Texas watching him.

"You'll be safe with them, with my brothers," Texas reassured me, but my belly didn't feel like I could believe it completely since I was sure he meant biker brothers, not blood related. He cleared his throat. "Trust me."

But I couldn't. I didn't know the guy. Instead, I said nothing.

His lips twitched and he nodded towards the dogs. "They're good."

Warmth rushed through me as I dropped my eyes to my babies. "Yeah, they are. The best, really." I licked my dry lips. "Um, do you need anything? A cool cloth? A drink? Pain meds?"

He grunted. "I'll take all of them." He paused a beat. "Please."

Darn, I probably should have asked him as soon as we got in. "No problem," I said softly, and then went down the hall to my bathroom. I closed the door after myself and called Denise.

"What's wrong?"

"I can't make it into work, honey. An accident happened right out front of my place, and I have to stay for… um, to give them answers. I'm so sorry to ask this, but can you go in and get the bread and rolls in the oven?"

"Of course, babe. I'm getting up right now and will be there soon. Do you want me to stop in—"

"No! Ah, thank you, though." I couldn't risk pulling Denise into this, not when she had a daughter to take care of. "Will Mrs Bishop be okay coming in to watch Mariana?"

"Yeah, she won't care. She's probably already up watching her shows or feeding her horde. Don't stress, okay? I've got this. I'll see you when you get in."

"Thank you, Denise, you're a lifesaver."

"Any time." And she would. She'd do anything for anybody in need. I hated having to do this to her, but I didn't know anyone else who knew how to do what I did. I'd shown Denise in case something happened, but now I felt guilty for asking her since she had Mariana to take care of. I would have to find a part-time or casual person I could teach who could fill in for me. Honestly, I'd been lucky so far. I hadn't been sick with anything, so I could keep the bakery up and running.

After grabbing what I needed, I made my way back down the hall and over to Texas. "Do you think your, um, brother will be able to get your bike off the road, or should I go out and do it?" I asked, handing him the pain medication and cool pack.

I went into the kitchen for the drink and brought it back out when he answered, "They can do it. They shouldn't be too far away."

The dogs jerked towards the door just before I heard another rumble of bikes.

I rested a hand against my stomach with the sudden swirling inside. I hoped it didn't follow through with anything, like a fart. Harley and Coco growled when we heard the heavy footfalls on the front porch. My heart beat so hard I was surprised I couldn't see it when I looked down at my chest.

"Honey," Texas called. "Relax, you got nothin' to worry about."

I hummed under my breath and only jumped a little when a loud knock dropped on the front door. The dogs started barking until I called, "Heel." Moving over to the door, I caught their eyes and pointed over near Texas. "Back." They shifted away from the door and sat in front of Texas. Sucking in a deep breath, I opened the door and gulped.

Satan, take me now.

In the door stood a man much taller than me, which wasn't hard because I wasn't the tallest person. He was tall, broad, bearded, with tattoos on his arms under his tee, and all I could think was that he had to be cold. I was also slightly scared by his intense eyes.

"Here for Texas," he stated. I nodded and moved to the side; it was then I realized there were four others with him.

"Fuck, Dodge, what're you doin' here?" Texas asked.

"Just got to town when Ruin got the call."

When the last one entered, I closed the door and shifted over to my dogs, who'd started growling when the man named Dodge got too close to Texas.

"Coco, Harley, here," I commanded from the doorway into the kitchen. They trotted over and sat in front of me, their eyes trained on all the men.

I took in the others, like they did me. Only when I saw a certain dark head of hair, my eyes widened for a second and a squeak escaped me before I could thin my lips and blank my expression. I quickly looked back to Texas.

Cody Marcus was in my house.

Cody bloody Marcus.

Snap me in half and stuff me down the toilet. I'd forgotten he was a part of the Hawks.

Oh Lord. Lordy, Lord, Lord. I was going to throw up. Right there in front of a bunch of tough bikers. I was going to blow chunks at their feet and probably all over my dogs. I could run and hide in my room until they're gone. I could—

"Honey," Texas called. I blinked and hummed. He smirked. "Didn't catch your name."

"Channa," I told him.

"Channa, sweet-arse name, honey."

I shrugged, running my hands over my babies' heads. A couple of the men chuckled, but I didn't dare look away from Texas.

"Channa, this here is Dodge." The bearded one with tatted arms. "That's Talon." Talon. I knew that name. I'd heard that name a few times. He was Cody's father…. I glanced at him and nodded. He tipped his chin up, and I ignored the fact he was nearly as good-looking as his son. "By the door is Ruin"—the one who wasn't Cody, but very noticeable with his dark hair and eyes—"and Coyote." Coyote? Coyote was Cody's club name, and I could see from his patch on the vest that he was a full member. He'd followed in his daddy's footsteps. Though I hadn't noticed a club vest on him when he'd been in the bakery, but he wore one now.

With a nod in their direction, I looked back to Dodge. He seemed the safest, even with those intense eyes. "You probably saw Texas's ride out the front. We'll need to move it—"

"Already done, babe," he told me. "You wanna tell me your side of the story?"

I nodded because I wanted them out of my house as soon as possible. I swear I could feel heat coating my body from someone's, or a few, eyes trained on me.

"I heard the bike, then a crash, and tyres screeching to a stop. I looked out the window to see Texas on the ground with three men around him. One held a gun on him while the other two beat him. I... I couldn't live with myself if I didn't do something."

"*You* went out there?" Ruin asked, shock clear in his tone.

Ignoring him, I told Dodge, "I tried to get them to stop, but when they started to take Texas to the vehicle, I sent the dogs out. The dogs got a few bites in which shocked them enough to leave."

Texas snorted. "It was a bit more than that."

I glared down at him. "No, it wasn't. I got him in here, gave him some pain meds, and called um... one of you."

"That was me," Ruin said.

"Right. Well, there we have it. Now is now."

"Texas?" Dodge turned to him.

"Ah, shouldn't you guys get him to a doctor?"

"We have someone comin'," Talon replied.

"But... I mean, I have to get to work." *So please leave. Please.*

"You gonna get in trouble from your boss?" Dodge asked.

"She works at the bakery a few places up."

I tensed because those words came from Cody Marcus.

Had he recognized me? I didn't think I had anything lying around the house he could have seen to know where I worked. Crap, he must have recognized me. Knowing he had made me giddy, yet it also brought the vomit feeling up again. I couldn't even look his way. When I'd glanced at Ruin before, I made sure my gaze didn't fall on him.

"Right, the bakery girl arguin' with that old guy."

Darn Stanley.

"You have someone who can fill in for the day?" Dodge asked.

"I need someone? I… why? Can't I just leave after you all and go about my day?" Were they going to hold me hostage for some reason?

"Channa, don't stress. We ain't gonna harm you," Talon said.

"Uh-huh," I mumbled, because I didn't believe him since they said I'd need someone to fill in for me. "I can't leave my business in Denise and Stanley's hands. Denise is baking right now for me, but I'll have to go in and help to get it out on time. And Stanley gets crabby if the place is too hot when he comes in to ice things. I don't have anyone else to help Denise with the lunch rush either." I was in a near panic. I couldn't leave my shop for the day. I just couldn't.

"It's all good, honey. You mind if we hang for a bit while we wait on Doc? We'll lock up after," Dodge offered.

They wanted to wait in my house. Without me there. With my babies.

I glanced down at them. My dogs were before any other worry. "It's okay. I'll wait."

"We'll take care of your dogs," Ruin said.

I shook my head. "No offense, but I don't know any of you, and my dogs are my life. I wouldn't even leave them with my neighbour, who I do know."

"Understood," Talon said. "Can you give us a minute? Then after Doc comes, we'll get outta your hair."

Dodge shot Talon a look, one I didn't trust. Yet what choice did I have? I nodded and turned to go into the kitchen, calling for Coco and Harley to follow.

CHAPTER THREE

COYOTE

*S*he was familiar, and I wasn't just thinking about how I'd seen her that day at the bakery. There was something niggling at the back of my mind. But now wasn't the time to let it form. We had other matters to deal with.

As soon as Channa was out of sight, we all shifted closer to Texas to speak low. Dodge was the first to ask, "Who?"

"That fuckin' new gang. They got it in their heads Hawks has stolen off them, but wouldn't say what. Didn't get all the information since the scene was interrupted, which was fuckin' good because they were gonna use me to give Hawks a lesson. They'd said they'd been watchin' the Hawks. Seen me and knew I was close to the Hawks. Thought I was the best option to deal with."

Texas hadn't even been patched into the club. Hell, he was only in town long enough to set up his second tattoo business. Fucking bad timing.

"It's time we have a sit down with these fuckers," I stated. The gang hadn't been around long, but if they thought they could just take charge and hurt any of us, they had another thing coming. I was ready to teach them a lesson, along with the other brothers.

Talon, who was the club president and my dad, dropped his hand to my shoulder and applied pressure. "We will." He removed his hand and glanced back down to Texas. "Where's it hurt?"

"Ribs. Think cracked or broken. The rest will heal quickly. Just worried about Ink It."

"We've got it, brother, you know that," Dodge said. Dodge was Texas's uncle, but since he'd been under Dodge's roof when he was just fourteen, Dodge went from uncle to his dad. "I'll stay around a bit longer and help out."

"What about Low?" Texas asked. Low was Dodge's old lady and also Texas's mum.

Dodge cursed under his breath. "She's gonna go crazy, you know that."

Texas sighed. "Yep."

Dodge smirked. "No doubt she'll get her arse here to take care of you." Texas groaned. I'd known Low for most of my life, so I knew there was also a chance she'd want to go and kick these guys arses for touching her boy. "Rommy as well," Dodge added. Rommy was Texas's sister and also very protective of her brother.

"Rommy can't take the time off," Texas said.

"Fuck, I know. I'll figure something out. For now, tell us what you meant earlier, when you said that wasn't all that happened."

Texas actually grinned. "Christ, it was damn amazin'. No kiddin'. That shit blew my mind."

"Spit it out then," Ruin demanded. Ruin also had a father in the club, Stoke. Ruin and I lived in Ballarat and were a part of the original chapter, where Texas would patch into the one Dodge was the president of. They belonged to the Caroline Springs chapter. But we were all family. All close and would do anything for the club to keep the peace.

"When I came to, it was to see her dogs going crazy, and then she was there kickin' arse."

"What do you mean?" I asked.

Texas chuckled low. "She was like a silent ninja. Her moves were from a damn kung-fu movie as she took them all down within seconds."

"No shit?" Ruin breathed.

"No fuckin' shit. She saved my damn life." He swallowed, his hand holding his waist. "I'm worried they'll want retribution."

Dodge and Talon shared a look before Talon said, "We'll keep an eye on things for her. Patrollin' won't be singular any longer. Two brothers at a time, no excuses."

We all agreed. Not only about the patrolling but

looking out for Channa. She did just risk her life for a brother, and we didn't want something happening to her because of it.

Channa.

Why did her name seem familiar?

The knock on the door had my thoughts shifting. The dogs barked and had just run back into the living room when we heard shouted, "No, heel. Come." Silence, and then they trotted back into the kitchen, and we heard "Who's my good babies? So brave and amazing." We all looked at each other. Texas was the only one smiling. That woman, the one cooing over her animals, had been the one to kick arse… it was hard to believe.

"Coyote, get the door," Texas said.

Blinking, I nodded and went to the door, opening it. "Doc," I greeted with a grin and leaned in to kiss my sister on the cheek. "Thanks for comin'."

Maya rolled her eyes. "Don't call me that."

"But you're our doc." After Maya finished high school, she went straight to university to complete a three-year degree for a Bachelor of Paramedic Science. She was now on her year of working as a student para-medic. We were fucking proud of her.

I'd taken a different route to my career, and with my parents' help, I opened up a Harley store. We sold, fixed, and did custom paint jobs, along with any type of decals customers wanted. I'd also been talking to a couple of brothers in Melbourne about opening a second shop.

"What we got?" she asked, stepping into the house. She paused when she saw Texas on the couch. I wasn't sure what had happened between those two, but they hardly spoke. Then again, most of the time he was in Caroline Springs and Maya in Ballarat. It could be distance, but I had a feeling it was something else. No matter how many times I asked, both of them pretty much told me I was imagining things.

Maya sucked in a breath and moved right over to the couch after receiving a kiss on the forehead from our dad, Talon. I closed the door, and they went on talking quietly, explaining what had happened. They wouldn't need me here for anything, so instead, I made my way through the living room and into the kitchen.

Only I paused when I turned the corner and found Channa with her ear up to the wall. Her eyes widened, and she stepped back, tripped, windmilled her arms, and then straightened with a blush on her cheeks and neck.

"I thought I heard a possum scratching in the wall," she tried.

I wanted to laugh, even smile, but I didn't because I didn't want her to think she was stupid for doing it. Hell, I would have done the same if I was in her shoes with strangers in her house and not really sure what was going on or what we'd do to her.

Leaning against the wall, I crossed my arms over my chest. "Huh, I don't hear anythin'."

She mimicked me by crossing her arms over her chest. "Must have stopped. The dogs were going crazy over it." I glanced down at the dogs who sat beside her, staring at me. "Well, they *were*," she added.

I happened to glance at her feet, which were nearly damn blue. "Your feet are cold."

Her brows dipped, and she looked down. "Crap." She went to the pile of folded washing on the kitchen table and grabbed some socks. As she put them on, she explained, "I didn't put shoes on when I heard the crash. I just rushed out there and—"

"Are your feet okay? Let me see," I said and started to walk over to her, but she moved around the table to have it between us. She panted out her breaths, her eyes wild and a little panicky.

What the fuck?

"No, they're fine. I'm good. It's all good." She nodded over and over. She let out a puff of air and then laughed. "See, all covered and getting warm. They don't hurt." She jumped up and down a bit.

Christ, she was weird, but in a funny way. I just didn't understand why she didn't want me near her. Unless she'd had a bad relationship or was in one now? The thought pissed me right the fuck off.

"You got a man?" I asked, a little harsher than I'd intended. I wouldn't be surprised if she was taken. She was cute. Short, but cute in her light blue jeans and tee. Her hair was straight, sitting just past her shoulders, and red—a dark red that went well with her light hazel eyes. Freckles touched over her nose and upper cheeks.

Yeah, she was damn cute.

She snorted, then kind of wheezed. Maybe she

couldn't believe I'd asked. "No, ah, yeah, no. I don't have time for that."

It was good information to know since we'd have to have her back until we got those other fuckers off ours.

"Anyway," she started, "um, how long until I can get to work?"

"Soon."

"Okay," she drew out. She went on to straighten things on the table and refold some clothes. I had a feeling she was nervous around me. "Do you… would any of you, I mean you and your mates, want a drink or something?"

"Nah, we'll be all right." I crouched and clicked my fingers.

The dogs looked to Channa. She smiled softly at them. "It's okay," she said.

Their tails swished back and forth as they slowly approached me, but then one of them jumped sideways and back again, overexcited. Chuckling, I curled my fingers through their fur at their necks and ran them down their backs. I got licks to the face for it.

"Harley," Channa groaned. "Sorry, he gets very excited."

Grinning, I nodded. "I can tell. I like his name. What was hers again?"

"Coco."

"Coco," I said, and her tail swiped the floor as she sat in front of me. Harley didn't like that though. He pushed in closer and licked my neck, making me laugh. I glanced up at Channa, her eyes warm until she saw me looking and went back to folding already folded clothes.

"Coyote?" Ruin called, coming around the corner. He chuckled. "Sorry to interrupt, since I see you're finally gettin' some lovin' off someone."

Rolling my eyes, I bit out, "Fuck off."

"They're gettin' Texas back to the compound."

With a final pat, I straightened and nodded. I started for the doorway, glancing back to say, "Comin'?"

She jumped and nodded, shifting around the table to follow us. In the living room, Dodge helped Texas from the couch, and I noticed Maya was already gone. She was probably on the way to the compound and meeting them there. I'd find out later just how bad Texas's injuries were.

"Channa." Talon caught her attention as he moved closer.

"Yep?" she squeaked. Clearing her throat, she added, "Yes?"

"We're concerned those guys will want to come back in the area, so the brothers of Hawks will be keeping a lookout."

I froze for a moment. Her eyes then widened in fear. She hadn't thought of the possibility of them returning. She blinked and shook her head. "I'm sure they won't—"

"We're keepin' an eye out." He stared.

"Okay," she whispered. Glancing down to her dogs, it was obvious she was thinking of them and not herself.

"Honey," Texas called, and a stab of agitation gripped me with his easiness with her. As soon as he had her eyes, he smiled. "Thanks for savin' my life."

"I didn't—"

"You did. I owe you one."

She shook her head, her hands landing on the dogs' heads, as if they comforted her with a touch. "No, you don't."

"I do. So if you need anythin' at any time, you call, yeah?"

Her lips thinned and she nodded, but I was sure she was just agreeing to get him gone.

Texas chuckled. "You're only agreein' now 'cause you don't have my number."

Her shoulders slumped at being figured out. I glanced away, grinning. I wasn't the only one.

"How about I give it to her before you fall on your face?" I asked.

"Thanks, Coyote. See ya, honey," Texas called.

Once they were out the door, Talon turned back to Channa. "Coyote and Ruin are on you today—"

She snorted, then giggled and mumbled, "That's what she said." She blanched, her hand shot up and covered her mouth before she dropped it and shook her hands out. She cleared her throat and tipped her chin up, even when she was blushing. "I'm sorry, please continue."

Ruin hooted out a laugh, while Talon's lips twitched, and I grinned.

The redness spread down her neck, but she didn't look away from us.

Yeah, she was definitely cute.

"Right. As I said, Coyote and Ruin have your back today when you go to your shop."

"What do you mean by having my back exactly? Like, from afar?"

"No."

"From outside the shop? Not that I think anyone needs to go to the shop. Those douches don't know I work there." She let out a huff of annoyance and put her hands on her hips. "I'm going to have to put my foot down. They won't come for me—"

"Can you guarantee it?" Talon asked.

She paused, biting her bottom lip. After she shrugged, she said, "I'm not 100 percent, but I'm a small inconvenience in their life. I'm sure they'll forget about me. Besides, the shop always has people around it during the day, *and* I can take care of myself, plus I have Coco and Harley to help me here."

"What happens if they do come back and bring more with them?" It was a low blow, but I had to say it because I knew she cared about her dogs more than herself. "Are you willin' to risk Coco and Harley because you're being stubborn?"

The room quieted; she swung her angry gaze to pierce me. I waited. We all did to see what she would say. See if she would continue to be stubborn.

She took a breath, glanced down to her dogs, and her

hands fisted before she nodded. "Okay," she said softly. Her gaze lifted, and she added, "But it doesn't have to be close, like right up my... ah, in my face?" Heat hit her cheeks once more. I liked how easily she blushed.

"No, it doesn't," I said with a small smile. She wasn't stupid; she wanted to be safe and would take the help we offered since it was all our fault in the damn first place. "From afar then, and only until we get this shit sorted." And we would, because no one deserved their lives being screwed over because of some trouble we were having. Sucked big time she was caught up in this, but she saved Texas's life. Even he said that. We'd make sure she stayed safe.

Her lips thinned. "All right."

"Good," Talon said. "Whoever takes over from Coyote and Ruin's shift today will always wear a club vest and patch. Trust no one else."

She nodded, suddenly seeming tired with her slouched shoulders, and yet frustrated, if her angry eyes were anything to go by.

The sooner we could get this shit sorted, the sooner she'd go back to her normal life. Without worry.

However, there was still something familiar about Channa, and I wanted to know why.

I'd find out, even if it took me some time, because I didn't mind being around her at all.

CHAPTER FOUR

CHANNA

I could feel my brave face faltering. What I really wanted was to run from the house screaming and crying. But before I could, Coyote and Ruin stayed around to give me Texas's number and help me lock up before I could make the walk to the shop. Nerves tickled my skin as sweat started to pool at the back of my neck and hands.

Cody Marcus, or as they called him, Coyote, had been in my house. He'd spoken to me. He'd petted my dogs. He'd tried to look at my feet. All right, that was a weird thing to think, but still. My brain was about to explode with an overload of Cody. Especially since, in the years I hadn't seen him, time had been very good to him in the looks department. Yet I wouldn't, *couldn't* go there because I didn't think he knew I was pee girl, which was the only plus side to this whole situation.

I didn't regret helping Texas because he would have been hurt in more ways than he already had been. Dead even. However, I wished I'd left him outside, called for help, and then locked myself back in the house. Although, with all of them being intense, I had a feeling they still would have gotten in.

At least they were nice enough to want to make sure I stayed safe because of their stuff-up. It hadn't even occurred to me the men would come back, and I wouldn't risk anything when it came to Coco and Harley, so the help was appreciated. I'd also decided to lock my babies inside until I could pop home to let them out on breaks, not liking the thought of them in the yard alone. The Hawks guys had put enough fear inside me over the thought of those men coming back.

The only thing I wasn't a fan of, besides the arse-holes, was it meant Cody would stick around in my life longer.

I wanted to scream, as there was a possibility I was being stupid and overreacting about the whole situation back in high school. Yet the mortification had cut me so deep it felt like it was still a gaping wound inside me.

At the bakery, I glanced to the bikes pulling to a stop on the other side of the road. I received a two-finger wave from Ruin and a chin lift from Cody. I couldn't bring myself to call him Coyote; it seemed weird.

My first stop would be the toilet. It sure felt like I

needed to poop myself from the way my belly had been coiling. It could also be from the worry of leaving Coco and Harley at home, but I just had to reassure myself they were safe inside. I did consider asking Stanley if I could stay at his place with my babies since he didn't live far from the bakery either. But there was a chance I'd end up killing him, since my emotions were all over the place. Unless I asked him to mind the dogs….

Gah, I don't know what to do.

"Hey, honey," Denise called as she put some baked loaves on the shelves behind the counter. "Everything get sorted?"

"Yes, all done." I wasn't going to tell her or Stanley what went on, knowing they would worry for me. Also, I didn't want them involved. "Sorry again about getting you in early. I think I'll have to hire a part-time person who knows how to do my duties, as well."

She hummed under her breath. Turning to me, she nodded. "It's probably a good idea. Not that I mind helping out."

I gave her a warm smile. "I know you don't."

She returned my smile with her own. "Good. Plus, if you hire someone, you might get a chance for some time off. No twenty-two-year-old should be working as hard as you."

Walking out the back, with Denise following, I told her, "But you know I love this. The bakery. I love running this place."

Taking an apron off the hook, I pulled it over my head and went to my workstation. Denise had already got the first round of rolls and bread out of the oven. I just needed to get the next set cooking.

"Honey, I know you love working, but how are you going to meet your better half?"

Snorting, I told her, "I don't need anyone. Besides, I'll just take Amos up on his offer when the time comes."

She let out a bark of laughter. "You deserve better than someone who loves you for your treats."

Lifting a tray into the oven, I turned and shrugged. "I'm happy. That's all I worry about, and making sure Bakery Bliss runs smoothly to keep Mum's and my dream alive."

As she passed me, her hand squeezed my arm. "She'd be proud of everything already, honey."

My heart clenched. "Thanks, Denise." Since Denise had come in for me, we were only a little behind. By the time we flicked the sign on the front door to Open, at 6:00 a.m., we had only a few things to complete. Denise stayed out the front to prepare for the morning rush of people on the way to work, while I stayed and finished what I had to. I needed to get the ovens off soon since my kitchen wasn't the biggest and did heat up a lot, even with the cooler mornings. Within another half an hour, I had the ovens off and the air conditioner on. I stood in the coolroom, drinking gulps of water from the bottle and taking in the frigid air for a moment.

A smile tipped up my lips. Yeah, I was happy with my business. Not many at twenty-two could say they owned their own shop, but I could. Like Denise said, I knew Mum would be proud, and that was all that mattered.

I didn't need a man to complete me. Well, it would be nice to have some bedroom time with someone, but I had a vibrator for that.

Since I had the door opened a little, I heard Denise call, "Channa?"

"Coming," I yelled back. Once I put my water on the shelf, I slipped out of the coolroom and stopped because I found someone scowling at me. Rolling my eyes, I said, "Don't give me that look, Stanley. You're in early, so you can't complain. Besides, I had a situation this morning. Denise had to come in for me, and things were delayed."

He dropped his hands on his hips. "What happened?"

"I'll talk about it later. Denise just called. She needs help."

"Fine," he grumbled. "But you'd better explain."

Some of it I would.

Moving through the doors, I grinned. "Morning, Bryson."

"Hey, Channa, how are you?"

"Good," I said, stopping at the counter. The shop had a few people waiting for coffees, but it wasn't overly busy.

"Denise called you out for me." His elbows touched down on the counter and he leaned into them. "What are you doing after work today?" he asked. Bryson worked at the gym just down the road. He'd been coming here since we opened, and we'd become friends. We'd even gone to the movies and out to eat a few times, but there was nothing between us. He'd tried to get me to join the gym again and again, but I knew I wouldn't have time, and I liked to work out in private. Eventually, he gave in, but in that time, we'd got to know one another and enjoyed each other's company.

"Any other day, I would say nothing, but I've had a rough morning. What were you thinking, though?"

The front door opened, and I glanced away from Bryson and saw Cody enter. His eyes were glued to Bryson. Strange, did they know each other? I offered a lame wave and regretted it right away. Thankfully, he didn't see it.

"Channa?" Bryson called.

"Sorry, what?"

"There's a new action movie out I thought you'd like to see, but we can go another day."

I moved my gaze over Bryson's shoulder again to see Cody glaring at him. I looked to Bryson again. "Um, sure, another day. That'd be good."

He straightened. "Great."

"Bryson, your coffee," Denise called.

Bryson winked at me, then turned. He froze when he spotted Cody close behind him. "Excuse me," he said, but Cody didn't move. Bryson narrowed his gaze, shifted around Cody, and moved down to the end of the counter.

Cody stepped close my way. "Two cappuccinos, one with sugar," he said, while keeping an eye on Bryson.

Did he have a crush on the guy? Was Cody gay? But then he wouldn't have glared at him... unless Bryson wasn't interested, I supposed. My heart dropped and mixed with my gut; it would be a damn shame if Cody was gay. Many women—and I wasn't saying I was one of them—would be disappointed if he wasn't on the market.

"Sure. Denise—"

"Got it," she called.

He grabbed out his wallet, but I waved him off. "No charge."

His gaze slowly slid my way and his smile was lazy. "No, Channa." Had he said my name before? I wasn't sure, and maybe I'd been too busy in my head to take it in, and I still didn't then because it sounded nice coming from his lips. Too nice. Like it would be easy to fantasise him calling my name while....

Nope. Nuh-uh. I wasn't allowing that to get to me and my body. Not him.

"Yes, Co—ah, Coyote." Crap, I nearly called him Cody. He didn't know I knew his real name.

He slapped a note on the counter. "No, Channa," he stated, his voice deeper than normal.

"Channa," Bryson called.

I glanced there.

"Channa," Cody said.

I looked at him.

"Channa," Bryson clipped.

I started to shift my gaze when a hand covered mine on the counter. I looked down to see Cody had slipped the note under my hand. My eyes shot up to glare at the smiling man.

I heard a curse, then Bryson called with a wave, "See you tomorrow."

"You got it." I waved, and then, as Cody was watching me, I placed his note in the Save the Gorillas tin.

He chuckled.

I paled. "Shit, I needed to give you change."

He laughed more, shaking his head. "All good, Channa."

I picked up the tin, tipped it upside down, but there wasn't a way to open it. "I could get a can opener."

His hands covered mine over the tin, which pulled my gaze up to meet his. Humour danced in his eyes. "Forget it."

"Two cappuccinos, one with sugar," Denise called.

He dropped my hands. "Better get back to it." I was still in some type of meltdown, maybe over his laugh, maybe from his touch. Whatever it was, I stood there like an idiot as he grabbed the takeaway coffees, walked to the door, and out it.

Denise sidled up beside me. "What was that?"

"Huh?" I asked.

"What was *that*?"

"Looked like they were trying to piss over her" came from behind us.

Denise and I turned to face Stanley, who stood just outside the doors to the back with his arms crossed over his chest. He said to me, "You've got some explaining to do. How'd you get the attention of the Hawks MC?"

My eyes widened. I quickly shushed Stanley and ushered him out the back by waving my hands that way. He stomped through, I followed, and Denise was behind me.

"I'll keep an ear out for customers," she said, stopping just inside the doors. "What actually happened this morning?" she asked me, then directed at Stanley, "And what do you mean the Hawks MC have their attention on her?"

"When I pulled around the back, I noticed two bikes out the front with their riders still on them. They had their eyes trained on the bakery. I didn't like it, didn't trust it, not until I saw one of them with our Channa."

It warmed my heart when he said *our* like they'd claimed me as their family. I guess I had with them as well. It was good to know they felt the same.

They both stared at me. "After the morning rush, we'll have a coffee, and I'll explain everything," I told them, just as we all heard the front door open.

"As long as you do," Stanley ordered in a fatherly way. I nodded, and Denise and I went back out front to deal with the morning customers looking for breakfast and coffee on the way to work.

As soon as it looked like things had settled, Denise called, "Stanley, coffee and explanation time." Denise shooed me towards a table. "Go sit. I'll bring the coffees over."

I didn't want to say anything to them about the situation, but I hadn't come up with a lie they would buy. I'd thought maybe I could say I owed the Hawks MC money, and they were watching me to make sure I didn't run from town. Only they would try and give me money and neither of them had much. I knew that.

Denise was a single mum; her ex didn't want anything to do with her when she told him she was pregnant and left her with no support. Since then, he hadn't paid a single cent towards Mariana. Denise had done it all on her own since her parents weren't around either. She was an amazing mum, worked at the bakery, and then at home, making soap and selling it online.

Stanley had been married, though never had children before he lost his wife when he was fifty. He'd never dated anyone since. I knew he used to be in the army, and maybe got a pension off them as well as his wage here, but I would never feel comfortable with accepting money from either of them, especially for a fake situation I would make up.

I considered pretending I was dating a Hawks member, but having them out front watching over the shop wouldn't help that suggestion, as they'd likely think the man I'd picked was a stalker.

There was only one option, and that was the truth. At least I thought it was. Even after I sat down at the table, I still wasn't sure which way I was supposed to go. What happened if the Hawks MC didn't want me to say anything? Maybe I could just tell them that.

I screamed in my mind, but it didn't help.

When Stanley and Denise sat down and Denise pushed a coffee my way, I sat on my shaky hands. I was nervous, but only because I worried what my mess would do to them.

"So?" Stanley asked.

"They like the front of Bakery Bliss?" I tried.

Stanley dropped his coffee to the table after a sip and crossed his arms over his chest. Denise just snorted and rolled her eyes at me.

"They want me as their girlfriend?" Dear God, these were lame. I didn't usually choke under pressure, but my brain was farting something shocking in my head and giving me nothing.

They looked at each other and laughed. That was just rude.

Stanley shook his head. "We're not laughing at what you said, more that you'll try lying to us when you're so shit at it."

"Hey" burst out of me.

"And even though the biker pissed on you in front of Bryson, you're just pulling our chains. Just tell us what's going on, kid."

"Fine." I sighed. "But I want you both to say you'll not worry and stay out of this first."

"Promise," Denise said quickly. Too quickly.

Stanley nodded.

"Say it, Stanley."

"Yeah, yeah, I promise."

"It's nothing too bad," I told them, and realized I probably should have started with that. "This morning there was a crash out the front of my house. A guy, who is friends with the Hawks MC, was jumped. They were going to… um, hurt him a lot. I had to do something, so I stepped in to help him." Denise's eyes widened and Stanley cursed. "It's okay. I got them to back off and helped the guy."

"Then why are they watching over you?"

I waved a hand around, trying to play it off with a snort as well. "It's nothing. They're a little concerned the, ah, bad guys will come back. They offered their help by keeping an eye out."

Stanley rested his arms on the table and leaned forward. "When you said you helped the guy, how did you do it?"

I glanced around and prayed for a customer to come in or for time to speed up and the lunch rush to start.

"Channa," Denise said softly.

"Well, um, you know. I shouted at them, told them the cops were coming to scare them off."

"Did it work?" Stanley asked. Had he actually been a police officer instead of in the army in the past because I felt like I was being interrogated?

"Yes?" I said.

Stanley glared at me. Denise pressed her hands over her heart. "What happened?" she asked.

Crap, I hated they knew me too well. I really had to find out how they could tell when I lied.

"I helped. That's all you need to know."

Stanley stood so suddenly his chair crashed to the floor. He started for the door. I raced after him and grabbed his hand. "Stanley, where are you going?"

"To find out all the information from them." He nodded outside towards Cody and Ruin.

"No. Leave them, please. I don't even know if I can tell you two."

"Bull. If you don't tell me, then I'm going out there."

"I kicked their arses with the dogs' help."

"Fuck," Stanley clipped and scrubbed a hand over his weathered face. "Any type of guy, but especially the bad ones, won't want to be seen getting their arses handed to them by some bird. They'll want payback." He shook his head. "Right, you and the dogs are coming to my place until this shit is over. They can watch you from there. No ifs, buts, or any damn shit." The more he got pissed, the more he swore.

My chest expanded in love but deflated quickly when I realized something and voiced my concern. "I won't risk you—"

"Kid." He sighed, shaking his head. "Make an old man happy and let me help you. I know the Hawks have got your back, which they damn well should since it's their bloody mess, but I'll feel a shitload better knowing you're under my roof and not in a house alone."

"So will I," Denise added.

I glanced between each of them and saw the concern they had for me in their pinched eyes and thinned lips.

"They said they'll get it sorted," I told them. "I don't think this will last."

"Channa, you've got the dogs, but I have a security system, guns, and a few other weapons."

My eyes widened. "Are they even legal?"

"Let's not worry about that. Keeping you safe is the main concern."

They wouldn't be happy until I was under Stanley's roof, and if I was honest with myself, I would feel safer with someone else in the house.

"Okay." I nodded. "I'll move in." And hope we didn't kill each other. It would be a good idea to hide his weapons in case he used them on me since he got annoyed so quickly.

"Good," Stanley grunted, and after a pat to my head, he went out the back again. The door opened and some customers came in, so Denise and I got back to work.

CHAPTER FIVE

COYOTE

"Do you reckon she's tellin' them what went on?" Ruin asked as we watched what was going on in the shop. It'd quietened down and looked like the employees were sitting down for a chat.

"Probably."

"Think we'll need to warn them about keepin' their mouths closed?"

"Hard to say. But I don't think she'd say anything to them if she didn't know them well. Honestly, they probably saw us, put her on the spot, and dragged it out of her. She wouldn't want anyone to know in case it brought drama to them."

When Ruin stayed silent for a while, I turned to him. He was staring at me, smiling.

"What?" I clipped.

"Nothin'." His smile widened.

"Spit it out, Ruin, or I'll kick your arse."

He chuckled. "Like you could."

I smirked. "You know I can." After all, I'd done it before when we'd been in the boxing ring.

"Whatever," he mumbled. Ruin removed his jacket since the sun was finally showing up from behind some clouds. "So…," he drew out, "you interested?"

"In what?" I knew what he was talking about. He'd already given me shit for storming in there—even though I'd just wanted a damn coffee—when we noticed a guy hanging all over the counter in front of Channa. The dickhead was some meathead who thought his shit didn't stink, and now he and Channa were going to see a movie together.

It didn't sit right inside me.

Surely, he wasn't Channa's type.

Not that I cared.

"You know what I mean. It's not like you're in a relationship. The one with Anna ended, what, three months ago?"

I shrugged. "Somethin' like that." Anna and I had been together for nearly a year, but towards the end, it'd felt like there was a missing piece. At first, it'd been good… no, great. But that had a lot to do with the chemistry, maybe. Yeah, we got along, but she kept harping at me to take her for a ride on the bike. We were dating, but I saved that spot for the one woman I knew I'd spend the rest of my life with. She was probably right when she said I'd doomed our relationship from the start because I refused to let her ride on the back, already knowing she wasn't a keeper. I'd felt like a dick for hurting her, but I couldn't help it. I'd known she wasn't the one, but I still enjoyed her company enough to keep her around.

Fuck me, I sounded like a damn bastard.

Though, she wasn't too upset when she slipped into a brother's bed the weekend after I broke it off.

"Are you interested?" he asked again.

Raising a brow, I questioned, "Why you askin'? Are you?"

"Maybe."

I clenched my jaw to stop myself from frowning. Why did I care who Channa dated? I didn't. Shit, I'd only met her a few hours ago. Yeah, she seemed like an all right kind of woman, but it seemed like I'd only just got rid of Anna. Plus, I'd gone and stuffed things up by having a club bunny suck me off one night when I was tanked. Since then, the bitch Genny wouldn't leave me alone. She thought I'd wanted more from her, and she'd been wrong. Now I had my own damn stalker.

Women were trouble, and I wasn't in the mood to add more trouble to my life.

Glancing away, I pulled apart my jaw and said, "Go for it." Those words tasted sour in my mouth. I ignored it though.

Ruin hummed under his breath, waiting for me to react. I didn't. He could think what he wanted.

My gaze caught movement down the side of the bakery. A man who looked in his sixties stopped at the corner of the building and waved us over. He'd been one of the two inside speaking to Channa.

Ruin and I shared an amused glance before heading over. When we stopped in front of the man, he dropped his hands to his hips and asked, "What are you going to do about the situation with Channa?"

"What do you know?" Ruin asked.

"That she dropped into your shit for helping a guy out. Now it could come back and bite her on the arse." He ground his teeth together, then sucked in a deep breath through his nose. "I've got her moving in with me. I have better security and enough weapons to protect her. I'll let the Hawks MC do drive-bys, but I have her back while she's in my house."

Well shit, what could we say to that? We were comfortable that he knew what happened, and Dad could hate it, but if this guy wanted to protect a woman who meant something to him, we wouldn't say no.

"Are you her dad?"

"No. That piece of shit—" He shook his head. "No, I'm not. But the other woman who works with us, Denise, we see Channa as our family. So if anything does happen, I'll bring hell down on you all."

I stilled. I got where he was coming from, but still.

"We understand your concern, but take care who you're talkin' to like that, old man. We'd never want to risk anyone or have anyone in our business, but if Channa hadn't helped us out, a brother would be dead. We have her back in every damn way so that the shit doesn't land on her."

He grunted and eyed us some more. "Good," he stated, and after that, he rattled off his address. "She works from three in the morning to two in the afternoon, so she'll be here. Then at my place the rest of the time. She works hard so she won't mind just heading back to rest after. She'll be here on her own until Denise and I come in. I usually stick around until four, finishing some things, but today I'll take her to her place to pack and then to mine to settle her in before coming back to finish what I need to. Denise is here on her own to close at six. Do we need to worry about her?"

"No. I'll get someone here just in case. Someone will pick Channa up at three in the morning to bring her to work. They'll stay in the shop until someone else is in there with her. Another brother will take her home at two and stay there until you're back. She'll be covered at all times. Same as the shop and even her house when she's not there. Once things are sorted and we know she's in the clear, things'll go back to the way they were for you all."

He nodded and his hand came out. I took it when he said, "Name's Stanley Penbrook."

"Coyote, and this is Ruin. Make sure whoever you see around wears our patch."

"I will. Better get back in before she knows I'm

missing or I'll get my arse chewed." With that, he turned and walked back down the side of the building.

"Ruin, Coyote" was called from across the road.

Killer and Vicious stood just outside a vehicle beside our rides. They were there to take over our shift. For some reason, maybe it was because I felt I owed Channa, I wanted to stay around. However, I knew it wouldn't be worth it. I needed to check on my business, get some rest, and take another shift.

"Hey," Ruin called, a smirk playing on his lips, and I knew he was going to give his brother-in-law shit.

"Killer, Vicious, how's the tribe?" I asked before Ruin could start.

Vicious snorted. "I only have one, and she's well." Vicious moved back to town with his old lady—Ruin's sister, Nary, about a month ago. Vicious was helping his woman open up a shelter for women in town. I wasn't sure if they'd stick around after it, but it was good to have them around. Even if they hadn't lived far when they were in Caroline Springs.

"Mine are good," Killer said. Killer was usually straight-faced and tight-lipped, but when it came to his twins, he liked to talk about them. His old lady, Ivy, or Chatter as we called her, owned a café in town. Not that she worked there much. Since they had the twins, both boys, they kept her ran off her feet instead. Killer had his own construction company with Stoke, Ruin's dad, but they still helped out everywhere they could in the club. Killer was also the enforcer for the Hawks MC.

"You better be treating my sister right, Vicious," Ruin taunted.

"Fuck off, Ruin."

Ruin grinned, shaking his head. "You know, she was just tellin' me the other day she wasn't happy in marriage—"

Vicious tagged the front of Ruin's tee and was in his face. "Another word, and I'll tell her about that woman you left crying at the compound."

Ruin's mouth snapped shut. He shoved Vicious off, who was now smirking. "It wasn't like that. The woman thought there was something between us when there wasn't."

Vicious shrugged. "Whatever."

Moving on, I said, "Talon filled you in, but things have just changed." I told them what Stanley had said.

Killer nodded. "We'll follow behind them, and when he leaves his place, we'll stay to keep an eye on her."

"We'll head to the compound before we split to do our own shit and let Talon know someone will have to patrol by her house every hour."

Killer sighed. "Fuckin' sucks we're back to patrollin' regularly, all because of these cunts."

I nodded. "Agreed. Let's damn hope they're smart enough to take a meet with us."

"So far Talon hasn't had any luck," Killer said.

"Fuck," Ruin barked.

"You two head off, get some rest," Vicious said.

Yeah, we'd already been up the night before when Ruin got the call from Channa. I was damn tired, yet I felt a tug towards the bakery. In a way, I wanted to stay, wanted to at least inform Channa we were going.

But I didn't.

There was no point in getting unnecessarily involved.

RUIN and I walked through the compound and greeted brothers on the way to the back office where I knew Dad would be. Ruin knocked on the door and when we heard Talon, who I pointedly addressed by his name rather than Dad when at the club, on the other side order, "Enter," Ruin opened the door and stepped in.

"Wildcat, how you doin'?" Ruin said, walking to my mum with his arms open.

"Touch her and die, Ruin," Talon snarled.

Mum laughed, probably thinking he didn't mean it when he actually did.

"I'm good, Ruin." She smiled, and then it grew when she saw me standing in the doorway. "Cody," she called and started for me, wrapping me up in a tight hug. Mum refused to call me Coyote, even though it was Ruby, my sister, who was a twin with Drake, who'd come up with it. When she was young and said my name, it always sounded like she was saying Coyote, and when Maya informed the family coyotes were cunning and smart, it stuck and became my club name as well.

Yet, to Mum, I would only ever be her Cody. She

wasn't my real mother, but I saw her as more of a mum than the biological one. Honestly, Zara was the best. It was she who made me want to find that someone special in my life. What my parents had together was strong and damn kickarse. Yeah, they fought and teased, but they loved each other something fierce.

"Hey, Mum," I said against her temple, where I kissed her as well. "How's Ruby and Drake?"

She slapped my arm. "How about you pop into the house and find out? It's been too long since you've come for a family dinner."

"It's been three weeks since I've come home."

"Three weeks, Cody. *Three* weeks. That's three family dinners you've missed."

"How about I promise to come to the next ten… when this stuff is over?"

She narrowed her gaze. "Ten?"

"Ten."

She turned to Talon. "When will all this, whatever it is, be over?"

"In a week or two hopefully."

She grinned. "Okay. I better go anyway. I have another meeting at the high school for Drake." She kissed my cheek, went to Talon and gave him a quick peck on the lips, which he didn't seem happy with since he pulled her into a longer one. Something I turned away from because when it was your parents, you just didn't need to see that shit. With a laugh, she waved to Ruin and left.

After she was out of earshot, Ruin and I gave a

detailed report. It was probably too soon for any of the gang members to show up for retaliation, which was why we'd have to be vigilant from now on.

"Are you two good to do the morning shift? Get her to work at three?" Talon asked.

"Works for me," Ruin replied.

I nodded. "I'm good."

"Griz and Stoke will be taking over from Killer and Vicious, so you'll be on after them." He was telling us so we knew who we had to look out for. "Go get some rest, Ruin. Coyote, want a word."

"I'm out. Coyote, I'll meet you at your place and we'll ride together, yeah?"

I tipped my chin up. "You got it." When the door shut behind him, I faced Talon again. "What's up?" I asked, shifting to sit in the seat opposite him and lifting a leg up to rest on my knee.

"Your mum's worried about you. She only recently heard you broke up with Anna—"

I groaned. "Dad." For me, whenever we were alone or at home, Talon was Dad, but in every other scenario, he was Talon. He understood why I called him Talon around the brothers. After all, it would seem weird if there was a situation and I was calling him Dad in front of everyone.

"Boy, you know how she gets. She thinks you're down in the dumps about the break-up."

"I'm not."

"I know. I tried to tell her that and about how Anna

moved on quickly, but she's thinking Anna broke your heart and she wanted me to check on you."

Laughing softly, I shook my head. "Honestly, I'm fine. More than fine. Anna wasn't it for me. She wasn't the one. You can tell Mum that. Business has just been busy. I'm still looking into openin' another place in Melbourne. I didn't realize three weeks had gone by without me being home."

He nodded. "I get it. You're young and got a shit-ton of things to do. I'll try and get her to back off with the worrying."

I snorted. "It won't happen. We both know it."

He grinned. "Yeah, we do. You still like living above the shop?" he asked. I'd moved above the Harley shop as soon as the second level got built a year ago.

"I do." I smirked. "You can tell Mum that as well."

He chuckled, leaning back on his chair. "Read right through that, huh?"

"Hell yes, because I know you'd know I'm fine living away from my parents at twenty-eight. You'd think she'd be used to it since I moved out when I was twenty-five."

"That's true. But she's never liked any of the places you've lived because then you're not home and protected."

I winced.

"What was that look?" Dad demanded.

"What look?"

"Like you know somethin' but don't want to say it."

Rolling my eyes, I asked, "You seriously got that from one look?"

"Boy, I know you. I know all my kids. What's goin' on?"

Shit. It wasn't for me to say, and honestly, I wasn't sure who'd be freaked out more between Mum and Dad.

"Dad, it's not my business to share."

He studied me for a moment with a scowl on his face. His brows shot up. "It's Maya. Fuck, is Maya thinkin' of movin' out?"

"I don't know what you're talkin' about." Fuck me, I was going to have to call my sister as soon as I was out of here.

"She is. Motherfuckin' hell. She can't. She's only twenty-one."

"Nearly twenty-two. I would have been gone around the same age if Mum hadn't guilted me into stayin' longer."

He nodded and ran a hand over his face. "Yeah, I get that. Maybe Kitten'll talk Maya into stayin' longer." He stood and started for the door. "Get some rest."

"Where are you goin'?"

"To talk to my woman."

Jesus Christ. Maya was going to kill me.

"Get some rest," he ordered again, shutting the door behind himself.

Quickly, I pulled my phone out. Maya answered after the third ring. "Hey, bro. Dad said you had to stay around and watch out for the woman who helped Texas out, how'd it go?"

"Good, but no time for that. I fucked up, Doc."

She sighed. "What did you do?"

"I didn't say anythin', but apparently Dad can read me and somehow he knows you're thinkin' of movin' out."

A pained groan dropped out of her. "Oh God. War has come."

"You're overreacting a bit." I cringed, knowing that she probably wasn't.

"Really?" she snapped. *"Really?* I'm overreacting? What about when Dad spoke to the basketball association because he thought our shorts were too short? Or when he didn't want me to go to uni? Then there was the time Dad nearly choked my first date as he threatened him to keep his hands to himself. How about when Dad tried to ground me for wearing a summer dress? When Dad—"

"I get it. Dad's a little overprotective."

She snorted. "Yeah, okay, we'll go with a little. He's as protective with me as Mum is with you. It's like they talked about this before we grew up and decided which child they'd protect more. Mum's cool with things I do when Dad isn't, and it's opposite for you." She groaned again. "I'm going to be living at home until I'm thirty."

"Shit, sorry, Doc." Though I couldn't help but smile since I was a bit protective of my sister as well. Her shorts for basketball *had* been too short; I'd heard guys talking about them. Plus, her first date was a douche, and I'd wanted to punch him on first sight.

"You're not sorry. I bet you're smiling crazily right now. You're nearly as bad as Dad. I'll get payback. You know that, right?"

Fuck. "Yeah, I do."

She cackled. "Good."

"Now, tell me the verdict on Texas."

She sighed. "Besides the bruises and cuts all over him, he has four cracked ribs."

"Damn. Did you and him talk—"

"I've got to go. Talk soon, bro."

I snorted. It was like that as soon as I brought anything up between them. "Yeah, yeah. Good luck with Dad," I teased.

"Screw you," she snarled and then ended the call. I couldn't help but laugh. But in the end, if she needed me to speak to Dad about her moving, I would. I'd help any of my family out when they needed it.

CHAPTER SIX

CHANNA

I hated my early mornings even more now.

It'd been a week since things had happened and I was *still* living at Stanley's. The Hawks MC were *still* protecting me, and they *still* hadn't heard from the gang leader for things to be settled. The only plus side was that nothing else had happened. From what I knew, no one suspicious-looking had been by my place or the bakery.

What had turned my early morning from mild irritation to hate was how I got to work. It wasn't on my own. *Oh no,* I wasn't allowed to. I had to be transported to and from work by a Hawks MC member, and in the mornings, it was always, *always* Cody and Ruin.

Ruin was fine; he was a jokester and was always

flirty and sweet, yet there was a seriousness beneath the surface.

It was the other man who rattled me in ways I hadn't been before. He watched a lot, was quiet, yet spoke when he felt it was necessary. He even sometimes asked questions, but it was his proximity that drove me nuts. He seemed to always be in the way, specifically because in the mornings, they refused to stay outside when I was on my own in the bakery in case someone came in from the back. No, they wanted to be up in my grill when I was baking.

In the first few days, I messed up a couple of recipes and felt like a moron. It put me behind, and I had to deal with Stanley when he came in complaining it was too hot. Though, the heat from the ovens helped me blame my red cheeks on the warmth in the room when Cody got too close.

"Mornin'," Cody greeted when I climbed into the SUV.

"Hey," I said and glanced in the back. "Where's Ruin?"

"Meetin' us there." He put his hand to the back of my seat and looked over his shoulder when he backed out. I'd asked the first time why he didn't just use the darn reversing camera. He said he didn't trust it. I gritted my teeth and tensed when his thumb brushed my shoulder.

Why was he doing this to me? Did he expect a reaction? It didn't make sense because other than these little touches, he didn't come across like he wanted more from me. He wasn't really flirty, like Ruin… just nice.

Although, I could just be reading into this more than I was supposed to. He could want to just be friendly. I hadn't been around him with other women present, so I didn't know what he was like with others.

Crap, I had to keep my emotions in check. It could all just be because *I* was attracted to *him.*

Right. I would steel myself, my heart, until this was over, and then I wouldn't see him again.

I could go another week or two like this.

I could.

"Got you a coffee," he said when he started driving and nodded down between our seats.

Stupid nice gesture. "Thanks," I replied. It was the first time he'd brought a coffee. Nope, I wouldn't think into it. Usually I made one at the shop, but he'd got it before even picking me up. Slyly, I glanced around to see if he got Ruin one, but I couldn't see a third.

The stupid nice gesture wouldn't work on me.

It wouldn't.

I took a sip of the warm coffee and shut my brain down. The bakery wasn't far, and as soon as I was in there, I could just get to work and forget he was even about.

At least I'd try.

Glancing out my window, my eyes widened, and I screamed, "Cody!" A vehicle slammed into the side. I heard Cody curse. The seat belt tightened as our car shifted, rolled. I put my hands out, but they were shoved back as an arm whacked into my chest. My head banged into the window, eyes slammed closed, glass shattered, and the seat belt pulled tight again before everything stopped.

Blinking dazedly, the first thing I noticed was that we were upside down. My whole body ached, but the worst of the pain was in my head and chest.

"Cody?" I whispered. "Cody?" My heart thundered in my ears, even over the ringing. Slowly, I turned my head to see Cody hanging there lifelessly. "No, no, no, no," I sobbed. Blood dripped from somewhere near his head and arm, down onto the roof.

Wincing, I reached around to undo my seat belt and cried out when it gave and I fell to the roof. A hiss escaped me when glass sliced my arms, but I ignored the pain and frantically got to my knees. Reaching out, I held my breath as I pressed two fingers to the pulse at his neck.

Oxygen rushed out of me when I felt a steady rhythm pushing against my fingers. I dropped my hand and sighed.

Thank you, God.

A scream tore out of me when something suddenly grabbed me from behind. It dragged me backwards, and I tried to grip something, anything, but my hands were slimy and everything I touched slipped through my fingers.

Still, I fought when I was free. I screamed, I kicked, I hit… until something hard was pushed against my temple.

"Remember me, bitch? Move and I'll shoot." He kicked me and I moved with it, rolling over.

My gaze landed on the man who'd held the gun to Texas. Tears welled, my throat thickened, and my body shook.

Was this it?

Was this where I died?

All because I helped a man, all because I wouldn't allow someone to die when I could stop it? Would I have changed my decision? No, no I wouldn't.

Three others stepped up behind him and utter terror burned inside me. It froze me. One person I could take on, even with his gun, but more? I didn't like my chances.

No.

No.

I couldn't, *wouldn't* sit around and take whatever they were about to do. I didn't go through what I had already in life and give up when things were good.

Licking my dry lips, I tipped my chin up and said, "Yes, I remember you." I laughed. "I remember I kicked your arse and you ran away like a twat."

His face reddened in anger. I was sure this was it. This was where I would be shot and killed.

However, a voice snarled from behind me, "Drop your fuckin' weapon and back away from her." My heart gave a hard leap at the sound of Cody's voice.

"You stupid, man? You shoot me, I'll kill her."

The men behind him pulled out more guns.

If Cody could shoot the three behind him while

protecting himself, I could take down the one in front of me. The one who got butthurt because a woman had beat him. Only how could I relay my message without saying anything?

Slowly, I glanced over my shoulder.

"Eyes here, bitch," the man snarled, then kicked me in the thigh. Wincing, I looked back and his gaze moved over me, back to Cody. "You're outnumbered." He smiled. "Go get him," he ordered. His other goons started around him, then froze. "What the fuck you doin'?" he asked.

They stepped back. I wanted to see what had their eyes widening, had them swallowing in fear. But I didn't. I had to keep my focus on the main threat.

"It seems you think you have the upper hand, arsehole. Try again." That sounded like Ruin.

"You're surrounded, motherfucker. Back away from Channa, now." What in the hell was Stanley doing there?

One of the men in front of me said, "That's a fucking rocket launcher."

Dear God, Stanley had brought a "toy" from his house. But how did he know something was going on?

The men in front of me all tensed when we listened to the loud roar of bikes coming our way.

"Do not fuckin' move," Cody ordered.

The other goons started cursing the main guy, but he ignored them and focused down on me. I saw it then, the clear decision in his eyes. Before the Hawks MC arrived, he was going to make me pay. The bikes drew closer; shouting started, especially when the man in front of me didn't look away.

His hand shook a little. He was shitting bricks. Right then I knew I would have to do something, and quick.

I slapped my hands to the ground, used them to pick up my body, ignoring the pain through me, and I pushed down to sweep my foot under his. He stumbled to the side but managed to jump it. I kicked my body up with all my might to stand before him. I punched forward, right towards his throat. Startled, he dropped the gun, his hands gripping his throat as he fought for breath.

Fury still blinded me. I hit him again and again, in the stomach, his shoulder. Kicking out my foot, I pushed, and he tripped backwards, falling to the ground. He rolled, reaching for the gun, and in the next second, someone dropped down on top of the man, restraining him.

As I tried to catch my breath, I rested a hand against my chest and took a step back. I noticed then others had surrounded us. Bikes were parked all around, and men from the Hawks MC were seizing the other douches. I'd heard their bikes but didn't realise they'd arrived.

How could I have not heard them surrounding us?

"Channa?" was called behind me. Turning, I spotted Stanley, along with Cody and Ruin, making their way over. I blinked; wetness touched my cheeks. My hands shook when I pulled them up to wipe it away.

"Fuck, kid, fuck," Stanley muttered, pulling me into his arms.

I sucked in a ragged breath and made a noise in the back of my throat. My whole body was shaking now. The adrenaline had worn off, and all I kept repeating in my head was how I could have died.

Only I must have said it aloud, because in the next moment, I was moved from one set of arms to another. A hand cupped the back of my head, and Cody's deep, gruff voice whispered, "You're all right, baby. You're fine, you're here. You're all right."

I nodded into his chest, but I couldn't stop shaking. My arms lay limp at my sides, and my body throbbed, some spots more painful than others.

"How'd you know?" he asked, but I knew he wasn't talking to me because Ruin answered.

"Wasn't far from here, heard the crash, and I just fuckin' knew. Called the brothers."

The hand at my head didn't stop from gently running up and down. It helped me catch my breath, helped me settle a little.

"What about you?" Cody asked.

"I always check from my window that you guys pick her up, saw her get into the car, but then something told me to keep watching. Caught a car following. Got some things together and came as soon as I could."

"Man, a rocket launcher?" Ruin said.

"It got the pissants' attention, didn't it?"

Ruin chuckled. "It sure fuckin' did. Good job, old

man." There was a pause, and then Ruin said softly, "She okay?"

"Yeah, just in shock," Cody answered.

Why was this time so different? Why couldn't I get a handle on it like I had done the first time? I looked weak. I was acting weak.

"You two get to the hospital," a new voice said.

I didn't want to go to hospital. I just wanted to go home, my actual home, and crawl into bed to sleep for a week.

Cody tensed. "Dad—"

"No, Cody. You were in a motherfuckin' crash. Hospital to get checked out. Ruin, you take them. Stanley, is it?"

And suddenly I didn't want to open my mouth to say I didn't want to go. Talon sounded a bit scary. Then again, I would love to open my mouth and say something, but it was like I was outside my body or an alien had sucked out my brain and it wasn't working any longer.

I just wanted to cry. I wanted to curl into a ball. I wanted to stop picturing the crash and the way Cody had been limp in his seat. How there was so much blood.

"Yep," Stanley replied, the word sounding light like he was smiling.

"You mind givin' them a lift?"

"Not at all."

"Dad, I don't need to—"

"For her, you go. Hear me?"

"I would have taken her still. *I* just don't need to see a doctor."

"You want me to call your mum? You got blood all over you, boy. Get checked over."

His hand at my lower back pressed in for a moment. He sighed, and I felt it brush over my hair. "What about the situation here?" he asked.

"I'll get your aunt onto it."

"Those fuckers?"

"They're goin' to the compound. Bet their fuckin' leader will speak to me now."

His chin briefly touched the top of my head; he must have nodded. "Keep me updated."

"Same goes for you. Ruin, take care of them."

"You got it, Prez," Ruin answered. "Let's go, guys."

"I've got her," Cody said softly with an arm around my waist. He wrapped the other around my arm closest to him as he led me towards another car. "I've got you," Cody whispered into my temple. Did he know my gaze had drifted to the car we'd been in? Did he know it kept replaying in my head?

I nodded as he opened the back door to the car for me. I slid in, wincing when cuts and scrapes pulled. He closed the door and walked around to the other side while Ruin and Stanley climbed in the front. Cody jumped in next to me, and I took a shuddering breath.

I had to push the crash back, push the man holding the gun to me away. I had to be strong.

"Is it over?" I asked quietly.

Cody took my hand. "It will be."

I glanced at him for the first time and saw the blood, saw the cut. Just as I reached out, I pulled my hand back. "Are you okay?"

"I'm fine," he told me.

I nodded again. It would be over. I would build up my wall inside me and block what I could out of the night… eventually. I would go back to how things were.

"My bakery—"

"Don't you worry, Channa. It can close for one day at least," Stanley said from the front.

He was right. "Can you call Denise for me?" I asked.

"Of course. Soon as we get in the hospital."

"Stanley," I called.

"Yeah, kid?"

"Did you really bring a rocket launcher with you?"

Ruin snorted, Cody chuckled low, and Stanley nodded. "Sure did."

A giggle escaped me when I pictured old Stanley with a rocket launcher on his shoulder, aiming at the bastards. Another laugh dropped from my lips, and suddenly lightness filled me. I relaxed back in the seat and shared a small smile with Cody.

It was over.

No more guns, no more arseholes, and no more car crashes.

It was over, so I had a right to feel better even when my body ached. I had a right to feel safer now I knew the Hawks men would deal with the rest.

"How does a person even get a rocket launcher?" Ruin asked.

I snorted, then laughed, holding my stomach because it hurt.

"I have my ways," Stanley answered, and then said nothing more when Ruin hounded him.

At the hospital, I thought they would call the police after we shared we were in a car accident. They didn't, and I had a feeling it had something to do with the Hawks MC and the people they knew. The cuts were cleaned, our heads scanned, and it turned out Cody had a concussion. Mine was just a bad headache from hitting my head. Though, I had bruised ribs and a bandaged arm where one of the cuts needed stitches. To my embarrassment, Cody had told them how I reacted after everything, and they were sure it was shock and nothing else. Since I was more back to myself as time went by, he believed them.

We were sent on our way with prescriptions of pain meds, which Ruin picked up from a twenty-four-hour pharmacy on the way to Stanley's.

"Are you sure I can't just go back to my place?" I asked once more.

"No," Stanley stated. "One more night at my place and then I'll get the dogs back to your house before I come into work tomorrow. Yeah?"

"Okay. Denise was okay about everything?"

"As I said, she was pissed, shocked, but she's fine. Are *you* sure you want to go back to work tomorrow?"

"Yes, I need to. You know I hate closing the place down." We pulled into Stanley's driveway and I saw another car sitting at the curb. The one Ruin said would be there for him and Cody to take when they left.

"You need to hire someone to help," Cody said from beside me.

I nodded. "I'm going to look into it soon."

He smiled. "Just rest today then, yeah?"

"I will…. Um, are you going to be okay? You should rest, but not too much, have someone check on you every hour if you do." I sounded like an idiot. I'd said everything the doctor had, so he didn't need me repeating it.

"I'll be fine," he told me.

We all got out of the car, and when Cody walked around to my side, he took my hand. My heart fluttered. "I'll come see you tomorrow—"

My belly dipped. "You don't have to. I'm fine now, and sorry for freaking out on you. It just got to me once I knew things were going to be okay."

"Don't apologize. I get it. Fuck, Channa, you were brave."

I glanced away and shook my head but didn't say anything.

"I'll see you tomorrow," he said again. I'd opened my mouth to say something when his finger landed on my lips. "Nuh-uh, I'll be seeing you, and then you can tell me how you knew my name."

Oh shit. "I-I don't know what you're talking about."

He smirked. "You do." With a wink, he dropped my hand and nodded towards the front of the house where Stanley stood waiting.

I didn't know what to say. I probably couldn't say anything anyway because I had to use all my energy thinking of a lie for when he popped in tomorrow.

Shit, again.

And just when I thought I wouldn't have to see him again and the past could stay in the past. Luck just wasn't on my side, and it seemed Cody Marcus was going to stick around a little longer.

CHAPTER SEVEN

COYOTE

*R*uin and I got into the car left for us. I sat in the passenger seat and stared at the house until Stanley and Channa went inside. Again, I thought about Channa, when she cried out my name, my *real* name, right before they crashed into us. How'd she know my name?

I was sure no one had said it that first night, and I was looking forward to seeing what she'd say since when I'd already questioned her, she'd looked like a deer caught in the headlights. Scared. Only nothing like she had been after everything that happened. Christ, she'd put fear in me when I'd seen her on the ground and the motherfucker pointing a gun at her, and then again when, after it all ended, she hadn't been herself.

Anger had me fisting my hands and clenching my jaw. Those cunts nearly had her, and on my watch. It was damn lucky she knew how to handle herself.

"You think she'll be okay?" Ruin asked.

"Yeah, eventually." And she would. I could tell when the shock had worn off and she started being herself again that she'd found the strength to move on. She was damn brave. Damn amazing.

"She kicked arse again. Was a sight to see."

"It was. Though, why did she learn in the first place? Not many women would want to learn self-defence unless there was another reason." I couldn't help but think it had something to do with her father. The way Stanley spoke of him told me he thought her dad was a pile of shit. What had happened?

"You're right. You think she has other troubles?"

"I think she *had* them, but not now."

"You wanna find out though, don't you?"

"I do."

"So…," he drew out. "You still reckon I can have a go at her?" My upper lip rose before I could blank my expression. Ruin started laughing. "Yeah, that's what I thought."

"Don't know what you're talkin' about," I said, ignoring the foul taste in my mouth.

"Brother, don't bullshit me."

"I ain't."

"Yeah right. She sure looked comfy in your arms."

"*Brother*, I was consoling her after all the shit she'd been through."

"Yeah, yeah. What a fucked-up situation. Never thought they'd be stupid enough to ram the damn car. Why now?"

"My guess? He was gettin' sick of waitin'. Probably thought he would take one of us on, but not two." I paused as a burning sensation started in my chest. "He nearly had her—"

"Brother—"

"No. He did. If I hadn't fuckin' woke up when I did, he would have shot and killed her."

"Coyote, don't go down that road. Things worked out."

Through my tight jaw, I snarled, "She shouldn't have been damn involved in the first place. Those fuckers have to pay."

"You know they will. Prez will make sure of it, and when we get to the compound, we'll find out more. But how're you feelin'?"

I snorted. My head was fucking killing me and my body felt like it'd gone a few rounds in the boxing ring. "Fine."

He chuckled. "I call bullshit again, but I'll let the prez deal with you."

No matter. I wouldn't leave the damn compound until all this crap was over, for Channa's sake. She needed to go back to her normal life. A life I could tell she was happy in. There could be a few changes to her life, like a few new people in it because I knew Ruin wanted to get to know her. Maybe he did want to date her. I also wanted to find out some things about her, and to do that, we'd have to spend some time together. The thought of that sounded good to me.

At the compound, I climbed out of the car a bit slower than I normally would. Yet, even with how shit I felt, I would still be there so I could get my own hits in on the motherfuckers.

We made our way into the common room. Even in the early hours a few brothers were hanging around on their day off with some club bunnies. To start with, the club didn't have women hanging about who were after a brother for the night because Mum hated it. Over the years, she'd been more lenient. She also trusted Dad completely. She didn't want to hold the brothers back from enjoying their lives.

"Trig," I called. "Where's the prez?"

"Office, I think. Glad you're okay, Coyote." A few others called out something similar.

With a wave, I said, "Thanks, brothers."

He saluted me with a drink. I glanced at Ruin, only he'd stopped by the TV and looked tense. "Ruin?" I called and then glanced at the screen. A guy was on stage singing something.

"Comin'," he said, and with a final look at the TV, he moved towards me.

"You know him?"

"Yeah, you should too. He's a year older than Swan and used to live next door to her. They were friends. A couple of years ago, he and his family moved to the US. Guess he made it big." He shrugged.

"How'd you know about that?"

He chuckled. "Griz was complain' to Stoke one day when I was over there, sayin' he hated the friendship they had, went on and on about it. He wanted to kick the guy's arse, even though he was a kid, because he used to look at Swan like she'd hung the moon for him. Bet Griz was happy when they moved."

"Huh, never heard of him. What was his name?"

"Lochlan Humphrey."

"It ain't ringing any bells."

"Doesn't matter anyway." He smiled and reached out to knock on the office door.

"Enter," Talon called. Ruin opened it and stepped through. I followed. Already in the office were Griz, Blue, Vicious, Killer, Stoke, and Cowboy. He was a younger member, just twenty-one—a good guy who helped me out at the business a lot.

"You should be restin'," Talon tried. I stared him down. "Yeah, I'd be the fuckin' same."

"Heard from their leader?" I asked.

"We're expectin' a call any second, since Killer used one of the guys' phones and sent a video of one of the captives gettin' worked over."

Fucking good. I knew they would have gone about it the right way. Killer wouldn't have shown his own face or his tats. He wouldn't have worn his cut in it either. Totally anonymous, but still, since they were fucking with us, they'd know where it would come from.

"They tell you anythin'?" Ruin asked.

Griz snorted. "Sang like cockatoos."

"You mean canaries," Cowboy said.

Griz glared. "What?"

"The sayin' is sang like canaries." When Griz just stared Cowboy down, he added, "But it doesn't matter what kind of bird it is."

Blue snickered; Stoke flat-out laughed.

"What did they say?" I asked.

"Sit before you fall down, Coyote," Talon demanded, nodding to the chair in front of his desk.

I wasn't going to be a fool and argue since I felt like crap, so I did.

"Apparently the main guy, whose name's Cub, was goin' after Channa on his own. He roped those guys into helpin' because he wanted payback on her since she made him look like a little pussy," Stoke explained.

"Did they say what they think we stole off them?" Ruin asked.

"All he said was that we'd have to take it up with their leader. But if that fucker doesn't tell us what it is, we'll do some more work on the guys we have. I want this finished by the time night falls," Talon said.

"Agreed," I stated coldly, just as some of the other brothers did.

The phone rang. We shared a look before Talon put it on speaker. "Speak," he ordered.

"This is Wolf. I'm the leader of the Takahashi family and see you have some of my men."

"I'm not sure what you're talkin' about," Talon answered. In case the phone call was compromised, he couldn't say too much. "But how about we meet and sort a few things out?"

There was silence for a few beats. "I'm out the front of the compound." The call ended. Shock rocked through me.

"He's got some damn big balls," Blue said.

"He does. Let's go see what he has to say." Talon stood, and we followed him outside. Others tried to join, but Talon told them to stay back. When we neared the locked gate, a lone man stood on the other side.

What the fuck was this? Did he think he was invincible? Unless his men were hidden somewhere close. I glanced around, like other brothers were doing, but didn't see anything out of place. This Wolf guy, who had an Asian background, didn't look like he belonged to a thug gang. A mobster one, yeah, with his crisp white suit, black shirt, and long jacket. His long dark hair was neatly tied at the back of his neck. His eyes were what told us he had confidence and something a little crazy in them.

"Talon, I presume?" He even didn't sound like a damn gang member. He spoke clear and correct.

"Yeah, and you're Wolf." Talon stopped just on the other side of the gate and crossed his arms over his chest. "You've come alone."

He nodded. "In good faith."

Blue snorted. "Good faith? After one of yours caused not one, but fuckin' two crashes *and* near deaths of some of ours?"

Wolf's jaw clenched. "Cub acted alone. He's… let's say… unruly. I never wanted anyone hurt. I only ordered him to ask questions, but he has something against your club that isn't a part of my gang. I reside in Melbourne and have a few members who travel from here to the city. Cub was one of them. It was lucky I was in town checking on them when the situation happened."

"You sayin' he went out on his own for all this shit?" Talon asked.

"Yes."

Talon's silence told us he wasn't sure whether to believe this guy. Still, Talon put his hands on his waist and stated, "He has to pay for what he's done. Two brothers are injured, and so is a woman who's under the club's protection. He was going to *kill* them all if he had his damn way."

"I wouldn't think he'd kill—"

"He had a gun to a brother's head. A gun to the woman's, and everyone who was there could see the intent in his fuckin' eyes. He was gonna kill them. If you don't believe that, I can give you the reports on the damn injuries. *No one* gets away with hurtin' anyone in Hawks."

His nostrils flared, and the hands at his sides fisted. "Fucking fool," he snarled to the ground. He looked up and met Talon's hard gaze. "He's yours."

"What?" Talon demanded, his brows shooting up in surprise. I wouldn't have seen it if I wasn't standing beside him.

"Do with him what you will. He acted alone, thinking he could climb the ladder by doing something foolish without consequences. He was wrong. Punish him however you choose. I don't want problems with the Hawks MC, just an answer."

Talon ignored the last part and asked, "The others that were with him?"

"Three, I believe?"

Talon nodded.

"They were stupid to follow Cub in the first place. Put fear in them, and then if they haven't done anything to anyone in your club, release them."

"You want us to teach them a lesson?" Griz asked.

Who the fuck was this guy?

"If you believe they need it, yes."

"Who the fuck are you?" Talon barked. "And what do you think we stole off you?"

He smiled. It was only slight, but still there. "As I said, I am Wolf. I control a large part of Melbourne, the women, drugs, and weaponry. I have seen what the Hawks MC can do. I want you to know we don't have an issue with one another unless you get involved in my business."

"Stay out of our territory and we won't," Talon warned.

He nodded once. "I have heard this and will abide by it."

Talon snorted. "Jesus, you've got some damn balls comin' here without anyone with you. Tell us what you think we stole and then this shit will be done."

"Mimi Takahashi."

"Mimi?" Ruin said, and I glanced at him. Hell, we all did. "She's a club girl."

Wolf snarled. "So, she is here?"

We all shifted our gaze back to him. "What do you want with her?" Talon asked.

"She's my sister."

"And?" Blue pressed.

A tick started at Wolf's temple. He breathed deeply through his nose, which seemed to help him compose himself. "Mimi disappeared. I have been looking for her. She needs to come home."

"When a woman becomes a part of the club, they're protected."

His upper lip rose. "She shouldn't have left in the first place."

"Why did she leave?" Griz asked. We wouldn't even bring her into this if she'd been treated badly in the first place.

"It is not what you're thinking," he said roughly.

"Then tell us, and we'll see if we bring Mimi out he —" Talon was cut off.

"Taro?" The word was spoken from behind us.

Wolf tensed. His gaze moved behind us. "Mimi," he whispered.

"What are you doing here?" Mimi asked. She stepped between Talon and Blue, her hands pressed to her body, one at her chest, the other to her stomach.

"Finding you."

"I'm not coming back."

"Mimi—"

"No, Taro. I told them I refuse. I know it brings shame to the family, but I won't do it."

Wolf glanced around at us, obviously hesitant to speak in front of us, and I couldn't blame the guy. Obviously, it was a family issue.

"I have control over the family now, Mimi."

She gasped, her hand moving up to cup her throat. "Father?"

Wolf clenched his jaw. "I would rather speak with you in private."

She drew in a shuddering breath and nodded.

"Come with me then," Wolf said gently.

"Ruin, you go with them," Talon ordered.

Wolf's gaze hardened when he speared Talon with it. "She is family. She does not need a guard dog with her when with me."

"She's also been Hawks for six months. She's family to us, and she left your family for a reason. I won't have her goin' on her own."

"Mimi," Wolf clipped.

Mimi turned to Talon. "It's okay, Mr Marcus. I'm sorry I brought this trouble to your doorstep, but I will be safe with my brother." It did sound like she trusted her brother, but there was still a situation with her family.

Talon shook his head. "Mimi, girl, you've been here for a while. You know how this works. You walked into this compound and became a part of Hawks. No matter where you're goin' or what type of situation it is, we'll have your back. Take Ruin. He can stand away while you talk. But I'd feel better with a brother there."

Before Mimi could say anything, Wolf did. "Thank

you for protecting her. Ruin is allowed to accompany us."

"Ruin?" Talon called.

"I'll follow behind," he said.

"Keep us posted," Talon ordered.

"You got it, Prez." And with a pat to my back, Ruin moved off to his ride.

Talon lifted his hand and waved. The gates opened slowly. Wolf stayed where he was, and then Talon confirmed, "Nothin' comes back to bite us on the arse with whatever happens to your guy?"

Wolf nodded. "Nothing." His hand reached out. "Mimi?"

Mimi smiled softly up at Talon as she pressed her hand on his arm. "Thank you."

"Darlin', don't do anythin' rash. Let us know what's goin' down, yeah?"

"I will, Mr Marcus."

He shook his head. "Told you a million times, call me Talon."

She grinned and moved over to her brother's side. Ruin's ride roared to life, and we all watched Wolf lead Mimi, with a hand to her back, towards his car.

"Safe to only have Ruin go with him?" Stoke asked. He was probably itching to follow and make sure his son would stay safe.

Talon turned to him. "Do you believe this Wolf guy?"

Stoke's jaw clenched. "Fuck. Yeah, I do." He ran a hand over his head. "If he was lookin' for trouble, he would have come guns ablazin'. He would have fought for his men. The only thing he gave a shit about was his sister."

"That's exactly what I got as well." He tapped Stoke on the arm. "Know it's hard to see them take charge of shit." Talon glanced at me and away. "But hell, they'll be taking over for us soon enough."

I snorted. "Nothin' will keep you away from here, old man."

The brothers chuckled. Talon grinned. "Besides your mum."

"Well, yeah." I left the "duh" part off. "We headin' in to find out why this fucker has a hard-on for Hawks?"

"We are. Then you're gettin' home, and I mean home, so we can keep an eye on you for the night."

"Talon—"

"Concussion, boy. You're lucky your mum's not here wrappin' you in cotton wool."

Blue laughed. "Give her time."

Wait, why wasn't she here hounding me? I whistled. "You haven't told her?"

The brothers chuckled, knowing how much shit Talon was about to get himself in.

"You wanna shut up and help deal with this cunt or do I ring your mum now?"

"I'll be fuckin' helpin'."

Talon grinned and hooked his arm around my shoulders. "Thought that'd be the case." We all started to head back in. Talon leaned in. "You doin' okay?"

I smirked. I knew it wouldn't take him long to ask

quietly. "Headache and a few pains, but I'll be fine. Want to get my hands on this guy."

He nodded. "Can't say I blame you. Now… about you and this bakery woman."

"Nothin's goin' on."

"Coyote."

The brothers had moved ahead, so I said, "Dad. Leave it."

He glanced at me, grinning like an idiot. "All right, I'll leave it after I say one last thing. When you know the right woman for you, don't leave it too long."

Jesus. I didn't know shit except for the fact that I wanted to find out how she knew my real name.

CHAPTER EIGHT

CHANNA

$\mathcal{A}$ll day nerves ate at me like fleas did dogs. I kept making mistakes and dropping things each time I heard the door open. I just wanted the day to end, but the lunch rush had only just finished, and I still had about an hour of things to do before I could get out of here.

Maybe Cody wouldn't even show. Maybe he was just being nice and wanted to check on me. Maybe if he did arrive before I left, I could sneak out the back door and run home.

Wait, I couldn't go home. He knew where I lived. But I had to go home because Stanley had dropped off my babies there.

"Thank you," I said to the customer after I handed

over the change. With a smile, she left the bakery, and I could already feel the heat of a stare on me. I was just glad it wasn't the one I didn't want. Though, this one I could do without as well.

Sighing, I glanced to the side and spotted Denise wiping down the coffee machine while she stared at me. She'd been doing it all day. It was sweet she was worried, but no matter how many times I said I was okay, even though my body still ached like a stripper's would after a hard night, she didn't believe me.

"I'm okay," I told her before she asked.

"Honey, I know I've said this, but you were in a car accident yesterday. You should be home resting. I can see the wincing and cringing with nearly every move." She dropped her rag and stepped closer. "I'm worried about you. How about I do tomorrow—"

"No—"

"Channa." She groaned in frustration.

"Denise, I love you, but you have a little girl to take care of. I promise I'm fine." Her lips pinched. Rolling my eyes, I adjusted to "Okay, I *will* be fine in a couple of days. This is nothing I can't handle." As long as it was truly over.

We both heard the door open, and my heart decided it was time to play with my gut—it dropped so fast.

"Channa, are you okay?" Bryson asked, striding over to the counter.

Slowly, my heart crept back up where it belonged. I smiled at Bryson. "I'm good, why?"

His head jerked back. "Why? You never close the

bakery." His eyes ran over me. "What happened to your head?" He reached out and gently ran a finger over the tape I had there covering the cut. "And your arm?" His fingers grazed the bandage.

Of course, it was then the door opened again and Cody stepped through. His eyes were hard, scary, and on us.

Laughing nervously, I grabbed Bryson's hand in mine and told him, "I just had an accident."

Bryson frowned before he glanced over his shoulder. He tensed, and we both watched Cody approach.

"Channa," Cody said, his voice a little growly.

"Um, hey, ah, Coyote."

Bryson snorted.

It was creepy how slow it took Cody to look at Bryson. "Somethin' funny?"

"Is that really your name?"

"Does it matter if it is? Because I don't really give a shit what you think." His gaze dropped to the counter, and I realized then I still held Bryson's hand. I wanted to drop it, I really did, but I didn't want to do it in front of Cody so he would think I was doing it for him.

Dear God, I just hurt my brain.

"Bryson," Denise called. Her eyes were a little wide. "I have a coffee ready for you."

"In a second," Bryson called back as his hand squeezed mine as he smiled. "I'm glad you're okay. I was worried about you. I tried calling the bakery, but no one was here, and it made me realise I didn't have your mobile number."

He didn't because everything we'd organized, we'd done it while he was at the shop for his coffee. I hadn't seen the need to give him my number, and I'd never asked for his.

I wasn't even sure why I was hesitating to give him my number now. We were friends. We hung out. It wasn't much, but we did. Denise and Stanley had my number and they were my friends also.

"Your coffee's gettin' cold," Cody stated.

Bryson ground his teeth together. "It's fine," he bit out. Rolling his eyes at me, he dropped my hand and pulled out his phone, passing it over to me. "Add your number in and I'll call about that movie."

Again, I hesitated, and I felt guilty for it. If Cody wasn't standing there waiting, watching, I probably would have added my number in right away. And that thought had me reaching for his phone with a small smile. I was being stupid after all. It didn't matter Cody saw me putting a number in a guy's phone. He wasn't anything to me, and Bryson was my friend.

I held it out for him. "There you go. It's saved under Coffee Girl."

He laughed. "Great. I'll text you later, then you'll have my number."

I nodded. "Sounds like a plan."

Bryson winked, dropped some cash on the counter, and moved to the end to pick up his coffee. "Later, Channa."

"Bye," I called, and Cody stepped in front of my line of sight.

Crap, I couldn't run, couldn't hide. I had to face him. I gave him a half-smile. "That was Bryson. He works at the gym and has been coming in here since we opened. We're friends." *Shut up, Channa, shut up.* I shrugged when he kept looking, and added, "Sometimes we catch up, watch movies, go out to eat. Not that we do it much because, you know"—I waved my hand around the shop—"I'm always here working." I nodded. "Yep, this bakery keeps me busy. I'm a busy little beaver."

"Channa," Denise called. I faced her, and she mouthed, "What are you doing?"

I widened my eyes, hoping she knew it was me screaming for help.

"Excuse me, Coyote, sir," Denise called. "Would you like a coffee?"

I sagged, mumbling something like, "I've just got to see if Stanley needs help. Be back." I fled through the doors like my arse was on fire.

Stanley looked over at me from icing a cake a customer had ordered for her husband's birthday. It was a penis cake, and usually thinking of such requests made me smile when customers did things like this for friends or loved ones. Only I didn't smile this time because I was too busy freaking out.

"What's up your arse?"

"Nothing." I snorted and walked over to the bench. "You need a hand?"

His eyes narrowed. "Do you want to wreck this cake?"

"No."

"Then I don't need a hand. Who are you hiding from?"

I laughed, only it wasn't a real one. "No one."

We both turned to the doors when we heard them swish open. It wasn't the only thing swishing; my belly did as well when Cody smirked.

"Ah," Stanley drew out. He rolled his eyes and went back to work after a nod to Cody.

"Channa, how are you feelin'?" Cody asked. He moved over to the wall and leaned there, resting back like he was in the mood for a long chat. I wasn't. I wasn't even in the mood for an itty-bitty one. However, I needed to make sure the mess was honestly over and I would be safe once more.

Suddenly, I felt dizzy as the blood rushed to my head. *Please, God, make things good.*

Instead of answering him, I asked quietly, "Is it over, really?"

He nodded. "Yeah, it is. He won't come after you again."

Did I want to know what happened to him? What did bikers do to men who tried harming them? Put on masks and stab them repeatedly? Did they stick knives to their hands and slash them open over and over…? I really had to stop watching horror movies.

I decided I didn't want to know what they did to him.

Sighing in relief, I felt tension drift from my shoulders. "Thank God."

I didn't know if I was supposed to feel guilty over

being elated that he couldn't hurt me anymore because I wasn't sure if he was still alive or not.

He had been going to kill us. End us. Guilt wasn't supposed to play a part in this scenario. I was supposed to be happy knowing he wasn't out there. That he'd been stopped from hurting me, Cody, and even my family—Denise, Stanley, the dogs.

Yet, guilt niggled away inside me.

"Channa," Stanley called. "Don't you dare."

"What?" Cody asked.

"She's feeling guilty for being happy about knowing he won't bother her."

"What? No, I wasn't." I laughed, the sound forced. "Please, I'm fine."

Cody straightened and took a step my way. "Channa, you don't need to feel guilty. He'll pay for what he's done—"

"I don't want to know how," I blurted, a little too loudly.

Stanley chuckled. "We're not in a damn movie or book, kid. They didn't kill him." He paused and looked over at Cody. "Right?"

Cody's grin was warm, and my belly fluttered, dammit. "He's alive."

"See," Stanley said.

Maybe I did watch too many shows and my mind got carried away.

"Though, we did teach him a lesson," Cody added.

"Like… maths or something?" I stupidly asked. I

wanted to kick myself for it, especially when Stanley *and* Cody chuckled.

"He's been handed over to the cops. They'd somehow found some things on him that he shouldn't have had. He'll be goin' to jail for a long damn time. None of his other friends will do anything either. You've got nothing to worry about or feel guilty over."

"Thank you," I said automatically.

He shook his head. "No thanks needed. We got you into the mess, so we got you out. Hell, we're the ones who are thankful to you."

Heat hit my cheeks. I picked up a tea towel and started wiping down the bench. Stanley shot me a look, one that said he thought I was a fool. I had to agree.

"Anyway," I started. "I better get back to work."

"Aren't you leaving?" Stanley asked.

I punched him in the arm. "Such a joker. I have a billion things to do."

"Channa," Cody said.

"Hmm?" I asked, still wiping at that invisible spot.

"Can I walk you home?"

I stilled. "Um, busy?"

"Channa, you still need to rest," Cody said. He was right, and I felt like a zombie, but I wasn't leaving the shop without protection for me against Cody. He'd ask questions, well *a* question, one I didn't want to talk about. Yes, it was probably stupid, but I couldn't help it.

However, I'd look more pathetic if I kept going as I was.

I nodded. "All right." I glanced at him and away.

Why did he have to be so good-looking? "I'll just get my things and we'll head off."

"Got it." He stayed right there.

"Um, I'll meet you out the front?"

He chuckled. "Okay." He walked to the doors and out them, and as soon as he was gone, Stanley turned to me.

"What the fuck?" he asked. "Are you scared to be around him because of what happened? He won't hurt you."

"I know."

"Then what is it? Shit, if it's because he's in a biker club, it shouldn't matter. I've done my research into them, and I'd be proud to have a son-in-law in their club because I've learned how damn fierce they are with protecting their women."

"I'm not his woman," I blurted.

He paused, then guffawed. "You've got a big old crush on him. That's why you're acting all stupid."

"I do not!" I near screeched.

With another laugh, he picked up his icing bag again and got to work once more. "Sure," he drew out.

"I don't. I knew him back in high school and he doesn't remember me. That's why it's awkward."

He shook his head. "It's that, but there's something else. Like you want to stick your tongue in his mouth."

"Stanley, I don't," I snapped.

He rolled his eyes. "Give the guy a break, kid. He's nice."

"I am not speaking to you about him. There is *nothing* between Cody and me. There never will be."

"You call him Cody, hey?" He grinned.

Shit.

"I'm going," I told him, grabbing my bag from my locker.

"Enjoy your walk," he taunted with a chuckle.

"Shut up, Stanley," I said and then slipped through the doors. After another thought, I stuck my head back through and said, "Thank you for helping me, Stanley. You know I love you, right?"

He froze, swallowed, and nodded. "Yeah, kid. I know because you can't stay mad at me. But right back at you."

My heart warmed. With a smile, I shut the door again only to turn and find Denise staring at me. "Bryson wants in your pants," she blurted.

"What? No, no he doesn't. Oh my God, Denise, don't put that in my head."

"I'd thought you'd see it eventually, and yes, he's treated you like a friend, but he wants you, Channa. I'm only saying this because I'm worried he's going to get his head knocked in by the other guy who's interested."

"Who?"

Her brows dipped, her head tilted, and the look she gave me told me she thought I was an idiot. Heck, I was getting that a lot lately. I'd even give myself that look as well, but I was honestly sure she was wrong about Cody. She didn't know our history; she didn't understand.

"Um, okay, I don't think that's what's going on with Cody. But let's table this for another day." I had enough to deal with on the walk home. I still hadn't come up with anything to tell Cody about how I knew his name.

"All right, I know you've been through a lot lately. I just thought you should know. Maybe, I don't know, warn Bryson or something."

I waved her words off and started for the door where I could see Cody waiting outside. "It'll be fine." It would; at least, I hoped it would. As soon as I had a talk with Cody, I probably wouldn't see him again since I knew things were heading back to normal.

Gulping, I pushed open the front door and walked out.

When Cody smiled, I stumbled a little. Cursing at myself, I said, "Hey."

His smile widened. "Hey. You ready?"

"Yep." I nodded. We started off down the path. At least with my house not being far, I might have a chance to skip over my reason for knowing his name by the time we got there. Unless he expected to come inside. Damn, would he?

"How'd you come to runnin' a bakery?" Cody asked, and I couldn't help but be surprised and happy he spoke of something else other than me knowing his name.

"Mum and I always loved baking." I smiled just thinking of her. "It was our dream, and after working hard, saving, it became a reality. We knew it wasn't going to be easy." We'd gone to so many banks for a loan and were rejected by most, except one, and that was all we needed. "But it was worth it," I told him.

"Where's your mum now?"

Sorrow stabbed at my chest. "She passed away two years ago."

"I'm sorry," he said softly.

"Thanks."

A hand grabbed my wrist and I was pulled to a stop just metres away from my house. I'd nearly made it. Glancing down, I saw his strong, large hand wrapped around my wrist. *Huh, it looks good there.* But nope, I wasn't going to think that way.

"Channa." His voice was deep, yet surprisingly gentle.

"Uh-huh?" I replied.

"Eyes, angel," he ordered, and of course my body reacted. I looked up. "Wanna tell me how you knew my name?"

Shit.

"No?" I asked.

He chuckled. "Sorry, but I gotta know."

Bite me on the arse.

Sighing, I bit my bottom lip and tilted my head to the side while my mind ran over all different scenarios. All of them were terrible.

Straightening, I nodded. All right, I could do this. I could. "I knew you from high school before I left. You saved me one day in the gym when I was humiliated. Thanks, nice knowing you. I have to go. Bye." I raced through my words and then swiftly made my way up to the front of my house.

I ran like a chicken. I'd be fine if I never had to face him again.

"Channa," Cody called.

Unlocking my front door, I turned and waved. "Thanks again. Later—I mean goodbye." There, that was final. I stepped through the door, shut and locked it before leaning against the wood.

Groaning, I dropped my head into my hands and cringed.

I *was* an idiot, a fool, and stupid.

Even my stomach was revolting and twisting over my actions. *I just ran. Ran.*

God, was he still out there? I couldn't even bring myself to look. Suddenly, I jumped when the dog door was attacked by my two babies fighting to get through first. I slid myself down to the floor, resting my back against the front door and waited. It only took seconds, but Coco was first, Harley close behind her as they rushed towards me.

"Hello, my babies," I cooed as they layered me in kisses. Others might get nauseous from the thought of dogs licking and jumping on them, but I loved it when they got so excited to see me. They were my family after all, and I was just as thrilled to see them. They even had me relaxing after what I'd just done.

"Mommy made the biggest fool out of herself," I told them.

Coco sat on her rear end studying me while Harley ran off to, no doubt, get a toy for me to throw.

Reaching out, I ran a hand over her head and down her back. "Looks like you'll be stuck with me forever. I just don't have the skills to get a boyfriend." Except, there was what Denise said about me having a chance with Bryson, but he wasn't who got my butterflies fluttering. Instead, they were interested in one man. I shook my head. "Not that I want to date Cody."

I didn't. And I would keep telling myself that.

CHAPTER NINE

COYOTE

$\mathcal{I}$ was damn amused by how Channa acted.
She seemed shy and uncomfortable, but I
was sure there was interest for me in her eyes. Hell, I
had to admit I liked her. I'd realized it even more since I
looked forward to seeing her. I woke up thinking about
her, went to work wondering what she was doing. But
for the life of me, I couldn't think what she meant about
school, and that shitted me. I'd saved her? In the gym?
Nothing came to mind. At least not right then, but I'd
figure it out while I gave her time, since it was obvious
she'd been embarrassed by what had happened back
then.

Making my way towards the bakery where my ride

sat, I pulled out my phone and rang the one person who could help jog my memory.

"Yo, bro, what's happening?"

"Doc." I smiled into the phone when she sighed. "Need your help on somethin'."

"Someone hurt?"

"No, nothin' like that. Do you remember a girl around your age in high school that left because of something happenin'? Somethin' I apparently helped her with, but obviously I never saw her again because I can't remember the situation at the moment?"

"Let me think for a second," she said. "While I'm doing that, let me tell you what happened here."

Fuck.

"Dad sat me down and gave me a lecture about moving out and not taking the opportunity to get my feet under me and save money to put to my future. Cody, it went on for an hour. One. Hour."

"How'd it end up?" I asked.

"I promised I would give it a thought and mentioned I'm not his little girl anymore. I've grown up."

Shit.

"How'd he take that?"

She groaned. "He had a tantrum, telling me I would always be his baby girl no matter how much I grow up. Just like Ruby." She took a breath. "Thank God Mum came in, and when they started having words, I slipped out."

"Have I told you how sorry I am?"

"You'll still pay," she said lightly. "Now, I do

remember a story that went around school. A girl from my grade—I was in year seven at the time—got played a prank on by some older kids. I felt so sorry for her. It was terrible. I think her name was Charline. No, that doesn't seem right."

"Channa?"

"Yeah, that's it. Anyway, the prank was so bad I heard she peed herself, but I don't know what happened to her. Why are you asking?"

It all came back. I'd heard something going on in the gym and had gone to take a look. A girl had been on the floor with others standing around her, mocking her. Some fucking boy, I couldn't remember his name, had got her to meet him there, but it was all a trick.

Fuck me.

The girl was Channa.

Christ, now that it clicked, I remembered the look of pure horror etched onto her face.

Grinding my teeth together, I clenched my phone to my ear. I wished I'd beaten those fuckers harder than I had.

They'd tormented Channa. Sweet Channa.

They'd fucked with her enough she'd moved.

"Cody?" Maya called.

But I couldn't talk because all I could see was what happened that day many years ago. I could have known her back then. I could have protected her more than I had. I could have prevented the shit situation.

Fucking motherfucker.

"Cody!" Maya snapped.

"Talk to you soon," I told her.

"Don't you dare hang up on me, Cody Marcus. Tell me why you're asking."

I stopped beside my ride and dropped my chin. "I didn't realise it was *her* that day when I helped her."

"Oh shit, that's right, you beat up the people who did it to her. How do you know her now?"

"It was her place Texas was in the other night. She helped him."

"I didn't think she was in town anymore."

"I don't know the full story yet."

"Cody… the incident probably scarred her in ways."

It had. Clearly, she was still plagued by it. To be embarrassed by it for so many years told me how much it'd stuck with her. My gut clenched.

"She'll be fine," I told Maya.

"Cody—"

"I'll make sure she's fine." No matter how long it took, I'd have her seeing past that point in her life and looking forward to a future—one where she'd never have to think about that time in her life again.

One way or another.

"Cody, all I want you to understand is that it may have happened years ago, but something like that can really stick with a person."

"I know that, Maya. I'll handle it."

She sighed. "All right, bro. Hey, maybe I could meet her one day? We travelled in different circles back then, but if you've got your boxers in a twist over her, I know she's someone I want to know."

"One day, maybe. Thanks for the info. I'll talk to you soon."

"Right, later."

"See ya, Doc." I hung up and put my phone away, fisting my hands at my sides. Turning towards the bakery, I couldn't help but think of what Stanley had also said. How Channa's dad wasn't the best. I wanted to know what he meant, because I had a feeling it wasn't good, and then on top of all that, she had to put up with adolescent dickheads.

If Channa thought she wasn't going to see me again because of what happened, she'd be wrong.

Each time I spent with her, I wanted to know more. I wanted to know it all, and I would.

WALKING INTO THE COMPOUND, I spotted Ruin making his way to the hall where the bedrooms lay. I wanted to see how he'd gone with Mimi and her brother. When I got to his room, I found him packing.

"Brother, what's goin' on?" I asked, resting against his door frame.

He glanced over his shoulder. With his usual smile gone, he put me on edge. Ruin resumed packing. "Headin' to Melbourne. Mimi needs someone at her back. Even when she doesn't want it to be me."

Mimi and Ruin had shared a night together. Ruin was being himself and had treated Mimi like a club girl, where he didn't want anything to do with her the next day. She'd been cut up, but he didn't notice like others did. Like I did.

Straightening, I asked, "What happened?"

"Mimi needs to go back to see her father. He's on his deathbed. Even though her brother's the one who took over the business, I heard her fear about going back because of their uncles. The brother promised to protect her, but I'll go as added security. Not someone from their side of the tracks."

"Prez agreed?" I queried.

"Yeah, eventually. I'll have some of the brothers up there as backup if needed, but I reckon I'll be right."

"And her brother was for it?"

He snorted. "He wasn't at first, but when she started fighting with me about me goin', he conceded."

Weird. Then again, there was a chance he saw what I had. That there was something that could grow between Mimi and Ruin. That was if Ruin got his head out of his arse before he lost his chance. Though, he might be if he was making himself her protector on this trip.

"Wish I could come, but until I find a manager for the business, I'm stuck here. I don't trust the employees I have to take up the position."

"I know, brother. Don't stress. I've got this situation under control."

"How long you think you'll be gone?" I asked, moving over to the bed and sitting on the edge.

"Aw, you gonna miss me, Coyote?" he teased with a smirk.

I rolled my eyes. "You wish. I was gonna celebrate the time I'd get on my own." All right, I might miss the fucker. We'd been around each other since we were in high school. At first, we'd hated each other and said some shit we shouldn't have. In the end, Stoke had taken care of Ruin's family when shit had gone down with a situation because of Ruin's dead dad, and since Ruin would be around a lot more because Stoke had married and had a kid with Mally, Ruin's mum, we put things in the past and became friends instead.

"Sure you will." He patted my head and I swatted his hand away, causing him to chuckle. "Though, I'm sure you'll be too busy with a certain baker girl."

Hell, maybe I would.

"Hmm, no comment? I'm takin' that as a yes, finally, and all it took was a night's sleep." He moved over to the other side of his bed and grabbed some shit out of his drawers.

"Thought you were into her?" I questioned, resting back on my hands on the bed.

Ruin smirked. "Brother, I was just testin' you. Saw the way your jaw clenched over her. Knew to stay away." He closed his case, zipped it, and dragged it off the bed.

"You takin' your Jeep?"

"Yep. Wolf should be here for Mimi. I'll follow them," he explained.

"How long you lookin' at bein' away?" I asked again.

"Mimi's wantin' it to be as short as possible." He shrugged. "A week, I'd say." He stepped forward, and I stood; we embraced in a one-armed hug. "Good luck with your woman." He grinned, slapping my arm.

I smirked. "Can't say she's my woman."

"Uh-huh." We moved over to the door.

"Be safe, brother," I told him.

He shut his door behind us and locked it before saying, "Thanks, you too."

As he headed off outside, I made my way to my own room. Each brother had a place they could chill in. It was good to have after a night of partying. Yet, I liked my home above the shop better because it was mine. Something I'd worked hard for, along with the shop.

Fuck, thinking of the shop, I had to get back there to shut it down and count the registers.

It had been a gamble opening a Harley store in Ballarat. But business was good. People drove from all over to visit the place. Hell, I'd had a customer in there the other day from South Australia, saying they'd heard about it and wanted to see what the rave was. He ended up buying a shitload of things that other Harley stores didn't have. Like the custom signs, which were made to look vintage, that Cowboy supplied for the shop.

When I got to my door, I pulled out my keys and inserted them in the lock, but found it already unlocked. Confusion dipped my brows; I swung the door open and cursed under my breath.

Stepping through, I demanded, "What the fuck you doin' in here, Genny?"

I didn't need this shit.

Genny, who lounged on my bed in lingerie, was a

club bunny who didn't take the damn hint when someone didn't want more than just a blowjob from her. Hell, that had happened two months ago after Anna and I had split, and Genny still pestered me like it was yesterday. I'd turned her down politely the first twenty times, but it was as if there was nothing in her skull since it didn't sink in.

Sighing, I ran a hand over my head and shifted out of the doorway. "Get out."

"Coyote," she whined with a pout. "Come on, baby, let me help you relax."

"No," I clipped, crossing my arms over my chest. "How long you been in here?"

She smiled. "I saw you arrive and thought I'd come and surprise you."

"How'd you get in?"

She giggled as she sat up, moving to the side of the bed, planting her feet on the floor. She spread her legs and ran her hand up to cup a breast. "I'm good at getting what I want."

I didn't feel anything but disgust.

What I also didn't like was the fact she'd got into my room. "*How* did *you* get in?" I asked again, dropping my fisted hands to my sides.

She didn't get a damn clue on my mood. With another pout, she cooed, "Aren't you happy to see me?" She slipped her hand under her panties and touched herself, leaning back on my bed to do it.

She had nothing I wanted to see. Nothing I wanted to know. She was trash compared to Channa. I wouldn't fucking have it. I'd been nice. I'd been calm, but I was about to lose my shit.

"No, I ain't happy to see you. I want you to leave, bitch."

She shook her head. "You don't mean that, baby."

"I do. Get the fuck out and never speak to or come near me again."

She grinned and shook her head again. "I can't do that. You need me, Coyote, and one day you'll see it. Then I'll be your old lady."

I didn't hit women, but I was considering it with this cunt.

Moving back to the door, I glanced out it. Genny must have thought I was going to close my door and have my way with her because she let out an excited squeal, then giggled before moaning, "Coyote."

I cringed. "Yo, Blue. Can you get the prez for me?" I called down the hall.

"You good?" Blue asked.

"Will be soon," I told him. He shot me a chin lift and went to get Talon.

Another shrill laugh from Genny sounded behind me. I faced her as she ground down on her fingers. She licked her lips. "Never done a daddy and son before."

Bile threatened. I screwed my nose up at her, but she just kept doing what she was with a smile on her face. Fucking sick bitch. I couldn't understand how she was seriously so dumb. She had to have a screw loose.

Christ, I didn't want to watch her any longer. I

moved back into the hall and closed my door. The last thing I heard was her saying, "I'll wait for you."

A few moments later, Talon and Blue were coming down the hall. Talon called, "What's up?"

"Found somethin' in my room I want gone." When they reached my side, I opened the door, and Genny was still there on the bed riding her fingers.

"The fuck?" Talon snarled.

"Stop," Blue ordered, and she finally fucking listened.

Genny pulled her hand free and licked her fingers. The three of us all sneered our disgust.

"She was in here when I got here."

Talon's gaze came to me. "You didn't lock your door?"

"Oh, I fuckin' locked it. She got in and won't say how. I've asked her to leave a few times, but she won't. Thinks she'll be my old lady one day."

Talon groaned, closed his eyes, and scrubbed a hand over his face. "I'm sick of this shit."

"What do you mean?" I asked.

Instead of answering, he looked back at Genny. "Get your shit and get the fuck out. You're banned from the compound. Banned from hookin' up with any brother. If I find out you have or you even tried, you'll be hearin' from Hellmouth."

Genny's eyes widened. Every woman knew not to fuck with Hellmouth. She'd threatened and scared a few club bunnies with a knife when the bunnies got too close to her man or any who was already claimed.

"Please, please don't do this to me."

"Genny," Talon barked over her cries. "Had too many complaints about you. Not only with not listenin' to the brothers, but from some of the bitches you slapped around thinkin' you owned some of the brothers. It's over. Get your clothes, your shit, and get the fuck out. We never want to see your face again."

Seemed I wasn't the only one suffering from Genny's crazy desires. The bitch needed to go. Christ, I was about ready to go back to how things were when Talon got rid of all the club bunnies for Mum's sake. Yet I knew the other brothers enjoyed them too much. It just wasn't my thing.

She stood, ran towards me with wild, crazy eyes, and gripped my tee, begging, "Coyote, don't let him do this to us. Please, baby. Tell him no. Tell him you want me."

Prying her hands free, I told her, "It ain't happenin' between us. Listen to the prez."

She stomped and crossed her arms over her chest. "No!"

"Blue, call Hellmouth," Talon said.

Her hands shot up in front of her. "Wait, don't do that. I'll go. I will." She spun back around, went to her clothes on the end of the bed, and quickly got dressed. She made it our way with her head hanging low.

"Hawks is off-limits to you, Genny," Talon said.

"Okay," she whispered with a sniff before she moved by us and down the hall.

"Blue, follow her. Make sure she gets out without

more trouble. Then let the brothers and other bitches know the situation."

"Got it, brother." Blue nodded before he left.

"You good?" Talon asked.

"Yeah, she just wasn't listenin' to me."

His hand dropped to my shoulder and gave it a squeeze. "Watch your back. Don't trust her, Cody."

"I will, and there's no chance of that." Though I doubt she'd do anything to go against Talon's words.

He gave me a shake. "Good. Now, how's things comin' with this bakery girl?"

Rolling my eyes, I shrugged off his hold and told him, "Nothin's happenin'. Got to go burn my sheets. Later, Prez."

I wasn't ready to talk shit about Channa to my dad. Hell, Channa didn't even seem to want to talk to me. Until I knew there was something amazing to grow between us, I'd keep my mouth shut, or else Mum and her women would be at the bakery by tomorrow.

I knew Channa wouldn't be ready for that. I wasn't even sure if she'd handle Maya paying her a visit. I'd have to wait and see how things went when I saw her next.

For now, I did have sheets to burn before I locked up the room and got back to work. I reckoned my employees could do with a treat. Maybe some cakes would go down well at work.

And I knew just the place to order them from.

CHAPTER TEN

CHANNA

*E*ven as I worked the following day, I still wanted to kick myself for the way I'd acted. I also considered finding Cody's number and calling him to say I wasn't who I'd been back then. And that I didn't pee myself when I got scared and that I was sorry for how I'd run off, but honestly, I was scared of what he thought.

Snorting to myself, I cleaned down my station and turned off the ovens since Stanley was due in a couple of hours. The phone to the bakery rang and before I got to it, it stopped. Denise must have arrived and picked it up out front. I made my way out there to flip the sign to Open and set out the chairs.

I saw her in the corner and gave her a wave. When she held her hand up in a stop motion, I paused.

"Hold on one second," she said into the phone. "The boss is here, so I'll ask now, but we don't usually do deliveries." She placed the phone on the counter and came my way. "Do you know the Harley store just off the main street?"

"Yes, I've heard it's popular."

Denise nodded. "It is. Well, they just rang and wanted to know if we could deliver two dozen party pies, sausage rolls, and the chocolate-chip cupcakes."

Holy wow, that would be a good sale.

"Let me check the stock we have," I told her and quickly headed to the kitchen.

"What's going on?" Stanley asked as he walked in the back door.

"You're early again. I'm starting to think you love it here."

He snorted, rolling his eyes. "Was bored and I got shit to do later. Though, maybe I should have waited since it's damn warm in here again." His gaze narrowed, and I grinned. "Anyway," he drew out. "What was going on?"

"That Harley store wants to order a whole heap of stuff. I'm checking if we have enough before I cook some more tonight. Since you're here, do you think you could deliver it?"

"The Harley store, you say?"

"Yes."

"Can't deliver it, sorry," he said, putting his things away.

"What? Why?"

"Was with a woman in the shop next door. If she sees me in the area, she'll kill me. You can take my car and deliver it."

"Are you serious? What did you do to her?"

"Nothing you need to know about." He tossed me his keys. "It's a good sale. You can't pass that up."

"I know, but I also need to be here with Denise."

He waved me off. "You've got a couple of hours before the lunch rush and I can handle the breakfast one with Denise. I swear I won't get pissed at a customer."

I nibbled on my bottom lip. "As long as you're sure?"

He waved at me. "It's fine."

"Okay, I'll tell Denise we'll do it. She's got the customer on the phone."

"I'll go tell her. You start boxing the stuff up."

Nodding, I said, "Thanks, Stanley." As I did, I couldn't help but think of the texts Bryson and I shared the previous night.

Bryson: Hey, coffee girl. Want to see that movie?

Me: I would like to, but I'm buggered tonight. Sorry, I really need to rest the next few days because of the accident.

Besides, I wasn't ready to see him after Denise said he wanted me. Not only would I be blushing through the whole thing, but I hated the thought of letting anyone down, and I worried that he did want something more than friendship.

Bryson: I understand. It's probably good you do rest. Can I ask you a question though?

My stomach had dropped when I'd read that.

Me: Sure.

The dots kept showing and disappearing again, and that had me feeling worse because I worried what he was going to ask.

Bryson: Actually, I'll ask you when we do go out. Talk soon, and take care, Channa. xx

He'd ended with two *X*s, and I couldn't help but stare at them. *X*s meant kisses.

I sighed at the thought. I really did have to talk with him, but knowing what was going to be said made me want to hurl. After I'd finished texting that I'd see him tomorrow for his usual coffee and I was going to get an early night, he hadn't replied. I'd worried I'd hurt his feelings because it did sound a little cold, plus I didn't put on any *X*s. If I had, I'd have been leading him on.

God, why couldn't I just be interested in Bryson? He was a great guy. Charming, funny, nice. However, I wasn't attracted to him despite him being good-looking.

Putting my thoughts aside, I went back out the front, passing Stanley on the way to check what time they wanted their order delivered. "Denise," I called, walking through the doors.

"Yeah?" She was down making coffee.

I smiled at the customer waiting for his order and asked, "What time was the delivery?"

"In an hour, which gives you enough time to get there and get back for the lunch rush. The owner, a guy, already paid for it over the phone with his credit card."

"Great. After I take these hot party pies and sausage rolls, can you refill it?"

"Will do, boss." She went on to serve someone else while I boxed the items.

The front door opened, and through the display window in the pie warmer, I saw Bryson entering. Hiding would be a chicken way out, and I'd already been enough of a wuss. I grabbed the last few party pies, closed the lid, and straightened.

Smiling, I said, "You're in early."

Bryson winked. "I am. I have the afternoon off since I started early, so I wanted to catch you before I left."

What did I say in return? That was nice? Thanks? Okay?

Thankfully, Denise spoke up first, "Bryson, want your usual coffee?"

He nodded. "Thanks, Denise." He turned back to me again. "Sweetheart," he started, his voice lower. "What I wanted to ask last night was if you'd go on a date with me?"

Dear God. Did he think my workplace was the best spot to ask me out? His smile was hopeful, and I really, honestly hated to reject him.

"Bryson..."

His smile dropped away and he nodded. "You're not into me like that?"

"You're a great friend." He winced, and I cringed. "I'm so sorry. I wish I was because you're an amazing man."

"It's okay, Channa. Listen, just be careful with that biker guy, yeah?"

"There's nothing going on between me and him," I told him, which was the truth.

He studied me for a moment, and then said, "There might not be right now, but he's into you, and I don't want you getting hurt. They're with a different woman every night."

Thinning my lips, I didn't like the way he spoke about Cody like that. He didn't know him. Then again, I didn't either, and Bryson could be right, but it wasn't for either of us to speculate.

"It's none of our business what he does or who. I have to get going for a delivery. I hope… I want us to be friends, Bryson, like we were, but I'd prefer you not to talk about a person you don't know because… well, Coyote is my friend also."

His brows dipped and he clenched his jaw. "I'll talk to you soon" was all he said before he walked from the bakery.

"Hey, your coffee," Denise called, but Bryson didn't stop. "What was that about?" she asked me as I picked up the boxes.

"He asked me out. I said no. He warned me off Cody. I told him there was nothing there and asked to be friends if he didn't speak of Cody in a way I didn't like."

She whistled. "Guess we'll see if he comes back."

I hummed under my breath. "I'll be back as soon as I can," I told her.

"No problem."

As I walked through the doors out the back, Stanley held the box of cupcakes. "I'll help you to the car."

"Thanks, Stanley."

Outside, after Stanley placed the box in the trunk, he straightened and said, "It was good you put that meathead in his place."

I sighed. "Stanley, don't be mean and call Bryson that."

He shrugged. "Coyote's better for you."

Oh my God, was he seriously giving me dating advice? "Stanley—"

"Nope, that's all I wanted to say. Get moving before the pies and shit cool. Not that they would. It's hot as hell out here. See you when you get back." He grinned, and it seemed a little evil. He turned on his feet and made his way back inside.

Groaning, I swiped a hand over my face. Already I wanted the day to be over. In fact, I couldn't wait to be home, lazing on the couch with a beer, snacks, and a movie from the eighties. That sounded like heaven.

The drive took me a little longer than I thought it would. What didn't help was the roadworks on the route I took. A few curse words slipped past my lips. A large car park was attached to the Harley building, which was handy. Another plus was that it wasn't so busy I missed out on a spot. At the trunk, I popped it open before reaching up and tightening my ponytail. A few stray red strands blew across my face as I made my way towards the large two-storey building.

The automatic front doors swished open, and I stepped into the air conditioning. Right in front of me was a large, curved desk where at least four registers sat. A male employee smiled at me when he looked away from the female employee beside him. Both wore CM Rides work T-shirts.

"Hey, welcome to CM Rides. Can I help you with anything?" the guy asked.

"I have a delivery from Bakery Bliss for the owner," I told him.

His brows shot up to nearly meet his hairline of messy brown locks. "Channa?" he asked.

"Yes," I said hesitantly.

"Hey, I'm Cowboy. I saw you the other night when the car crash happened. I'm a member of the Hawks MC."

Oh....

"Um, hi?" I offered.

The woman said, "Hi, I'm Clary. I'm just here filling in for the day. If you just wait a moment, I'll call the owner down."

Strange. I didn't really need all those details.

"No, it's okay. I just have to drop these off. He's paid already over the phone." At least Denise had told me it was a man who owned the store. I placed the boxes on the desk and took a step back.

"Wait a moment, I'm sure the owner would like to thank you," Clary said with a friendly smile.

"I'm sure he's busy, plus I have to get back to the bakery—"

"Channa?" came from behind me. Turning, I spotted Texas just inside the doors. With a wide smile and arms open, he walked right up to me and enveloped me into a warm hug. "Been meanin' to come see you," he said into my hair.

"That's okay…. Um, you've healed well." Even in the two weeks since I'd seen him, the bruises had faded a lot on his face. "How's the ribs though?" I asked, stepping back from him.

"A lot better, thank fuck." He curled an arm around my shoulders and led me back to the desk. "Heard about the crash. Glad you kicked some arse again and the brothers got there."

Smiling, I looked up at him and said, "Me too. It's good that it's over."

Texas grinned down at me. "It really is, honey."

"Well, it's been good to see you, but I really do have to get back to work," I told him. Nodding to Clary and Cowboy, I'd started to shift out from under Texas's arm when Clary's hand dropped down on mine.

"Just a moment, the boss will be down. He wanted to see you."

Okay, something was weird here.

Texas started chuckling. I nudged him. "What's so funny?"

Smirking, he shook his head. "Nothin', darlin'."

When "Channa" was called, I glanced to the side, then froze.

Cody Marcus was headed right for me.

"Sorry, have to go." I waved and ignored Texas's chuckle when I quickly said to Clary, "Please tell the boss thank you for the business. I hope he enjoys them."

She smiled softly. "You can tell him yourself."

"I have to go—"

"Channa," Cody said, closer now. "Thanks for bringin' the order. I'm sure the employees will love them."

Wait... what?

Slowly, I turned to Cody again. "You're the owner?"

His grin was lazy and cheeky. "Sure am, angel." His gaze shifted to the man beside me. "Wanna take your arm off her? She's still healing from the crash."

Wait... I was?

A headache started to form. Texas snorted beside me. "My arm is fine where it is."

Cody's jaw clenched and his nostrils flared.

I scrubbed at my forehead. "You called for an order?" I asked Cody as he stopped in front of me.

"I did. Thanks again. The staff will love it." He took my hand and stepped back, tugging me to move with him. I did because I was still in a daze. Had Denise known it was Cody on the phone? She must have because she would've had to have taken his name from his card. Why didn't she tell me? Hang on… maybe Stanley knew Cody owned this store as well, which was why he had me coming here.

Were *my* employees trying to set me up with Cody Marcus?

I was going to kick their arses because suddenly I remembered how I'd acted the last time, and my face bloomed with heat.

Cody's lips twitched. "Wanna take a look around?"

I drew my brows down. "Um…."

Cody tucked my hand in the crook of his arm. "Come on. It won't take long."

"I think I'll come," I heard Texas say.

"Tex, I need to talk to you for a moment," Clary said. But all I could do was look up at Cody because he was grinning down at me.

"But—" Texas started.

"It can't wait," Clary quickly said.

"I have to get to work," I whispered.

Cody nodded once. "You'll be back there for lunch." He glanced behind me. "Cowboy, take the stuff to the break room and feed the horde."

"Got it, Coyote."

Cody led me around the desk as I asked, "How many employees do you have?"

"Around ten on each day."

Holy wow, that was a lot. As we walked and Cody explained items he held in the store, I noticed a few looks from said employees as we passed by. When we stopped by a set of stairs at the far end of the shop, I asked, "Storage upstairs?"

"Storage out back along with deliveries. Upstairs are a couple of offices, but behind that is my home."

My heart tap-danced around in my chest. Cody lived here. Right up those stairs were his living room, kitchen, *bedroom.*

"Oh" was all I could manage. I hoped my hand didn't leave a sweaty imprint on his arm, his *firm* arm when I removed it because all of a sudden, I felt very hot. "Well, um, I better go back to work."

"I'll walk you out." Turning, I dropped my hand from his arm and waved it discreetly to air it out. "But," he added, which had me facing him again, "before I do, I wanted to talk to you."

Stop, drop, and roll.

All I could think of was the saying the firemen taught kids at school when your clothes were aflame, and I wanted to test it out. Maybe I'd roll under something where I could hide.

"You don't need to look so scared. It's nothin' bad," he reassured me with a soft smile.

Still, I was in panic mode, and obviously he could see it from my erratic breathing and wide eyes.

"Right," I squeaked, and then cleared my throat. I nodded and tried again, "I, ah, should apologise for how I acted—"

He stepped closer, and all words vanished from my mind. "You don't need to apologise, angel. I remember what happened, and you were a victim of a scene that shouldn't have happened but did because of some teen fuckers."

I wanted to cover his mouth. I didn't want him to talk about it, but what he said was sweet to hear, even if it freaked me out.

"You've got nothin' to be embarrassed about, and, angel, I hope one day you'll not see that situation when you look at me."

Dear God, he was amazing.

"Um…."

He shook his head. "Don't say anything, babe. Let's move past that and become friends. If you want?"

I wanted. I was afraid I wanted more, but friends would work. At least I thought it would. I'd also pray I wouldn't see what happened in high school every time we saw each other.

I swallowed and nodded. "That sounds good. Friends."

His grin was big. "Great, angel." He took my hand in his and moved us in the direction of the front door. "Lookin' forward to tryin' your treats, Channa, but I'll walk you out and hope there'll be some left by the time I get back in."

"You'll have to tell me if you like them."

He winked. "Will do."

Near the desk, I waved to Clary, Texas, and Cowboy. I received a chin lift from Texas with a sweet smile, a grin from Cowboy, and Clary waved back wildly, but her eyes were on our joined hands. I hoped she didn't think too much of it. Friends held hands, right?

I mean, I would hold Denise or Stanley's hand. Probably.

"Which one?" Cody asked.

I pointed over to Stanley's car and explained, "Stanley lent me his car for the delivery."

"Good of him."

"Yeah, he's a good guy. Grumpy, but good."

Cody chuckled, and I missed a step. His hand tightened around mine more. "I'm good," I told him. "Must have been a loose stone or something."

"Must have been." His lips twitched. At the car, he took my keys from my hand when I pulled them out of my pocket and unlocked the door before he opened it for me. "I'll see you soon, yeah?"

Would he?

"Sure?" The word came out as a question.

He chuckled again. "You will. Drive safe, angel," he said, handing me my keys, and then, *then* he leaned forward and pressed his lips to my cheek. "Later."

"B-Bye," I called once I got myself under control. I watched him until he disappeared inside and then I slipped into the stifling car. Pressing a hand to my fluttering stomach, I breathed out a ragged breath. Friends kissed each other's cheeks.

God, I had a feeling being Cody's friend was going to kill me.

CHAPTER ELEVEN

COYOTE

Christ, just being around Channa had me wanting to keep her, to know everything there was about her. I couldn't get over how cute she was with me, scared, yet interested, and yeah, I was sure she was interested by the way she looked at me sometimes —and with how nervous she could be.

It was hard to resist sliding my mouth from her cheek to her lips, but she wasn't ready for that. Hell, I wasn't sure I was either. I needed to make sure Channa and I got along on a friendship level before moving on to more.

Walking through the doors, I eyed a smirking Texas. "We gotta talk," I told him.

He snorted. "Thought so."

"Bossman, those party pies are the bomb," Cowboy said around a mouthful of food.

Shit. I had to have some before they were all gone. "We'll get some food first." I started towards the back rooms where the stockroom was, along with the breakroom.

I stopped when Clary commented, "She seems sweet, Cody."

Fuck me.

Sighing, I faced my mum's friend, who was here helping fill in as an employee called in sick, and said, "Clary, can I ask a favour?"

She smiled. "Of course."

"Can you not tell Mum about this?"

Her smile disappeared. "Cody—"

"Please. Channa doesn't need to be visited by Mum and her crew yet. All I'm askin' is for you to hold off."

She thinned her lips, and I knew it was to hold back her grin. "All right, I'll hold off... until you two are dating."

"Clary, I ain't sayin' that's where Channa and I are headin'."

Texas scoffed.

Clary clapped her hands in front of her. "All good, my lips are sealed. Go get your food from your gal before it goes."

"Clary, she's not—"

Texas's hand dropped down on my shoulder and shook me a little before it dropped away and he said, "Brother, I wouldn't even bother."

Goddamn it, he was right. Clary would take what-ever she wanted from what she thought she saw between Channa and me.

Blowing out a slow breath through my nose, I nodded. On the way to the breakroom, Texas said, "Know what you're gonna say, Coyote. See your interest and can't say I blame you."

I rubbed at the back of my neck. "Shit, brother, I don't even wanna admit I'm interested in case I jinx things."

He nodded, grinning. "Can understand that. She's somethin' special, brother."

Smiling to myself, I couldn't help but agree. "Yeah, she is. Gonna take time and see where it leads."

"Will you have a hissy fit if I ask that if it don't work out, let me know?"

"Texas," I bit out.

He chuckled. "Take that as a yes."

A few others were around when we entered the breakroom. I went straight for the boxes and grabbed a plate from the pile that Cowboy must have set out. I piled it with the three items, as did Texas.

Oh fuck, I thought after the first bite. I wasn't just pulling anyone's leg and bragging about how good Channa was, but that first mouthful of the party pie, then the sausage roll was like damn heaven. I'd never had one as good.

Glancing up, I caught Texas glaring at me as he bit out, "You lucky fucker."

Laughing, I grinned like a fool because I did feel lucky.

I SAT in my ute after work with the air conditioner blasting, since it was one of those rare hot days even when we were getting close to winter. The heat was a reason I wouldn't leave my ride sitting out in it all day long. And while I waited for the cool to kick in, I thought about my plans for the night. It was just past seven. I could get back out of my car, go upstairs, and make something for dinner. Only that didn't appeal to me. All I could think about was seeing Channa again. However, I knew she had early nights; I wasn't sure what time she went to bed, but a quick visit would be okay. Hell, I was already in my car with the plan to see her; I might as well follow through.

By the time I pulled up out the front of her place, I knew this was where I'd wanted to be. Even my gut, which swirled like crazy, was thrilled at the thought of seeing her.

When I knocked on her door, I heard the dogs before anything. Then they quieted just before the door came open an inch.

"Cody," she whispered, and the door came open more. "Are you okay?"

Jesus, she was pure sweetness. "Yeah, angel. Just popped by to tell you your treats were a hit at the shop."

Her smile was radiant. She pulled the door all the

way open and said, "That's great." She paused, unsure what to do or say next, and I suddenly felt awkward for coming, but then Channa added, "Um, did you want to come in?"

I nodded. "Sure." When I stepped through the doorway, the cool air hit me. But what drew my attention more were the two dogs sitting on the floor waiting for attention. "Hey, Coco and Harley." At their names, their tails wagged, and they slowly crept forward while Channa closed the door.

"I'll just go get changed," Channa said.

Looking up from patting the dogs, I took in her clothes. Fuck me. She wore tiny sleep shorts and a fitted tee. I could tell she didn't have a bra on by the peaks of her nipples sticking out. Her curves were on full display and my hands ached to touch them.

Bloody hell, I'd been attracted to women through my life, but nothing like this.

"You're good," I said, even though my dick had started throbbing. I ignored it, wanting Channa to feel comfortable with me.

"I'm in my pyjamas," she confessed softly, as if I hadn't guessed.

"Babe, be yourself. Be comfortable." *And I'll try not to be the lowest of all douches and check you out every chance I get,* I added silently.

She rocked back and forth on her feet. "Thank you. I might just grab a cardigan." She smiled and darted off down the hallway. Jesus, I hoped the cardigan was old, ratty, and large on her to cover her legs also because they were something to look at.

I heard her approach and straightened from the dogs once more. Thank fuck my prayers had been answered, and she was in a long, green, woolly cardigan. It had me hiding my smile that she picked a big, thick cardigan in this heat. Then again, her house was near Antarctic temperatures from the air conditioner.

I asked, "You work every morning, angel?"

She waved to the couch, and we both sat down with some space between us. The dogs groaned as they lay on the floor in front of us. Harley rested his head on the top of my boot, which had me smiling.

"I do since I'm open every day. However, good news, I got home today and organised myself enough to place an ad in the newspaper for a baker."

"That is good news. You work too damn hard."

She rolled her eyes, pulling up her legs to sit cross-legged. Once more, thank God for that cardigan since it covered almost all her skin.

"What about you back in the days when you started your business? I'm sure you worked crazy hours as well."

Chuckling, I said, "Back in the day? Babe, you make me sound old."

She shrugged with a teasing grin. "Well, if the shoe fits."

Snorting, I shook my head. "Only six years older than you. I ain't so old." I winked, and a blush hit her cheeks.

Damn, what was she thinking about? Might be best I didn't know. "To answer your question, yeah, I did work my arse off when I first opened. I can understand it."

"When did you open your store?" Her hand shot out. "Wait, have you had dinner? Would you like a drink?"

Of fucking course my gut took that moment to growl like a damn beast.

Channa laughed and it sounded sweet. "I've already eaten, but let me make you something."

Christ, could she get better? Probably.

"Don't go to any trouble," I told her.

"Relax, it's not." She grinned. "I do like cooking as much as I do baking." She stood. "Um, do you want to come into the kitchen while I do it?"

"Sounds good, angel." I followed her in, with the dogs not far behind us, and I dragged out a stool at her counter. As she pulled out some ingredients, I explained, "After high school, I knew university wasn't for me, and ever since I was young, I've loved bikes."

She smiled as she diced up some veggies and chicken breast. "I guess that had something to do with your dad being who he is."

I winked. "Got it in one. Growin' up around the Hawks MC, I lived and breathed the club, bikes, and a family life that was bigger than just our own." The indent in her brows told me she was confused. "The club, babe, it's one big family. Uncles, aunts, pain-in-the-arse cousins. Even though we're not blood related, we're still connected as a family would be."

She'd paused cutting and stared down at the board. "That sounds amazing."

"It is. Yet, there are times when it isn't. But it's like that in all families." She nodded and turned to the frying pan she'd set out on the cook top behind her. She seemed a little upset, but if I was to guess, it'd be because the only family she'd really had died. There were Stanley and Denise, but it wouldn't have been the same as her mum. Christ, I'd be a fucking mess if I lost either of my parents. I wanted to damn hug her. I wanted to take her in my arms like I had after the car crash and protect her from the world.

Fucking hell, that was some strong shit to feel for a woman. No other had brought these instincts out.

"So how did you come about having a Harley store?" she asked.

Blinking, I cleared my throat and said, "Bikes were life for me. I loved riding, fixing, and designing up new decals for them. I took the ideas to my parents and they helped me get where I am today. At first when I got out of school, I did an apprenticeship with Dad in mechanics, and he taught me about running a business. Now I'm lookin' at openin' a store in Melbourne."

Over her shoulder and with a sweet smile, she said, "That's amazing, Cody. I'm glad it all worked out. You even do the decals. I saw some sticker sets at the shop and admired them."

"Yeah, got a printin' set-up in the warehouse. Another brother puts together those custom old signs hanging on the walls in the shop. They sell really well."

"Even better."

"How about you, babe? What's your story?"

She tensed. Her whole body froze while the food sizzled away in the pan. I'd hoped she'd want to open up, but I realised it was too soon, and we weren't at that stage yet.

"Fuck, that smells good," I said, giving her an out. It was up to her if she took it or not.

She turned with the pan in hand and slid the chicken stir-fry in the ready-prepared bowl. "Hope it tastes as good as it smells," she offered with a thin-lipped smile.

I pulled the bowl towards me and took a forkful. Flavour burst into my mouth, and I groaned. "Damn good," I said, still chewing.

She seemed lighter after my comment, but it quickly faded. "You know what happened in high school," she uttered. I nodded, not daring to say a word. She sucked in a breath. "Well, after it, Mum and I moved just out of town. I went to a different school and we started over our lives. One full of love and cooking." She glanced away, down to her dogs as they got close to her—sensing their owner was in a mood I expected. "Before what happened at the school…." She closed her mouth and gripped the bench, staring down at it. A tiny, mild laugh escaped her. "I don't know why I'm telling you this." She shook her head. "Maybe we should save it for in a year or two." She waved her hands in front of her with wide eyes. "Not that I'm saying we'll be friends for that long. I just—"

"Channa," I called.

Her lips snapped shut. "Hmm?"

"Relax, angel. Nothing you say or do will… let's say, put me off gettin' to know you, okay?" She'd been so close to opening up to me, but then it was as if she felt it'd be too much for me to understand or maybe handle. Or perhaps she didn't want to burden me with her past. One day I'd get her to understand I'd listen no matter what it was.

"Um, sure?"

She didn't sound sure.

I pushed the bowl back and patted my gut. "Best meal I've had in ages." I gave her a sharp look. "Don't tell my mum that. She'd kill me."

Laughter bubbled up and out of her. "My lips are sealed." She placed the bowl in the sink and leaned back against it again. "When will you look at opening another store?"

"Since we're already in April, maybe towards the end of the year. Get through winter first. Though, I ain't in any rush because this one keeps me busy enough. I'm going to look at hiring a manager soon. Train them up so I can take time away from this store to dedicate it to the new one. When the time comes."

"You're smart, Cody Marcus."

Goddamn, my name sounded good on her lips.

"Sorry, you don't mind me calling you Cody, right?"

"Not at all, angel." *In fact, if you could do it every damn second of the day, I'd be in bliss.*

"Are you sure? Maybe I should stick to Coyote."

"Channa." When I had her gaze, I made sure she understood. "Like you sayin' Cody over Coyote, yeah?"

"Sure," she drew out, and once more, it sounded like she wasn't sure.

I smirked. Damn, she was cute. She'd find out soon enough what I meant by her, and only her, calling me by my real name. "So, what's your favourite thing to make at the bakery?"

"That's a hard one." She bit her bottom lip while she thought, and I wanted to be the one to take that lip between my teeth to suck on it. Yeah, it was impossible to ignore the attraction I had for her. She cocked her head to the side, then shrugged. "I like many things and trying different recipes. Mum and I used to experiment all the time in the kitchen." She clicked her fingers. "I've got it. My all-time favourite thing to bake is shortbread. It's fun and creative. I have all types of cookie cutters, and it's easy to decorate them. More than cakes and anything else, which is why I have Stanley." Her eyes widened. "Oh my God, I just rambled on about things you didn't need to know or care about."

"Babe, I want to know all things about you. We're gettin' to know each other. It's what friends do."

She dragged her top teeth over her bottom lip and nodded. "Okay."

I smiled. "Okay."

"Do you like shortbread?" she asked.

"I do. Would love to taste yours one day."

Goddamn, a blush hit her cheeks, and I wanted to know her thoughts. "I'll make you some one day."

"Sounds good, angel." I glanced at the microwave. I'd been here for an hour already. The time had gone fast. Too fucking fast. But I had to get out of there so Channa could get some shut-eye. "What time do you usually go to bed?"

"About nine, but I can do later when necessary."

Good to hear she wanted me to stay. "Another night I'll take you up on that, angel. But you gotta get as much rest as you can after the shit you've been through."

Her shoulders dropped. Why did I get a sweet feeling in the gut knowing she was disappointed I'd be going soon? At least I fucking hoped it was that and not me bringing up the shit she'd been through. Standing, I walked around the counter, and the dogs shifted aside when I got close to Channa. It was good they'd accepted me, let me get close to their master.

Channa sucked in a shuddering breath. Her eyes widened a little when I reached out and pulled her into my arms. With one hand around her waist, I used the other to cup the back of her neck and glanced down to capture her gaze. I didn't miss the way her chest rose and fell.

I'd give my left nut to kiss her, to taste her, but it was too soon.

"We'll catch up soon, yeah?"

"Yes," she breathed out.

"Good." Leaning in slowly, I pressed my lips to her cheek and felt her shiver.

Goddamn, my restraint was lessening. I had to get out of here.

Pulling back, I turned just as her mouth touched mine. She gasped and pushed me back, her face burning. "That was meant for your cheek," she told me and lifted her hand to wipe across my mouth and then just held it there. "We'll just wipe that away and forget about it." She faked a yawn. "Will you look at the time? I really have to get to bed." Using her other hand, she tried to shove me to the side. When I didn't move, she walked around me and into the living room, mumbling about how tired she was.

Channa stopped at the front door and opened it. When I got closer, her hand shot out. "Night."

Chuckling, I took her hand in mine to hold, but she shook both of them up and down hard. "Night, angel." I tugged her close with her hand in mine. "Though, this handshaking isn't gonna stick. Good try though." With a wink, I walked out the door and waited for her to close it. Immediately I heard the locks kicking in.

Everything this woman did drove me crazy. My cock was half-hard from just feeling her lips on mine, even briefly. My chest felt bigger than normal. That I didn't understand, and hell, I felt like a damn woman in those romance books Mum read, which I sneaked a peek at, when they said their gut was swirling with butterflies.

CHAPTER TWELVE

CHANNA

*E*ven a few days later, I couldn't believe what had happened. I could have left it at the hug, or when he'd kissed my cheek. But no, of course it couldn't work out like that. I had to be an idiot and think that he thought friends could kiss cheeks, then I'd be the best damn friend and do it back. I just about swallowed my tongue, along with my heart, when our mouths touched. Though, Cody didn't seem to think I made things worse when I wiped it off like an idiot. In fact, he laughed and left all good-natured like, while I beat myself up for the rest of the night and didn't get a minute of sleep.

"I think he'll be in today," Denise said.

Spinning to her, I demanded, "What? Who? No. I

don't think so. He's busy."

She paused putting donuts into the display case from the tray she held. "Who are *you* talking about?" She grinned. "Whoever it is, sounds juicy. Spill."

I snorted. "No one. I'm not talking about anyone."

Stanley walked through the doors from the back. "Are we talking about Coyote? She's got a big old crush on him."

"Stanley!" I snapped and quickly glanced around to the few customers sitting at our few tables. Thankfully, they weren't paying us attention.

Stanley rolled his eyes. "It's pretty obvious." He handed off the tray of cookies to Denise and took the empty one she had.

"Oooh, please tell, Channa. I'd thought the first day you saw him you acted weird when you hid. Is there some past we don't know about?"

"Well—"

"They knew each other in high school," Stanley supplied.

Sighing, I glared at Stanley as he made his way into the back with a smirk. "It was more like I knew *of* him, and one day he saved me from a bullying situation," I explained as I put on some gloves to prepare the rolls for the lunch crowd who would come in within an hour. "I left school and moved out of town, so we hadn't seen each other since. Until that day in here."

"When you hid."

"Yes, when I hid. I knew he wouldn't know me, but I didn't want to risk it. That scene in high school cemented itself deep inside me, and I couldn't get over the humiliation."

Denise walked closer. "And now what's going on with you two?"

"We're friends. Well, becoming friends after everything that's happened."

She smiled. "And you like him?"

"As a friend, yes."

"But Stanley said—"

"Stanley is seeing things that aren't there. Anyway, who were you talking about earlier?"

"Bryson. He hasn't been in for a few days. I have a feeling it'll change today."

Well, bugger. I hadn't even noticed, and now I felt guilty for it. Then again, my mind had been consumed by work and Cody.

"Yeah, maybe," I said with a shrug. "Here, let me take that tray out the back and I'll grab some more pies."

"No problem." She smiled.

Was I supposed to text Bryson in the last few days to make sure he was okay? I didn't know if friends did that after their male friend wanted to date but the woman wasn't interested. God, I sounded like an idiot even in my head.

"Stanley, you're a man," I said, taking the tray to the sink.

"Last time I looked, I still had a penis."

"Well, thank God it hasn't fallen off." And why in the heck did I say that?

Stanley snorted. "What do you need, kid?"

"You know how Bryson asked me out—"

"Don't stress over that meat—" I shot him a look. He amended with "Ah, that guy. He'll get over his heart shattering."

"I didn't shatter his heart," I told him snippily.

"Uh-huh."

"I was going to ask, should I have texted him to check on him since he hasn't been in?"

"Nope."

"Why?"

"I'm rooting for Coyote."

Dear God, why did I ask Stanley for advice?

"There is nothing going on there."

He laughed. "Shit, you're funny. Go on and get, or I won't finish my work."

Grumbling under my breath, I grabbed what I needed and went back out the front.

"Here she is," Denise said with a smile.

I froze because in front of the register was Clary from Cody's work. She wasn't alone either. A tall, slender, yet fit man stood beside her with a beaming smile, as well as a woman with gorgeous long dark brown hair and a warm grin.

"Channa, hello," Clary greeted.

"Um, hi, Clary."

"I was just telling Denise I got to try your food at Cody's shop and wanted to bring some friends with me."

"She's right, buttercup. She went on and on and on."

Clary nudged the man in the side. "This here is

Julian."

I nodded, smiling. "Hello."

"Aren't you just delicious!"

My brows dipped, confused by what he meant. However, Clary pulled my attention away when she said, "And this is Zara."

Zara… why was that name familiar?

"Hi, Channa, it's a pleasure to meet you."

"You also." At least, I think it was. "Thank you for dropping by. What can I get you all?"

"Let me take that while you serve," Denise said, removing the tray from my hands.

"Thanks," I told her, and faced Clary, Julian, and Zara, who were all talking about what they should get.

Julian stepped closer. "I don't know what these two want, but I would kill for a skim milk latte to go with one of those apple turnovers."

"Skim milk, Julian?" Zara questioned.

"I've got to balance it out, SIL, or your brother will have some extra love handles to grab on to."

Zara rolled her eyes. "I don't need to know what my brother holds on to."

Oh, Julian was gay and dating Zara's brother. It was sweet how close they were.

Zara went on with her order. "I would love a hot chocolate and a pink donut, please."

I nodded. "No problem. What about you, Clary?"

"I'll also have a hot chocolate, but I want one of those mini raspberry cheesecakes, thanks."

"Got it. Are these to take away or have here?"

"We'll grab a seat," Julian said.

"Sounds good. It won't be too long."

"I'll get the coffee and hot chocolates," Denise offered.

"Thanks." I plated their cakes and had started around the counter when the front door opened. My belly twisted in guilt when Bryson stepped through.

He gave me a small smile, which I returned, one a little bigger because he was my friend. We weren't close, but I'd still class Bryson as a friend.

I deposited the plates onto the table. "There you go. I hope you enjoy. Denise will bring out the drinks too." I smiled.

"Thanks, cutie-pie," Julian said.

"Channa," Bryson called.

I glanced over at him, and he beckoned me over with a wave of the hand. "Sorry, I'll come by when I can."

"No worries," Zara said.

Bryson stayed by the door, which was strange. Usually he'd make his way straight to the register and wait there if I was busy. Taking the few steps over to him, since Clary and the others had picked a table near the door, I stopped at his side and said, "Hey. It's good to see you."

"You too. Always, Channa."

My stomach revolted and my smile died.

"Look, before you say no, just hear me out, yeah?" Bryson asked.

"Of course." I felt I had to give him that, and I just

prayed it wasn't about going out on a date again.

"You and I get along really well."

I nodded. "We do."

"I think the more we get to know one another, the more we'll see there could be a connection between us—"

"Bryson," I whispered.

"No, I've been thinking the last few days that this was what we needed. Time outside of here to see if we could go somewhere."

My heart hurt because I hated this. I really did. "I'm sorry, Bryson, but I can only see us as friends."

He shook his head. "You won't even give us a chance?"

Was I being mean if I said no? I could give him a chance, but that could lead him into a false hope. God, I didn't know what to do.

Bryson sighed. "Just think about it. For me. Have a few days and really think about it."

"Okay," I muttered.

He grinned; his hand reached out and gripped my upper arm. "Thank you." He leaned down and kissed my cheek. I wanted to move away from him, and I hated that I did because he was such a nice guy. "I'll talk to you soon." He went out the door and I stood there staring after him.

Why did a kiss on the cheek feel different with Bryson than it had with Cody?

"Are you okay, Channa?" Clary called.

Turning, I plastered on a smile, which I knew didn't

reach my eyes, and replied, "I'm fine. Thanks for asking." I hooked a thumb towards the counter. "Better get back to it."

Instead of staying behind the counter, I walked out the back of the shop.

"What's wrong?" Stanley asked.

"Huh? Oh, nothing." I waved him off and went over to the sink to start the dishes. We had a dishwasher, but that was for the smaller items.

"By the way, your phone's been making noises."

"Thanks." After I filled the sink, I checked my phone in the locker. Seeing who it was had me smiling and my heart gave off an excited extra-hard thump.

Coyote: Hey, angel. Haven't had a chance to drop by but wanted to check in with you. We'd had each other's numbers when I started staying at Stanley's, but we'd never texted one another.

Coyote: You're probably busy with work. Would it be cool if I came to your place with pizza at six? Let me know when you can and what type of pizza you eat, if you're up for a visitor.

Why couldn't my body react like this to Bryson? Someone who I knew was interested in me for more than friendship? But then again, it was probably better to stick with friendship with anyone, at least for a while for the business's sake. Shaking my head, I quickly altered his name to Cody.

Me: It would be great to see you! Did that sound too forward? Too keen? I quickly deleted it and went with: **Pizza sounds great. I eat anything but**

anchovies. I hit Send before I second-guessed myself again.

It chimed in my hand.

Cody: Great, see you then.

Did I text back or leave it? I knew if I texted, there would be a chance I'd say something stupid, so I dropped my phone in my bag and turned with a smile.

Stanley grunted. "I'm guessing that was your beau."

"I don't have a beau, Stanley. It was just a friend."

"Uh-huh. Well, whoever it was made you smile."

"Whatever," I grumbled, causing Stanley to chuckle. Ignoring him, I walked back out the front, and since it was still quiet, I made my way to Clary's table, after saying hello to Amos, who was at the coffee end of the counter.

"You seem to be in a better mood, sugar lumps," Julian commented.

Cocking my head to the side, I asked, "What makes you say that?"

"You went out the back frowning, but now you're smiling. Did your man upset you before, but he's made it better now?"

"Julian," Zara clipped low.

"My man?" I asked.

"Yes, the one who was by the door?" Julian said.

"Oh, he's not my man. He's… um, a friend."

"You didn't seem too happy with what he was saying," Julian commented and then took a sip of his coffee.

"Julian, stop being nosey," Clary ordered.

Laughing, I told her, "He's fine. Bryson, the friend, wanted to, um, see if we could be more than friends. It was awkward since I'd already told him I didn't want to date."

"Date just him or date at all?" Julian questioned.

I wasn't sure why I was talking to them about this, but I did feel comfortable around them. It was weird. Usually it took me a while to warm up to people. Maybe what helped was that Clary and Cody knew each other.

"Date him. He's asked me to think about it at least."

"Interesting." Julian smiled. "Why don't you take a seat for a little while?" He moved the seat next to him out with his foot. I guess since I was the boss, I could take a break or two.

"Sure." I sat down and nodded to their empty plates. "Was everything okay?"

"It was amazing," Zara said. "We tried a little of each other's. I'll be spreading the word to everyone about here."

My chest warmed. "Thank you. I really appreciate it."

Julian waved a hand around. "Anyway," he drew out. "What made you so happy after being out the back?"

His persistence made me laugh. "A friend is coming by tonight with pizza. Anyone can get happy about pizza."

"That's true," Clary said.

"A guy or girl friend?" Julian queried.

"A guy friend, and yes, before you ask, we are only

friends." I smiled.

He grinned in return. "My little dumpling, you've already got me pegged."

"Channa," Clary started, gaining my attention. "How did you come about owning a bakery? You must be, what, twenty?"

"Twenty-two actually. Mum and I always loved baking. It was our dream to own our own bakery. We made that dream come true."

"Oh, is your mum here?"

My smile dimmed a little. "No. She passed away."

Julian and Clary gasped. But it was Zara who reached across the table to lay her hand on mine. "I'm so sorry to hear that." She smiled gently, pulling her hand away. "I just bet she would be proud you kept this wonderful business going."

"I'd like to think so."

"Channa, baby," Amos called from the door. "Marry me?"

Laughing, I shook my head. "Not today."

He pouted. "One day, mark my word," he declared before he walked out and let Mrs Brickston step through with her cart before he closed the door.

When I glanced back to the others, they all stared at me with puzzled looks. "That's Amos. A regular, and he only wants me for my cakes."

They laughed. I felt a hand on my shoulder and looked up. "Hi, Mrs Brickston, how are you today?" I stood and moved beside her, taking hold of her forearm.

"I'm good, Channa. I just wanted to drop by and give you some jars of my homemade jam." She reached into her cart with her weathered, arthritic hands and pulled out a jar, then another, and handed them to me.

"Thank you so much, Mrs Brickston. I look forward to trying them." Glancing to the counter, I called, "Denise, can you get Mrs Brickston her usual?"

"On it," she replied.

"Mrs Brickston, I'll go and get you a box of treats. You take a seat and wait right here." I pulled out my seat next to Julian and guided her into it. "Mrs Brickston, this is Julian, Zara, and Clary. Now they're new friends, so don't go telling them anything too bad."

She cackled at that and patted my hand. "I'll try not to."

Smiling, I nodded. I knew I'd left her at the right table when I heard more laughter coming from there as I boxed up some cakes before I went out the back and did another box of cold pies. These would last her the week.

Mrs Brickston had been dropping by every second week for the last two years, and she always offered me all types of things she made from home. I didn't mind at all giving her cakes and pies in return. She was such a sweet soul. One day her daughter had dropped in with her and tried to pay for the food I gave her, but I refused it. We had a good bartering system going, and the jams she made were always delicious.

Making my way out the front, I grabbed the other box and made my way around the counter. Denise was already at the table talking to them and no doubt giving Mrs Brickston her coffee.

The table quieted when I approached. "Here you go, Mrs Brickston." I placed the boxes in her cart and pulled the top over it. "Now, did you want to stay longer, and I can walk you home after the lunch rush, or would you prefer to head out now?" She lived down the street and I liked to make sure she got home safely.

She smiled up at me. "I'll just finish my coffee and we can get going, Channa."

I nodded. "No problem."

"If you like, Mrs Brickston, we could walk you home. We're leaving shortly," Zara offered.

"That would be lovely. Then Channa can get ready for the rush."

"Are you sure?" I asked. After all, she'd only just met them. Then again, she probably felt as comfortable as I did around them.

"Positive, dear."

"All right." I mouthed, "Thank you," to Zara, and then said, "I'd better check everything is sorted for lunch then. It was nice seeing you, Mrs Brickston."

"You too, Channa."

"And it was great to see you again, Clary. And meet you, Julian and Zara. I hope you'll stop by again."

"We will, pumpkin," Julian said. Clary nodded with a smile.

"Have a good day," Zara said.

"You also," I called over my shoulder as I got back to work.

CHAPTER THIRTEEN

COYOTE

Even as I pulled up out the front of Channa's house with a damn flutter to my gut, I couldn't get the phone call I had with Mum out of my head. There was just something about it that seemed suspicious.

I'd been sitting in my office going over some paperwork when Mum's name had flashed over the phone.

"Hey, Mum, what's happenin'?" I'd asked.

"Oh, nothing much, Cody. I wanted to know if you could come to dinner tonight?"

First of all, she usually texted me about dinners. Her calling about it had me puzzled.

"Can't, Mum. I've got plans."

"Really? What type of plans?" Secondly, her voice

had taken on a different, higher tone when she'd asked that.

"Just seeing a friend for dinner."

"Oh, that sounds nice. What will you be eating?"

Usually she wouldn't ask something so specific. "Pizza. Why all the questions, Mum?"

"No reason," she'd said, a little too quickly.

"Okay," I'd drawn out. "Was there somethin' else you needed?"

"Nope." The *p* had popped from her lips. "But how has life been?"

My brows dipped. "Good. Busy with work. Drake texted me the other day tellin' me about gettin' into a fight at school. You know it wasn't his fault. He didn't start it."

"I know. It's all been sorted. You Marcus boys are always defending people in the right way. His poor friend, though."

She'd spoken the truth. I would've done the same because I felt bad for Drake's mate. My brother had saved him from a group of idiots bashing the shit out of him because he was gay. They'd said they'd caught him looking at their junk in the toilets. Drake knew it was a bunch of bullshit and took matters into his own hands when he'd seen the way his mate was injured.

I hadn't thought that shit still happened nowadays, but then again, there were stupid fucks in the world.

I'd shifted the conversation. "Okay, so this call isn't about Drake. Has Ruby done somethin'? Maya?"

"No, I was just checking in with my boy. God, can't a mother do that?"

"Yeah, Mum. Course you can."

"Good. Now, I better go. Have a *good* night, Cody."

"Will do."

While I'd known I'd have a good night since I was seeing Channa, there was something about that call that put me on alert. I'd have to go and visit Mum to see if I could get a better reading off her.

Grabbing the pizza boxes, I climbed out of the car and found Channa already on the front porch waiting with a sweet smile. Fuck me, just the sight of her had my heart feeling thicker and beating a bit harder. She wasn't in her pyjamas tonight, unfortunately. Actually, it was probably good she wasn't. Instead, she wore jeans and a tee, and I noticed when I got close, her feet were bare.

"Hey, angel." I grinned. Leaning in, I kissed her pinking cheeks.

"Hi," she said softly, and it went straight to my cock, causing it to jerk.

"You ready to eat?" I lifted the boxes a little.

"Sure am. Come on in." She moved to the door and stepped through, shifting to the side for me to enter and then shut the door. "Do you want a plate?"

"Nah, I'm good. You grab one if you want."

"I'll be fine…. Wait, you didn't get a whole pizza for me, did you? I won't eat a whole one, sorry."

"All good, babe. Save what you don't for tomorrow."

"Thank you." She took the box I held out to her, and we both sat on the couch.

"Where's Harley and Coco?"

"I locked them outside. They'll hate me for it, but it saves them staring at us while we eat. I'll let them in when we're done."

Chuckling, I nodded. "Fair enough."

She opened the box. "Meat lovers, awesome. What did you get?"

"Same. Can't go wrong with it."

"That's true."

We both took our first bite, and I stilled when she moaned around her mouthful. Jesus Christ, I'd love to hear that sound when I was inside her. I shifted on the couch and ate some more pizza, hoping it'd distract me.

"This is good," she told me with a warm smile. "How was your day?"

"I had a customer come in wantin' to know if there was anythin' in the store that could be used as a sex toy."

She sucked in a breath and started coughing. "What?"

Grinning, I patted her back until she settled. "Yeah, the woman asked Cowboy. He's the younger Hawks member and damn shy. He ran to me for help to deal with her."

Her brows dipped. Had me wondering if she didn't like the thought of me having to deal with the sex-crazed woman.

"Um, how did it go?"

"I told her nothin' in the store would be appropriate for what she wanted it for."

"I think I'm scared to ask what she wanted it for."

I snorted. "You should be, but I'm gonna tell you anyway, 'cause I'm just the sharin' kinda guy. She wanted something to shove up her husband's arse because he gets off on anythin' Harley."

Her nose screwed up and she faked a gag.

Damn cute.

"That's…. Okay, I could have done without hearing that."

"Hey, I'm hoping if I share, it'll get outta my head."

Channa giggled. "Well, I hope it helped. But I'm blaming you if I can't get it out of my head."

I grinned. "Fair enough." We continued eating and talking about our days, and I couldn't help but notice how comfortable I felt around her. I liked talking to her. Liked telling her about my day and hearing about hers.

Once we'd finished eating, we went into the kitchen. Channa deposited the boxes in the recycling bin, and I let the dogs in. They were excited. Harley jumped around stupidly while Coco, the gorgeous girl, sat before me with her tail wagging. I made sure to pay her a little more attention. Harley didn't like it, so he raced off to get some from his momma.

"Oh, guess who got some emails about the job opening?" she said, leaning up against the counter. When Harley dropped a toy at her feet, she bent to pick it up, putting her arse on display.

And what a view it was.

One I wanted to touch. I quickly turned away and said, "That's good news. How many applied so far?"

"Three. But one I'm not too sure about."

Standing, Channa gestured back into the living room and then handed me a beer. I made my way back to the couch, but someone got there first.

"Harley, off," Channa ordered. He paused for a moment until Channa clipped, "Harley."

He quickly jumped down and sat at her feet while Coco sat *on* mine. I caught Channa's warm eyes when she took in the scene. "She really likes you."

"And I like her," I said, patting Coco's head. "What were you saying? How you weren't sure about one?"

"Yes. I don't know what it was, but even in the email he sounded like he was looking down on me, and…." She trailed off, looking towards her front window.

"What?" I asked.

Shaking her head, she said, "Nothing. Well, I just thought I saw someone, but I mustn't have."

"I'll take a look."

"Cody, you don't have to."

I rested my hand on her shoulder. "I want to." I was out the front door quickly and did a look around the whole property of her house. I didn't see anyone, but I noticed footsteps in the front garden. Only I didn't want to stress Channa over it as they could have come from her. They looked female. Before I went back in, I took another look around, but once again, I saw and heard nothing out of the ordinary.

Channa was at the door by the time I got back. "Everything okay?"

"Yep, didn't find anyone."

She smiled. "See, I told you I was probably seeing something. Could have been a possum."

"Better to be safe than sorry. Precious cargo in this house."

She opened her mouth, then closed it, and red coated her cheeks. "Um, okay."

Grinning, I took her hand and pulled her inside. But just in the doorway, I stopped. "I better hit the road. We'll do this again soon."

"Okay," she whispered, looking everywhere but at me.

"Night, angel."

"Goodnight, Cody."

Leaning in, I pressed a quick kiss to her cheek and waited a beat to see if she'd try and kiss me. She didn't, which I'd already suspected since she'd been so flustered the last time.

"Reach out in text if you need anythin' or just want a chat, yeah?"

Her smile turned soft. "I will."

"Lock up after me."

She laughed. "I will."

I tapped the door frame and walked out the door. I waited until I heard the locks engage before moving off to my car. It was early enough for a visit home. I knew my family would still be up and awake. The twins, no doubt, causing havoc.

"Knock, knock," I called, entering through the front door. I could hear music, no doubt coming from Ruby's room, some cursing, probably from Drake playing some Xbox game, and then voices towards the kitchen.

"Is that my boy?" Mum called. She walked down the hall from the kitchen with Dad and Maya following. "What are you doing here? I thought you were out with a *friend*."

"I was, but it ended, and I thought I'd drop by." When she got close, I hugged her to me and kissed her head. She was short, just like Maya and Ruby were.

"Always nice to have you drop in," she said and glanced around me.

"What are you lookin' for?" I asked, greeting Dad with a slap to the back and Maya a hug.

"Looking for your laundry bag."

Chuckling, I said, "Don't have any." I'd only dropped off my laundry a few times before I bought my new washing machine.

"Ruby, Drake, come see your brother," Dad yelled.

"Fuck!" Drake bellowed—he probably just got killed in his game.

"Drake Marcus, enough of that language," Mum yelled, and slowly turned her glare to Dad. I hid my grin behind my hand and walked over to the couch. Maya quickly followed in case Mum was about to lecture Dad for the billionth time.

"Come on, Kitten. He's sixteen—"

"Sixteen, Talon. *Sixteen.* Not eighteen, not legal enough to drink. Until he is, I want to curb the swearing."

I caught Drake out the corner of my eyes turning and trying to sneak back to his room.

"Drake! I see you. Come here and hug your brother," Mum demanded. "And what do you say?"

"Sorry for swearin', Ma. But Dad's right—"

Dad groaned and palmed his face. "Boy, no."

"Your dad's right? Your *dad's* right? So you think I should just let you swear, smoke, do drugs, and drink?"

"Kitten, how in the fuck is swearin' the same as doing drugs and drinkin'?" Dad asked.

She opened her mouth and snapped it closed before glaring at everyone. "I'll think of something, and when I do, you'll all hear about it." She pointed at me and ordered Drake, "Hug him, then go get your sister. I'm sure she'll be deaf by the time she's twenty with that music."

Drake shuffled over, bent, and gave me a quick hug. "Hey, bro," he said.

"What's up, loser?" I teased, ruffling his dark hair.

"You're the loser, and not much since the last time we talked. I'll go get Ruby." He added under his breath, "Before she gets chewed out."

"I heard that," Mum said.

Drake groaned and quickly disappeared down the hall again. Mum and Dad sat on the couch opposite Maya and me.

"How was your pizza tonight?" Mum asked.

I raised a brow at her. "Good, why?"

She shrugged and looked around the room. "Just wondering."

I shook my head at her. Yeah, she was acting weird. Turning to Dad, I asked, "You heard from Ruin?"

"Yesterday. You?"

"Same. Seems to be takin' longer than he thought," I said.

Dad scowled. "Yeah. Stupid fuckin' dicks." He was right to call them that. Ruin had told me what happened when he'd gone with Mimi to see her father and uncle. I thinned my lips at the thought. It would be better for everyone when her father did die.

"I expect him to be gone for another few weeks," Dad said.

I nodded just as Ruby's music switched off. It was only moments later when she walked into the living room with a smile.

"Hey, Cody," she said, leaning down to give me a hug, which I returned before she moved to sit on the floor near Mum.

"You gotta get better taste in music, kid," I told her.

She stuck her tongue out. "Yungblud is the best singer."

Dad snorted. "I'm about ready to tear my ears off if I hear that 'Parents' song again."

Ruby rolled her eyes. "You're just getting old, old man."

He reached over Mum and gently clipped Ruby in the back of the head. "Enough of that 'old man' shit."

Ruby giggled. Dad settled back into the couch, putting his arm around Mum, who snuggled into him with a smile on her face. As they went on talking, I took in what was in front of me. A family who loved each other unconditionally. I wanted that for myself one day, my own family. My own woman who gave me shit, who told me what for, who loved me like I was the only reason she kept breathing.

Maya nudged me in the ribs. "You off with the fairies?"

Snorting, I said, "Somethin' like that. What were you sayin'?"

"My brilliant idea."

Oh shit.

"What?"

"It ain't so brilliant," Dad commented.

Maya glared at him and turned back to me. "That I could move in with you instead of some of my girl-friends."

Hell.

"Ah… I don't know if that'd be a good idea."

Maya frowned. "And why not?"

"'Cause he don't want his style cramped when he brings home his chicks and his little sister is there," Drake said, coming back into the living room. He sat on the couch arm near Dad.

Dad chuckled. Mum frowned.

"Come on, I wouldn't get in your way. You have, like, three extra rooms."

"Maya," Ruby started. "He's Cody. Do you really want to clean the bathroom after him?"

"Hey, I'm not that bad."

Ruby scoffed. "Yeah right. You're just like Drake, and I have to share one with him. Some days I want to wear a hazmat suit in there. Besides, the spare rooms are near his. Do you want to hear the stuff he gets up to in there?"

Drake started moaning obnoxiously. Dad roared with laughter while Mum reached over him and smacked Drake on the thigh.

"Enough of that." Though her lips twitched.

Maya sighed. "Yeah, I guess I didn't really think it through."

"There's no hurry to move out," Dad said.

If I didn't change the subject, things were about to get rowdy. "Anyway, what else has been goin' on?"

"Ruby has a boyfriend," Drake answered with a smirk.

"Drake!" Ruby yelled.

"What the fuck now?" Dad said.

Goddamn my idiot brother and his shit-stirring ways. Still, Ruby was too young to start dating.

"Honey, is this true?" Mum asked.

"No… yes." She groaned. "He asked me out, but I haven't given him an answer yet."

"It's a no," Dad and I said at the same time. We shared a grin.

Ruby whined, "Why?"

"You're sixteen," I said.

"You're too young," Dad clipped.

"Now, hold up," Maya started. "If Drake came home and said he had a girlfriend, would he be allowed to date her?"

I snorted. Dad chuckled. "That's different."

Mum slowly turned to Dad. "It's different? Haven't we already been through this with Maya when she started dating? There is no double-standard bullpoop in this house. Cody brought home a girl when he was fifteen. Ruby is sixteen. If she likes this boy, then we're giving her permission to date him."

Ruby leaned back against Mum's leg and the couch, crossing her arms over her chest and looking damn smug with that satisfied smile.

"Fine," Dad said.

"What? No," I barked.

Dad's hand came up. "No, it's fine. He just has to come to dinner here first before any said dates."

"No!" Ruby screamed. "You'll all scare him off."

Grinning, I said, "Tell me when and I'll be here."

"Now, Ruby," Mum said, "I think it's a good idea, and then you'll know if he's really interested in you. If he is, he won't be scared off so easily."

"Darn it all," she snapped and stood. "Fine. I'll ask him."

"And you do this before you even agree to date him," Dad said.

"Fine." Ruby glared. "I'm going to bed." She stomped

off, only to turn around to hug and kiss Mum, Dad, Maya, and me. When she passed Drake, she hit him in the gut and then ran for it. She couldn't stay shitty; she was too nice, which was why all we wanted to do was take care of her.

Even with all the crap we gave each other, and all the disagreements, I still wanted this for myself one day.

CHAPTER FOURTEEN

CHANNA

In the next few weeks, a routine seemed to settle in where Cody would drop by every couple of days and we'd eat dinner together. And not only had I made a few deliveries to his shop, but also to his dad's mechanic business. It was there I found out that it adjoined the compound of the Hawks MC.

But tonight would be different, a change in what had fast become our norm. I was going to his house. My nerves felt like they were eating at my insides in delight. Yet that didn't stop me from wanting to puke.

Then again, he always made me feel like this whenever I saw him or knew he was dropping by. The man was going to be the death of me. Especially since we'd stayed completely in the friend zone. Although I wasn't supposed to want more. The business was supposed to be my main priority. Yet I couldn't help but lie in bed each night thinking of him. Thinking of ways, that if I could be bold enough, I would make the move straight into an area my heart wanted me to take us.

I'd imagined kissing him, hugging him, loving him in ways we'd both be naked and enjoy learning one another's bodies.

Cody Marcus consumed my thoughts constantly, to the point where I made sure Bryson understood we could be nothing more than friends. I'd been honest with him and told him I was attracted to someone else. Of course, he'd guessed who. That was when, in a text, he told me I was a fool and to have a nice life. I couldn't help it; I'd cried because I hated hurting others. I hated disappointing people. Since that happened last week, I hadn't seen him in the shop, and I felt bad for thinking it was for the best.

But... if he wanted to ruin a friendship over this, there was nothing I could do about it. I'd told him I wanted to stay friends, and I did hope that with time, he would still want to be. I would just have to wait and see.

Getting out of my car, I leaned back in for the bag of Chinese takeout I'd said I was getting and my handbag, which I hooked over my shoulder. I knew the nerves wouldn't settle. My belly would continue feeling like a trapeze act with all the flipping and twisting.

The store was still open, and I smiled at a grinning Cowboy as I walked by the counter. I got a few more looks as I continued on and then up the stairs, where I stopped to knock.

It only took a few beats before Cody pulled the door open, his mouth stretching over a smile. "Hey, angel." He leaned in and kissed my cheek. My heart shifted as if it wanted out of my body and into his.

"Hey," I said, a little too softly.

He took the Chinese bag from my hand and nodded over his shoulder. "Come on in." When he took my hand, my heart skipped a beat.

Calm down, Channa. Friends hold hands.

"The offices are at the front here," he explained on the way. I nodded, taking it all in. When he pushed through some doors, it opened into a large living, dining, and kitchen.

"Oh wow," I said. My mouth dropped open when I noticed the floor-to-ceiling windows to the right of the massive space. "Such a view." I let my hand slip from his and walked over to take in the space outside. It looked over a large part of Ballarat. Turning to him, I smiled wide. "No wonder you wanted to build and live up here. It's beautiful."

He grinned with a nod. "I think so."

"It really is." After a final look, I faced him as he made his way over to the kitchen. And what a kitchen it was. Okay, I was completely jealous of the marble granite counters, the stainless steel appliances, the double oven, and the white wooden doors that opened to a walk-in pantry. "I could have an orgasm over this kitchen," I said without thinking and slapped a hand over my mouth. I didn't miss the choked sound Cody made. "Sorry," I mumbled. "It's just amazing, your kitchen."

Cody cleared his throat. "Right… ah, I suppose it's a good kitchen."

Removing my hand, I fought the blush, but of course my body wouldn't listen. Shaking my head, I told him, "Good doesn't do it justice." Walking over to the counter, I couldn't help but run my hands over the smoothness.

When I glanced up, Cody was watching my hands through hooded eyes. While I didn't have much experience, I thought I saw heat in the depths of his gaze. Interest.

Oh wow.

Was it for me or his counters?

His gaze rose and didn't change. I swallowed thickly. "Um, dinner?"

"Yeah," he said lazily. "Dinner." When he turned to grab some plates, I took in a shuddering breath and blew it out.

Maybe Cody didn't just want to be friends with me. That thought had my head spinning, my heart racing, while a sweet little tingle throbbed in my pussy.

Could Cody and I be more?

As I watched him dish up two helpings, I couldn't

help but think about how much I'd enjoyed getting to know him over the last few weeks. We'd gotten closer for sure, and I liked the direction our friendship was taking. And while I'd be happy if life stayed as it was, if the heat I thought I saw when he cast his gaze my way was real, then I wanted to explore that.

"Here you go, angel." He slid the plate across to me and picked his up. "Did you want to stay at the counter you love so much or eat on the couch?"

Another blush crept forward. "I don't mind."

He chuckled. Nodding to the stools where I stood, he said, "Sit. We'll eat here and then watch a movie, yeah?"

"Sounds good." Once I was seated, I took a forkful of beef and black bean.

"Glad you suggested Chinese. Hadn't had it in ages."

"I love this place, so I hope you do too. But next time, I'll cook that filet mignon with flavoured beans and scalloped potatoes I raved about a few days ago."

"Deal." He grinned.

We ate in comfortable silence for a bit. Until I remembered something I wanted to mention to him. "I've been meaning to tell you. Clary was in the bakery again and she's given me the name of another baker since all those others didn't work out." They'd been terrible. Some in attitude, but others, when I'd given them a trial, even for a couple of days, were useless. I honestly didn't know if their references gloated just to get rid of them.

When Cody didn't say anything, I glanced his way and found he'd paused.

"Cody?"

"Clary's been in the bakery?"

"Yes. Hadn't I said anything before?"

"Nope. It's good she's helping you find someone, and I hope it'll work out. We've both needed luck in that area." Which was true. Cody hadn't found a manager as yet either. I blamed his good looks when he'd said half of them had been women and weren't really interested in anything to do with bikes. I'd figured they'd been too keen to get into his jeans or on the back of his bike. Just thinking of it again sent my stomach dropping. Cody caught my attention when he asked, "But can you tell me if she's had others with her?"

"Yes," I said hesitantly.

He groaned, placing his fork on the plate to scrub a hand over the back of his neck. "Do you know who?"

"Um, yes." I nibbled on my bottom lip, unsure if I should tell him since he seemed to be getting worked up about it.

"Who?" he clipped.

I pushed my plate away and straightened my shoulders. "I'm not sure if I should tell you. It's obvious you're getting annoyed by something."

"Oh, I am. But it's better you tell me so I can wring her neck."

"Whose?' I demanded.

He took a breath. "Angel, I promise no harm will actually come to them."

I studied him, and he seemed more relaxed. "Okay, but I don't understand what the big deal is. They've been nothing but nice to me. They even walk Mrs Brickston home when she's in when they are."

He nodded.

"All right, well, there's Clary, Julian—" He groaned. "—and Zara."

"Fuckin' fuck," he cursed.

"What's wrong with them?" I snapped, standing and putting my hands to my hips.

"Nothin's wrong with them. Except their meddling ways."

My brows dipped. "I don't understand."

Reaching out, he took my hand and guided me forward. Between his knees.

Oh dear.

My nipples hardened at the close contact, ready and waiting for attention. *Down, girls.*

"Babe…" He snorted and dropped his head forward onto my shoulder where he shook it. When he straightened, he smiled, and I noticed in this position, we were the same height. "Can't fuckin' believe them."

"I mean, I know Clary had worked at your shop, but…."

His hands shook my hands that he held between his. "Clary is a friend of my mum's."

"So…?" I drew out. "It's not okay for her to come to my bakery?"

"That ain't it. Angel, my mum, she's Zara."

My eyes widened. "What? No, she's too young to be."

"Well, she's actually my stepmum, but I don't see or want anything to do with my real mum. Zara's been it since I was thirteen."

Oh.

Well…. Oh, his mum was in my store.

Wait, why was she in there?

"Next time they're in, call me. I want to drop by."

That would mean Julian was Cody's uncle.

Were they in there to check me out? To make sure I was the right kind of friend for Cody?

He gave another shake of my hand, and I looked up into his eyes. "Don't stress over this. Clary would have seen you at the store and… she would have…. Fuck it. Clary would have seen something between us, and she wouldn't have been able to *not* say anythin' to her posse. I'm surprised it was only those three. Did they give you shit?"

I was still stuck on the part of Clary seeing something between us.

So there was something between us? Did I ask?

"Channa, babe, did they give you any shit?"

"Um, no. I mean, they asked some questions, but I thought they were nice."

"How many times they been in?"

"At least once a week. They like my cakes." At least I thought they did. "I think they do anyway."

He smiled. "They would or else they wouldn't have

come back after the first time they saw you. No doubt you would have won them over with your kindness and charm."

I snorted. See, that wasn't very charming. "I doubt that."

"Don't worry. I'll deal with them."

"What do you mean?"

"They're being overprotective. Fuck, babe, I'm twenty-eight. I don't need them to look out for me."

"But why would they need to look out for you with me?"

I jumped slightly when he cupped my cheek. "Babe" was all he said, and it didn't explain anything.

However, when he leaned forward slowly, his eyes flicked down to my lips and up again. My ears rang, my body shivered, and I licked my suddenly dry lips.

My heart sang for joy when he pressed his lips against mine. Once, twice, and I made a noise of complaint when he pulled back.

"That's why they were checkin' you out."

Huh?

"What?"

He smirked. "Clary saw somethin' between us."

"Something?" I asked stupidly, but my brain wasn't firing.

"Yeah, angel."

I had to confirm, just to set myself right. In a quiet voice, I asked, "Do you mean… are you, well, interested in me more than friends?"

His smirk grew into a smile. "Are you with me?"

"Cody," I whined. Already I was near having a panic attack with how bold I was being.

"Channa," he mimicked.

I blew out a breath and then nodded.

"Yeah?"

"Yes."

"Good, 'cause I am too."

I dragged my top teeth over my bottom lip. "What does that mean, then?"

He leaned in again and touched his mouth to mine. Against my lips, he said, "It means we see where this could go. It means we're gonna watch some TV or a movie and take things each day as it comes." Another kiss to the corner of my mouth. "You good with that?"

"Yes," I whispered. I was more than okay with that. Now that I knew Cody was into me, I felt like I was floating on a cloud. Heck, I felt like Jasmine in *Aladdin* when they were flying through the sky on the carpet and seeing a whole new world again. It might have sounded cheesy, but that was where I was. In one big, cheesy moment, I felt giddy, and I couldn't stop smiling.

"Good," he stated. He stood, dipping down to kiss my shoulder. "Let's get this cleaned up and set up on the couch. But, babe?"

"Yes?"

"I expect you to sit by me this time."

Heat hit my cheeks. "Okay."

His smile was smug. "Okay."

After we boxed up the leftovers and put the plates in the dishwasher, we made our way towards the couch.

Cody sat first. He took my hand, spun me around, and pulled me down to sit right next to him where he could curl his arm around my shoulders.

"This good?"

It was perfect, amazing, and sent my pulse racing, but I didn't tell him that. Instead, I nodded and gave him a shy smile.

"You know what this also means?"

"What?"

"You've got to come to dinner with me to my family's place."

Oh heck no.

"I'm busy," I blurted.

He chuckled. "Nope, you ain't gettin' out of it."

I wasn't even sure how I was going to face Zara, his mother, the next time I saw her. To go to a family dinner would surely send me crazy from the amount of fear that was already building.

"I'll have to check my schedule." God, I sounded lame.

"Angel, I'll have your back."

Shifting to capture his gaze, his gorgeous eyes anyone would fall into, I said, "I'm not good with a heap of people."

"You own a bakery and see a heap of people all day."

"In small intervals. This is dinner with your family. Your sisters, brother, father, and mother." I scratched at my arm. "Look, I'm already breaking out in hives."

He chuckled and took my hand in his. "Channa, I'm not talkin' about tomorrow or the next day, but if this is goin' where we're seein' each other all the time, I want you to know my family. They're a big part of my life."

They were. I knew this from the way he spoke about them. Though, he'd never said his mum's name before.

"All right, Cody, but not too soon."

He tugged me close and kissed the tip of my nose. "Okay, angel."

CHAPTER FIFTEEN

COYOTE

$\mathcal{W}$ ithout sounding like a total girl, I swore I saw sparks fly when I first touched my mouth to Channa's. I'd wanted to take things slower, build up to it, but I couldn't resist kissing her there and then. And even though it'd been a couple of days since that first kiss, and we'd shared other brief kisses, I still couldn't get the first one out of my head.

Shit, how could I be so far gone when we hadn't even taken the kiss from a small touch to one full of desire and heat? But I was, and I needed to change that soon. It didn't help that we'd only seen each other once after dinner at my place.

My phone rang behind me, from where I stood looking out over the view Channa loved so much. I was supposed to be working, but I wasn't focused. All I wanted to do was go to Channa and kiss her like I wanted. I had a need to take her mouth, to claim it.

Picking up my phone, I smiled at the name on the screen. "Angel."

"Hey," she whispered, and it put me on alert.

"What's wrong?"

"What? Oh, nothing, but you said to call you when your, um, mum was in next. Actually, I'm surprised they're in again so soon."

I snorted. "Probably want to pry outta you what you've been up to. I'll be there in ten," I told her.

"Bye," she uttered and ended the call. I quickly grabbed my keys and bolted out of there like my arse was on fire. I hadn't confronted Mum and her posse yet, and I was looking forward to doing it. On the drive, I imagined many ways about what to do and say. In the end, I strolled up to the front door and opened it. My eyes landed on Mum, Clary, and Julian right away.

Channa stood at their table with a flushed face. Julian was the first to notice me. He let out a squeak, gripped Mum's arm, and tried to drag her under the table.

With my arms crossed over my chest, I watched Mum fight Julian's hand away.

"What's gotten into you?" she demanded.

Julian stood and walked behind Mum's chair. Probably in the hope she'd save him from my wrath. Then again, he seemed like the innocent party since he was mouthing, "It's her fault," and pointing down at Mum.

"Zara," Clary said, and I glanced there to see she'd also noticed me and looked a little pale.

Both Channa and Mum looked my way.

"Oh shit," Mum muttered. She didn't like to swear, but it was obvious she knew how much hell I was going to give her.

We had an audience, with a few customers, along with Denise and Stanley standing behind the counter.

Dropping my arms, I moved closer to the table. "Anythin' you wanna say, *Mum?*"

"Well, you see, I found this lovely little bakery, and I can see you also did."

I raised a brow.

"Now, Cody, it's not what it looks like," she tried.

"And what do you think I think it looks like?" I asked before turning to Channa and smiling. "Hey, babe." I leaned in and kissed her cheek while winding my arm around her waist.

"Hi," she replied, a little too high.

Smirking, I shifted my gaze back to the three nosey people. "Clary, I remember askin' you not to say anything."

"Will you look at the time? I've got to go." She stood and bolted for the door. I let her go.

Julian tried to quietly sneak out from behind Mum. "Do not move," I told him.

"But you let Clary go."

"She, I can understand. She would have been burstin' at the seams to say somethin'. But whose idea was it to come here?"

"Zara's," Julian said.

"It was not!" Mum cried. She thumbed to the man behind her. "It was his. I said no, Julian, we can't go to the bakery under false pretences, but he was all for it."

"Doesn't surprise me."

"Hey, it was nothing like that. I'm an innocent, sweet man."

"Who hounded Channa for information."

Julian snorted and rolled his eyes. "I was just getting to know her. Weren't we, Zara?"

"I'm not saying anything," Mum replied.

Julian stomped his foot, always the dramatic one. "I'm not taking all the blame for this."

"And what is this?" I asked.

"To see your woman and get to know her, since you obviously won't share her," Julian explained.

"Right. I'm layin' down the law now, and if either of you don't listen, there'll be hell to pay. Not only will I bring Mattie and Dad into it, but I'll keep everythin' else in my life secret."

Mum gasped. "Cody."

"Mum, you know I love you, but you and your posse need to butt outta my life until I'm willin' to share shit, yeah?"

She stared at me for a beat, then sighed. "Fine."

"Julian?"

"Got you, captain. And might I just say, you're so much like your daddy."

Shaking my head, I said, "Now promise this shit won't happen again."

"Promise," Mum said.

"Promise." Julian nodded.

Groaning, I scrubbed a hand over my face. "Both of you raise your hands so I know you ain't got your fingers crossed and say it again."

"Oooh, he's smart. Damn it," Julian said, but he raised both arms and promised again.

"Mum?"

She rolled her eyes and brought both hands up where I could see them. "Promise. Now, how about you both come to dinner tonight?"

Channa made a noise in the back of her throat and her eyes were wide. I wanted to chuckle at how panicked she looked but didn't. Instead, I tightened my hold around her. It was also in case she decided to run.

"I don't know," Channa said.

"Please, come," Mum begged. "We need the extra female advantage since Ruby, my youngest daughter, is bringing a date for dinner."

I tensed. "That's happenin' tonight? She didn't wait long to ask him."

"She likes him, Cody, and I need you, your father, and brother on their best behaviour."

"Sure," I drew out. I was going to make this little punk's life hell.

"See." Mum pointed at my face. "That evil look right there is why we need more women in the house to smooth things over." Mum glanced back to Channa. "Please, or else I fear for this young boy's life."

She was being a bit dramatic; then again, probably not.

"Okay," Channa whispered.

"Angel," I said, gaining her attention. "Don't let her pressure you into it."

"He's right, Channa. It's honestly okay if you don't make it."

Channa nibbled on her bottom lip for a moment. "No, I would love to come. Thank you for inviting me." Her hand gripped my side, telling me how nervous she was.

Mum beamed and clapped her hands. "Great." She stood. "I should really introduce myself properly. Channa, I'm Zara Marcus, Cody's mother. Behind me is Julian Jacobs, Cody's uncle and my brother-in-law."

Channa laughed. "It's good to meet you."

"Can I just say—" Julian started.

"No," I clipped.

Julian rolled his eyes. "Well, I'm going to because I'm sure your precious woman here would want to hear my sound advice."

"Sound advice? Probably crazy," I muttered into Channa's ear, causing her to giggle. I didn't miss the way Mum was watching us with soft eyes.

"I heard that," Julian complained. "Anyway, ignore my nephew being a douche canoe. I was going to say that you, my dear Channa, have wonderful taste in men." Julian shrugged. "But now I'm going to take it all back." He huffed, glaring at me.

Chuckling, I said, "Come on, Julian, you still love me."

He shrugged. "Get back to me on that. Now, I must be off. Mattie should be home soon, and we'll get some alone time before our girl gets home." He wiggled his brows. "You know what that means," he teased.

"Julian," I groaned.

Julian threw up his hands. "I was talking about sleeping. We'll take a nap together."

"Sure," Zara drew out. Channa just seemed amused by everything, but I really had to rush this up so we weren't holding up her time.

"I'm not that perverted," Julian whined.

Both Mum and I laughed.

Julian grinned. "Okay, maybe I am." Julian walked around the table and drew Channa from my arm into his. "Now, my sweet scone, I won't get to see you tonight. We have plans to see a movie. So, I wish you all the luck in the world."

"Luck? I'll need luck?" Channa blurted.

I pushed Julian back and put my hands on Channa's shoulders. "He's teasin' again. You'll get used to it."

"Oh, okay." But she didn't sound sure.

I tugged her back, so her body hit my chest, and wrapped my arms around her chest. "Relax, babe," I whispered into her ear and felt her suck in a deep breath.

She nodded. "I look forward to dinner," she said to Mum. "Please, will you let me bring dessert?"

Mum smiled. "I would love that. Thank you." She

reached out and took Channa's hand. "I'll see you tonight. Six."

"You will."

They said a quick goodbye and left. It was close to lunch, so I knew I had to get out of there. Channa turned in my arms, her hands going to my waist. I liked her touch. Liked it a fucking lot. I also liked the way she stared up at me—shy and sweet.

"Dinner, hey?" I said with a smirk.

"Looks like I'll be doing it sooner than later."

"You don't have to. Promise no one will be mad."

She laughed. "How can I say no when it looks like Ruby might need an extra pair of hands to keep you Marcus men on track?"

Frowning, I told her, "That little punk had better treat her right."

Channa smiled. "It's cute how protective you are of her."

I heard the door open behind me and ignored it. "You think I'm cute?"

"Very."

I hummed under my breath. "That's good to know. Now, how embarrassed would you get if I kissed you here and now?"

Her cheeks reddened. "Maybe a little, but I wouldn't mind."

Grinning, I slowly lowered my head but stopped when I heard yelled, "Are you fucking kidding me?"

Turning, I saw that fucking meathead who wanted in Channa's pants standing inside the door. He stomped towards us with a pissed-off look on his face. I tensed. My hands fisted at my sides.

"You have got to be joking, Channa. This fool, this fucking piece of trash? You're picking him over me?"

I went to open my mouth, but before I did, my tiny woman moved in front of me. *Me.* "Don't you dare talk about Cody that way."

Meathead waved a hand my way. "He's a biker, Channa. An outlaw."

"He's a good man," Channa defended.

"Bullshit, he's into illegal shit all the time. Hell, he's probably got women on the side while he gets his sugar from you."

Channa reached out and slapped the fucker. Meathead's hand shot out. I didn't know if he was going to hit her or just try and get her away from me. But I wouldn't have him touching her. I flicked my hand out, grabbing his wrist. "Don't fuckin' touch her."

He glared. "I wasn't going to hurt her."

My hold tightened. "I don't give two shits. You never reach for my woman."

He snorted and tried to shake my hold off. It didn't happen. "Fucking have her. She's nothing but—"

I pulled him to me. Our noses near touched, and I growled low, "Say whatever you want about me. I couldn't care, you pissant motherfucker. But never say anythin' about Channa. Never. You wanna try me? Go ahead. But I'll drag you the fuck outside and beat the shit outta you."

He snorted, but it quickly changed to a small groan

when I tightened my hold on his wrist more.

"Try me," I snarled, staring into his eyes.

He stayed silent for a beat before shaking his arm again. "Let go and I'll get the fuck out of here."

I loosened my hold, and it was lucky he took a step back. "Good choice."

"Whatever," he bit out. He looked to Channa. "You'll get hurt."

"No, I won't," she said clearly as she moved into my side and wound her arm around my waist. I rested mine across her shoulders, grinning at the dumb cunt.

He shook his head with a scowl on his thick head and turned, walking out of the bakery. It'd better be the last time Channa ever saw him.

I brought her around, so we faced each other. Clapping started, and I snorted when I spotted Stanley over the counter doing it. "That's what I'm talking about." He looked to Channa. "You picked well, kid." With that, he walked through the doors into the back room.

Denise was smiling so damn wide I was surprised her face didn't crack.

"I'm sorry," Channa said, bringing my attention down to her.

"What for, angel?"

"For that episode."

"Babe." I smirked. "You can't help you're a wanted woman. Men just gotta know you're taken now." Dipping down, I brushed my mouth over hers. "I've taken up enough of your time at work, and I gotta get back to finish shit before dinner."

Channa groaned, her nose screwed up from it. "Don't remind me."

"Seriously, angel, if you're not comfortable, we can cancel." She opened her mouth to probably tell me no because she was such a sweetheart, but I kissed her nose, and her lips snapped shut. "Just think about it for the rest of the day and call me later, yeah?"

She nodded. "Okay."

Looking around at the customers, I dropped my hands from her and announced, "Sorry about the disruption. I'd like to shout you for a coffee and cake."

"Boy," an older woman said, "don't you dare. This was the most action we get."

Channa whispered in my ear, "They're from the retirement village down the road."

"Damn right it was," another lady said. "You picked right, Channa."

"Thank you, Mrs Smith."

"Appreciate it, ladies. You all have a good day."

A few called out to me, but I turned to Channa, and with a final quick kiss to the corner of her mouth, I made my way towards the door. Glancing back, I caught her watching my arse. She lifted her gaze, saw me grinning, and blushed.

"Later, angel."

"Later, Cody."

If Channa did decide to come to dinner, she'd be nervous. I hoped I'd make her comfortable enough to get to know my family. I wanted them to know her and who she was. Because she was something special.

CHAPTER SIXTEEN

CHANNA

*E*arlier I called Cody saying I wanted to go to dinner, but now I wished I could eat those words. Or rewind time. And all because I couldn't settle. Even my babies looked at me strangely when I'd paced around my house, fretting about what to wear and if I'd brought the right desserts. What happened if they didn't like Mars Bar cookies or mud cake? Then I would look like a fool, and I'd try to eat them all so they didn't feel guilty.

Cody's hand slid to my knee, and I realized I was bouncing it. "Angel, you'll be fine."

"Uh-huh," I mumbled, biting at my thumbnail for something to do. My belly was ready to revolt the coffee and sandwich I'd had for lunch. I turned to Cody in the driver seat. "You would know. Does your family like Mars Bar cookies and mud cake? Because if they don't, that's okay. It means you'll have to let me eat them all so they don't feel bad for me bringing something terrible."

"Babe—"

I straightened. "Wait, do you even like cookies and mud cake?"

"Channa." He chuckled, squeezing my knee. "Can't say I've ever met anyone who doesn't like cookies and mud cake. Everyone's gonna love it. If they don't, I've got your back, babe. I'll eat the damn lot myself."

My body warmed. Cody Marcus was incredible.

I took his hand in mine. "You're amazing, you know that, right?"

He grinned. "I do now, and right back at ya, angel. Not every woman would worry about the dessert they bring for dinner with her man's parents."

I liked the sound of hearing Cody saying he was my man.

"What are you smilin' about?"

"That even though how we haven't *kissed* kissed, you still call yourself my man. What happens if I'm terrible at it? Heck, you could be a snooze in the kissing department."

His hand shot across me to hold me back in the seat as he slammed on the brakes and pulled over to the side of the road. In the next second, my seat belt was undone and I was hauled over the centre console and placed on his lap.

"Cody," I gasped. "W-What are you doing?"

"Proving we're both good at kissin'," he said and cupped the side of my face. He gently nudged the tip of my nose with his before touching his lips to mine in a brief kiss. My heart hammered in my chest. If it kept up, I wouldn't be surprised if I passed out.

I slid my hand up to the side of his neck and gripped as he dipped back in to scrape his teeth over my plump bottom lip. A whimper escaped me. My nipples hardened and my clit pulsed. I shifted a little, and Cody hissed out a breath when I moved near the hardness he had under his jeans.

"Cody," I whispered.

"Fuck," he replied, and then I melted against him when he kissed me harder, hotter, and licked over my top lip. I responded by opening my mouth under his. I gripped him tighter against me when the kiss turned up a notch. Our tongues tangled, our mouths moved, our bodies rubbed, and I couldn't get enough.

Even though I'd teased, I knew, *knew* he would deliver me the most perfect kiss I'd ever had.

We broke apart, both breathing heavily. I rested my forehead against his shoulder and hugged him close while he leisurely ran his hands up and down my back.

"Fuck," he clipped. "We better go before we're late… or we could cancel and continue this at my house?"

Laughing softly, I shook my head. "I would love to continue—"

He lifted me and placed me back on my seat. "Seat belt," he ordered, his tone rough, and I liked it a lot.

"But," I added, resting my hand over his on the steering wheel, "I can't back out now. It's too late and would be a bit suspicious."

"I don't give a fuck." He closed his eyes and dropped his head back with a sigh. "But I get it. All right, dinner it is then."

Smiling, I put my seat belt on and told him, "At least we know we're compatible in the kissing department."

"Hell yes we are. Though, I knew we would be, babe." He continued driving along the deserted and dark area and then turned onto a driveway.

"Were we seriously that close to the house?"

"Yep."

"And you would have turned back if I'd agreed?"

He smirked. "Fuck yes."

Laughing, I dropped the mirror down from the sun visor and checked my thoroughly kissed lips. I looked a little dazed and a lot red, but I couldn't change that now. I just hoped my cheeks would cool enough by the time I got to the front door of the beautiful ranch-style home.

My door opened, and I jumped. "Ready?" Cody asked.

"No… yes… no?"

He chuckled and held out his hand. After undoing my seat belt, I took his offered hand and got out of the car.

"I'll grab the desserts from the back," Cody said. He went to the Esky in the back tray of the ute and opened it, grabbing out the two boxes of cookies and mud cake. Maybe I went a bit overboard.

"What's wrong?" Cody asked. He hooked the boxes under one arm and circled my waist with his other, steering us towards the house.

"I think I made too much," I told him.

"From the feel of it, yeah." I slapped his stomach. "*But* once you see the Marcus men eat, you won't think it then."

At the door, I fought for control of my stomach and what it contained. I prayed I didn't throw up in their house.

"Angel, knock for me, then open the door and head in."

My eyes widened. "I'm not stepping in first," I whispered in a slightly panicked tone.

Cody grinned. "Why not?"

"I'd feel awkward, especially since no one answered the door. I can't just make myself at home like that."

"Babe, how can you head straight into danger but not a house where you'll be safe?"

"Because" was all I said. I didn't think when danger happened. I just acted.

"Fuck, you're cute. All right, I've got the door, but you gotta promise you'll walk in with me?"

"Of course," I said. Had he known I was on the verge of running into the surrounding bush and hiding for the night?

Snorting, he slid his arm from my waist, and he knocked. Before anyone called out or came to the door,

Cody opened it, took my hand, and pulled me through the door.

I froze.

Cody started laughing.

"I'll get it," someone called, and I heard footsteps rushing our way from somewhere, but I didn't dare look away from the scene in front of me.

"Fuck, it's just you two. Get in here and close the door," Talon ordered, and he placed the knife he'd been sharpening down on the coffee table and stood. A knife that obviously belonged to a set. A large set of big knives. Ones I saw clearly on the table.

"Oh, hey, Cody. Wait, who's this?" someone asked, and just as I blinked slowly and turned my attention the young girl's way, she glanced at her father. "Dad!" she screamed, stomping her foot. "What are you doing? No, just no, go and put them away."

"What's goin' on?" A male version of the young girl stepped into the living room and grinned. "Awesome, you went with the knives."

"Drake, shut up! Dad, you are not threatening Dillon with them."

"Dillon? That's the douche's name?" Cody commented, and I elbowed him.

"What is with all the yelling?" Zara asked as she walked down the hall behind the living room. She wiped her hands on an apron and smiled warmly when she spotted us. "Channa, Cody, you made it."

"Are we late?" I blurted.

"Mum, can't you see why they're late? They've been

making out in the car," Drake announced, and my cheeks flamed to life. Drake chuckled. "Can't say I blame him. You got a babe there, Coyote. Good on you." Drake shuffled forward with his hand outstretched. "Hey, I'm Drake, the better brother. One you can trade up to whenever you want to get rid of this loser." He lifted his other hand up to the side of his head in a phone action. "Call me."

I choked on a laugh.

Cody slapped his brother's hand away and thrust the boxes at him. "Take them to the kitchen before I kick your arse, dickhead."

Drake, not seeming to fear for his life, grinned and winked at me. "Will do, bro."

Ruby moved forward with her hand out to me. "It's nice to meet you, Channa. I'm Ruby. Cody's little sister, and twin to the idiot in the kitchen."

"Nice to meet you," I said, and added in a whisper, "Good luck for tonight."

"Thank you," she mouthed, and I turned to Zara, who stepped close to bring me into a hug, which I found sweet. A pang of loss for my mother also touched my heart. As soon as Zara finished saying hello and hugging Cody, Ruby grabbed her hand and turned her to face Talon. "Mum, did you see what Dad's doing?"

Zara's eyes widened. "No!"

Cody brought an arm around my chest and pulled me back into him, where he leaned close and whispered, "It's a madhouse, but I wouldn't change it."

I wouldn't either if I were him. Even though my

pulse raced with all the action going on, I loved every second of it.

Talon grinned, and I could imagine many women would swoon over it. "Kitten," he purred. "I'm just playin'. If the little punk can't take it, then he ain't for our baby girl."

Zara's eyes softened a little when Talon called her kitten, but she shook her head. "Honey, we are not coming across as the crazy family in front of *two* guests. Did you even say hello to Channa?"

"Hey, Channa," he said with a chin lift. "Good to see you again."

A knock sounded on the front door. I tensed. Ruby's eyes shot wide and filled with horror as she stared down at the knives.

"Dad, hide those knives," Ruby hissed. Talon crossed his arms over his chest and smirked at his daughter. "Mum," she whined.

"Talon Marcus," Zara snapped low as she walked over to him.

Another knock sounded on the front door.

Drake raced from the kitchen. "Wait for me."

"I'll get the door," Cody said, and I caught the evil glint to his eyes. Drake rubbed his hands together, while Talon just kept on grinning. The whole thing was starting to worry me.

"No!" I blurted a little too loudly. "I'll get the door," I told Cody and shoved him back out of the way. Ruby seemed pleased by this, but I wasn't sure if I was just holding off the inevitable. Swallowing thickly from nerves for not only me but Dillon, I opened the front door and stuck my head out. "Hi," I greeted the young man dressed in jeans and a black shirt holding two bunches of flowers. He was good-looking, even with his long hair. I could understand why Ruby didn't want this to fail. Especially when he smiled shyly.

"Hi, I'm Dillon. Here to have dinner with Ruby."

I nodded and leaned a little further out.

"What's she sayin'?" Talon asked behind me.

"Channa," Cody warned.

"Whatever they throw at you, just take it on. They won't hurt you or the women will kill them."

He gulped and looked a little pale now. "Okay," he whispered.

"Great." I opened the door and explained, "Don't worry, Dillon, this is my first time here for dinner with the family as well. I'm dating Ruby's older brother, Cody."

"She's makin' him relaxed. Get her to stop," Drake complained.

Dillon stepped through the door, and I closed it after him. "H-Hi," Dillon said. He held the first bunch of flowers out to Ruby. "These are for you."

Ruby blushed and took the flowers with a soft smile. "Thank you." She turned to her family. "Mum, Dad, this is Dillon."

Zara got closer, and Dillon thrust the second bunch out to her. "Thank you for having me, Mrs Marcus."

"It's a pleasure, Dillon, and so nice to meet you," she

replied, taking the flowers. I didn't miss the way his hands shook.

Dillon stepped closer to Talon. "It's nice to meet you, sir."

Talon didn't move or uncross his arms from his chest. He kept staring at Dillon with a glare. "Is it?"

"Ah… yes?"

"Huh."

"Talon, take his hand now," Zara snapped.

Talon did and shook it. From the slight wince Dillon showed, I knew the grip was tight. He tugged Dillon closer. "See those knives?" He nodded down to the table. Dear God, he wouldn't threaten a child, would he?

Dillon shakily said, "Yes."

"Good. Now, you know who I am?"

Dillon nodded.

"You know who Ruby's older brother is?"

Dillon glanced back to Cody, who stood with his arms crossed, glaring at poor Dillon. He nodded and shifted his gaze back to Talon when he said, "And you know Ruby's twin?"

"Yes."

"Dad, stop it," Ruby tried.

"Talon," Zara warned.

Talon ignored them and went on. "All you gotta remember is that *this* family is a part of the Hawks MC. We know how to make a body bleed with those knives. We also know how to make a body disappear."

Oh my God.

"O-Okay."

"You gonna treat Ruby with respect, right?"

"Yes, sir."

"Good." He dropped Dillon's hand and stepped back, curling his arm around a glaring Zara.

"We'll be keepin' an eye on you," Cody added, and I reached over to smack him in the stomach.

"Yeah," Drake piped in.

"Lord." I sighed. "Stop freaking him out." I shot my own glare at Cody, who smirked.

Zara clapped, gaining attention from all. "Channa is right. Leave Dillon alone, and let's go and eat. Dinner is ready."

"Since the kid was late," Talon said, raising a brow at Dillon.

"Sorry, sir. Dad had to stop and get petrol on the way."

"Why didn't you leave a bit early to be on time?" Cody questioned.

Rolling my eyes, I shook my head at them all. "Dinner sounds amazing, Zara."

"Yes, it does. Come on. All into the dining room."

Ruby took Dillon's hand, which all the Marcus men scowled at, but she pulled Dillon down the hall after her mum, and they whispered together along the way.

When all Marcus men looked to me, I took a step back. "What?"

Drake winked before he fled down the hall. Talon smiled and shook his head. "Welcome to the family, Channa." He walked off after that.

I turned to a grinning Cody. "What?" I asked again.

"Angel." He stepped up to me and hugged me close. "You fit in here perfectly."

My heart expanded.

"Cody," I whispered. He couldn't say that; we hadn't been together long.

He shook his head. "Nah, babe. You do, and I fuckin' love it." He dipped and took my mouth in a hard and heavy kiss that had me losing all thoughts. I just held on for the blissful ride.

"Mum, they're busy pashin'," Drake yelled from somewhere.

Groaning, I dropped my heated face to Cody's chest, which shook from his laughter.

"Leave them at it, kid," Talon yelled back.

"Dear God," I complained.

Cody squeezed me to him. "You'll get used to it all."

Pulling back, I nodded and said with a smile, "I know." Because I did. Already, even with the nerves, I admired the way their family clicked. How uncaring they were when they showed how much they loved and protected with every fibre, even in front of anyone. Yes, they could be a little over the top, but it was in an amusing, albeit scary way.

I wanted that. A family of my own like that, and I couldn't help but think it would be amazing to have it with Cody.

CHAPTER SEVENTEEN

CHANNA

We walked into the kitchen and caught Talon asking Dillon, "Do you want a beer, Dilbert?"

Ruby sighed and palmed her face. Dillon fidgeted and said, "It's Dillon, sir, and no thank you. I'm not old enough."

"You sure, Dilip?" Cody asked. "We let Drake have one in this house."

"I can?" Drake asked, giving things away. I hid my smile in my shoulder. Drake cleared his throat and leaned back in the chair. "I mean, yeah, I am."

"His name is Dillon," Ruby said in a low, irritated voice.

Zara smacked Talon's back after she dropped a tray

of meat onto the table. He smirked up at her, and as I sat, I caught the sweet look they shared before his arm curled around her waist, and she bent to capture a quick kiss.

Drake gagged. "None of that at the table, guys." He turned to me, his eyes shining with mischief. "Unless you wanna see how a real man kisses?"

Cody, who sat beside me, went to stand, but I gripped his arm and told Drake, "Cody's already shown me. I'm fine."

Cody laughed and put an arm around my shoulders. "Burn, brother."

Drake rolled his eyes. He didn't seem to mind since he was still smiling.

"Everything looks delicious, Zara," I said, taking in all the salads, plus baked potatoes, to go along with the meat.

"Thanks, Channa." She sat beside Talon and waved at the table. "Everyone, eat up."

We did. Well, I was going to, but Cody grabbed my plate from under me and asked, "Anythin' you don't eat?"

The sweet move got me all gooey on the inside. Smiling, I said, "I'll eat anything. Thanks."

He winked, and I happened to look around the table and caught Zara's pride shining in her eyes for Cody.

"Where's Maya tonight?" Cody asked.

Zara jolted a little, blinking, but it was Talon who answered, "She couldn't get outta her shift. But she should be home around ten."

"We'll have to jet around eight thirty. Channa's gotta be up at three."

"In the mornin'?" Drake asked, shock evident in his tone.

Laughing, I nodded, and as Cody placed my full plate down in front of me, I explained, "I own and run a bakery. I have to be up early to do the baking."

"No shit," Drake said in awe.

"Drake," Zara warned.

"Yeah, sorry, Mum. But I mean, I tried the stuff in the boxes before and they were the bomb. Can I come to the bakery one time?"

"Me too," Ruby said.

I glanced to Zara. She smiled. "It's fine with me."

"I would love to have you in there. But there's no paying for food."

"Wicked, free food." He pointed at Cody. "Bro, you picked damn well."

Cody chuckled, rested his hand on my neck, and applied pressure. "I think so."

"Hell yeah."

"I'd like to come as well," Dillon said quietly.

"We can go together," Ruby announced, and Dillon beamed at her. It faded as soon as he saw Talon leaned forward in his seat, glaring.

Since I was new as well, I felt I had to come to the rescue. "That would be great, Dillon." I smiled and heard Talon's snort. I then added, "I'll organise with Zara when the best time would be."

"Awesome," Drake replied. Ruby gave me a sweet

smile and mouthed, "Thank you." It seemed I was definitely in her good graces.

"I'll make sure to be there as well," Cody put in, before leaning into me and kissing my temple, where he whispered, "Know what you're doin', angel."

Turning to him, I widened my eyes and said, "What?" There was no way I was going to tell him when Zara and I would set it up for. Dillon was being a champ putting up with the overprotective men in the family already. I was sure he'd love some time with Ruby without them around. Well, besides at school.

Cody smirked and shook his head at me. I turned back to my food, but I didn't miss the look Cody shared with his father. One I didn't understand but wished I could read.

The meal was amazing, and in the end, I didn't need to worry about dessert. Everyone loved the treats. The company was even better, and I couldn't believe how comfortable I felt sitting and getting to know Cody's family.

It wasn't until we were sitting in the living room, and after Cody and I helped Zara and Talon clean up when we all heard a crash down the hall.

"You motherfucker," Drake yelled.

"Drake, stop it," Ruby screamed before there was a thump.

Zara and I shared a look of horror before all of us were up off our seats and making our way down the hall. All I could think was poor Dillon.

Talon entered first, then Zara, and I heard her gasp.

Cody followed in, stopping just inside the doorway to what looked like a games room with a pool table, bean bags, television, a big one at that, and some pinball machines. Cody hooked his arm around my waist and pulled me in front of him.

My attention went to the kids in the room, and my eyes widened. What I expected to see wasn't it. Dillon was in one piece. It was Drake who had a bloody nose.

Dillon's gaze dropped to the floor. "Sir, I'm sorry."

"Don't you dare apologize," Ruby said. "Drake was being a dick."

Talon crossed his arms over his chest. "What the fuck happened?"

No one said anything. Ruby looked from Dillon, who wouldn't meet anyone's gaze, but swallowed over and over, to Drake, who was staring at Dillon.

"Someone had better say somethin'," Cody warned.

"With respect, I don't tattle," Dillon said, and he finally looked up, but it was to glare at Drake, who snorted in return, crossing his arms over his chest, just like his dad.

Ruby groaned and threw a hand out in front of her. "Drake was being a dick," she repeated. "Saying things like I had a heap of guys interested in me, that Dillon wasn't anything special, just like I'm not. Told Dillon I'd probably have a new guy in a week because I get bored. Dillon didn't like it—not that I would. I'm not like that."

"I know you're not," Dillon muttered. "That's why I got angry."

Ruby nodded and took Dillon's hand in hers. Ruby

explained, "Dillon punched Drake when he wouldn't shut up. Drake didn't get the hint, said more, and Dillon hit him again."

Zara looked up at Talon; so did I. He studied the three of them before he nodded. "Drake, watch what you say."

Drake smirked. "You got it, Dad."

Was this planned? Talon wouldn't have his son test Dillon, would he? I glanced up at Cody and found him fighting a grin. Heck, maybe he had.

Zara cleared her throat and shot Talon a scowl before asking, "Does anyone need ice?"

"Yeah, I do," Drake said, still smiling.

"I'm good," Dillon said.

"It's always the quiet ones you have to keep an eye on," Cody commented and looked down at me.

"What does that mean? I'm not quiet. I don't...." When I caught everyone looking at me, grinning, I said, "Forget about it." There was no point arguing. If they wanted to think I was quiet and a badarse underneath like Dillon, then they could. Still, I couldn't help but be proud of Ruby's guy.

Cody chuckled. "We're gonna head off," he announced suddenly.

We were? "We are?"

"Yep," he said, and when his eyes dropped down to me, I caught their look, and it said he wanted to kiss me. It was definitely a good time to go because I was all for more kissing. His grin was sinful. "Say goodbye."

"Um, goodbye." I waved lamely, not looking away from him.

It was Talon's deep chuckle that had my cheeks burning and turning back to the room. I rushed forward so I didn't die of humiliation and hugged Zara. I had a feeling they guessed as I had what Cody's intentions were.

"Thank you for dinner," I told her.

"Thank you for coming. We'll talk soon."

"I'd love that."

"Bakery day," Drake shouted with a whoop.

"Let's get you some ice," Zara said, gripping the back of his neck and pulling him out of the room.

"Later, beautiful," he called.

"Bye, Drake."

Ruby moved forward and gave me a hug. "Thanks for your help tonight."

"Any time," I told her.

Dillon nodded at me with a small smile. "It was nice meeting you," he said.

"You too. I hope you'll come to the bakery." He nodded again before Ruby pulled him back over towards the couch where the television sat on the wall.

Facing Talon, I was at a loss on what to do. He was Cody's father, a biker, and a little intimidating. Did I pat him on the arm and say "see ya"? Or was I supposed to hug him like I did Zara?

In the end, I moved towards him and gave him a slap on the arm with a kiss on the cheek while I blushed and said, "Thank you for not putting fear in me for dating Cody."

He stared me down, and I backed up a step. "Wait, *you're* dating my son?"

What the heck?

Cody laughed and took my hand. "Don't scare her, Dad."

"Darlin', you got nothin' to worry about. I've seen you kick arse. I know I have to watch what I do and say when it comes to you."

Okay, I puffed up with a little pride over that. "Well… good."

Both men laughed, and it was my turn to lead Cody out by his hand, so I didn't say or do anything else to have Talon think differently.

In the car, I asked, "Do you think Dillon will survive your family?"

Cody snorted, reaching for my hand to hold on my thigh. "I think he may look shy, but there's something hiding underneath. Something that'd kick Drake's arse in his own house, even with Mum and Dad there. He can handle it."

I hoped he could. "They're sweet together," I commented.

"Angel, I don't want to think about how sweet my sister is with a guy."

Laughing, I said, "Fair enough. I'm just glad your mum isn't the same with me. Overprotective in a scary way."

"Not in a scary way, just overprotective. Else she

wouldn't have shown at your bakery to check you out."

I grinned. "That's true."

"Channa," he said, but then no more.

"Yes?"

"Gotta ask you somethin' and need you to be honest."

My throat dried up because my mind went straight to the thought that I'd done something. My hand tightened on his, and I nodded. "Of course."

"Shit, it ain't anythin' bad. In fact, it could be good, but… I'm fuckin' this up." He brought our joined hands up to kiss the back of my hand. "Angel, only if you're comfortable with it, I wanna stay the night at your place."

My heart went *ka-boom* and then swooned.

He was asking me, and he was crazy if he thought I'd say no, because it meant a lot more kissing time. Maybe even a little more.

My stomach swooshed in a whirlwind of butterflies.

Even though I would be nervous, and there was a chance I'd make a fool of myself by swallowing my tongue, I nodded. But he didn't see. His jaw tensed, and I realized I'd taken too long to answer.

"It's all good," he'd added. "I won't. I'd never want to rush, and I wasn't even talking about—"

Reaching out, I pressed two fingers to his lips. "Cody, I'd love for you to stay." Under my fingers, a smile grew. A big one. A satisfied one. "As long as you're okay with me leaving early to bake?"

"Babe, it's who you are and what you do. I'm just

damn honoured you'd have me in your bed."

"You're a damn charmer, Cody Marcus."

He grinned. "Only with you."

I doubted it, but I wouldn't think of our pasts. I wouldn't linger and worry. He was here with me, and that was all that mattered.

He parked out front of the house, and we got out, meeting at the front of the car, where he took my hand as we shared a smile, causing my heart to flutter. Inside, we were mauled with love and kisses from Coco and Harley. Though Coco was more discreet about it and only mauled us when we gave her some loving.

"Do you want a drink or anything?" I asked, heading for the kitchen.

"I'll grab a beer, babe, but I can get it." He wound an arm around my waist and kissed my temple. "I'll drink it while I play with the dogs out back." He moved to the refrigerator, took out a beer, and opened it. Since I was still stuck on the one spot, he brushed his lips over my neck as he walked back to the door where he unlocked it and stepped outside, whistling for the dogs. They ran after him, knowing they were about to have fun.

Could Cody get any better?

Heck, all I wanted to do was head to bed and get some romance on, but I knew I had to take care of my babies first. Yet, there he was doing it for me. So, what did I do with my time?

Wait… had I shaved my legs?

Oh God, I hadn't. When I'd showered, I didn't think they'd needed doing, but they absolutely did. I couldn't have Cody running his hand up my leg and it feeling like I was grating his skin off. That was if he did run his hand up my leg, but it wasn't a risk I was willing to take.

Rushing through getting out the dogs some dry food and filling their water bowls, I then raced into my bedroom to grab sleep shorts and a tank top before filing into the bathroom. I trimmed my pubes, praying Cody didn't walk into the bathroom in that moment while I was bent over with an electric razor trying to make my vagina more appealing. I quickly went over and locked the door before I got back to it. As soon as I was done, I turned on the shower. I had never showered and shaved so quickly in my life, and I cursed at the few cuts I made in my haste. I dressed and stood in front of the mirror. My hair was damp, my face clean of makeup, and I didn't know if I needed to apply more or not.

"Channa," Cody called, with a knock to the door.

"Y-Yes?" I squeaked and cleared my throat. "Ah, yes?"

"You comin' out anytime soon?"

I hadn't been that long, had I?

"It's been an hour," he answered my unasked question. I palmed my face and slunk my way to the door. Once I unlocked it, I flung it wide.

"I'm so sorry for leaving you waiting. I was… I just… um…."

He curled an arm around my waist, dragging me close, and I noticed his shoes and socks were gone, since I was looking down. He touched his nose to my neck, taking in a deep breath. "You smelled good before, but angel, whatever shampoo you use, I want to bathe in it."

A shiver swept over me—from his rough tone, from his warm hands on my waist, and from how close he was. He pulled back, our eyes meeting, and slowly he leaned in. When our mouths touched, my body heated. When we opened, to taste, to tease our tongues against each other's, I gripped his arms and held on to just feel him.

And I did.

I felt his hands as he slid them to my bottom and gently squeezed. I jumped, and Cody caught me with ease while I wrapped my arms around his neck and trailed kisses down his jaw, his neck, and back up again.

I rocked up and down against him while his fingers slipped under my shorts, touching my heat. He groaned and I bit into his neck with a moan.

"Fuck, angel." His fingers glided over my wetness, since I wasn't wearing any panties under the shorts. "Damn wet for me."

"Yes," I whispered.

"Christ. We don't have to do anythin'—"

"I want to."

"Thank fuck." He grinned when he slowly dropped my legs to the floor, and I realized we were now in my bedroom.

"The dogs—"

"Already fed."

Running my hands up his chest, I caught his sharp intake of breath. "Thank you."

"Anythin'."

"Anything?" I asked with a smile. I definitely had something in mind, and I wouldn't… well, I didn't want to become shy about it because I really wanted to see him without a top on. My pussy throbbed from the thought of his golden skin under my hands.

"Yeah, angel."

Scraping my top teeth over my bottom lip, I asked softly, "Can I take your tee off?"

His grin was wicked and had me melting. He cocked his head to the side and asked, "As long as I can with yours?"

My belly lit with fireworks of pleasure. "Deal." I dropped my hands to the hem of his tee, then paused. "Wait… we should get a certain talk out of the way first."

He stilled and jerked his head back in confusion. "Talk? Now?"

"Well, yes. I have an IUD in and have always used protection. There was only one other guy, and I didn't really like it—" His hand covered my mouth.

"Angel," he groaned. His jaw clenched. "Good to know, but I'd prefer not to know about the other guy. Obviously he was a dickhead who didn't know shit, but if I have more information, I'm gonna want to hunt the fucker down and kill him."

Whoa, he sounded serious.

Really serious.

"Okay," I mumbled behind his hand. "D-Do you mind if… I mean… I would like to feel you for the first time."

His gaze darkened, his chest rumbled with a growl, and he nodded. Shifting his palm to the side of my neck, he said, "Always been smart. But I got tested not that long ago. We're safe, and I'd love to be bare inside you."

Um, yay. "Awesome," I stated with a stupid smile and then dropped my gaze to my hands still at the hem of his tee. I would have taken it slowly, but I was never good at unwrapping anything leisurely. Cody chuckled when I whipped it up and off him with a fling. I stared, I may have drooled a little, and I touched… oh yes, I touched his smooth, warm, amazing skin at his chest, his arms, his shoulders, and stomach, which quivered under my fingers.

"You're drivin' me crazy, angel."

His fingers brushed over my sides where he'd gripped my tank top, and I giggled. Wide-eyed, I slapped a hand over my mouth, but it was too late. His grin turned into a smirk.

"Ticklish?"

I shook my head, only to laugh more when he tested my lie. "Stop," I yelled. "Please," I begged. With all the commotion, the dogs decided they wanted in on it and raced into the room.

"Bed," Cody ordered, and they did, though they looked pretty pissed. I felt bad for a millisecond until Cody took my attention when he cupped my cheeks and brought my gaze up to his. "Need you on the bed as well, angel."

My belly swished and my knees knocked, but I managed a nod.

However, when I went to step back, I stopped because Cody had a tight grip on my top. His eyes heated when he glided my top up my body. Cool air hit my warm skin and I shivered. But it was far from cold and had everything to do with the way Cody's eyes roamed over me.

"Fuck," he uttered, hands reaching out. On his first touch, my heart fluttered, causing my belly to swirl. I bit my bottom lip as his fingers ran over my sides, but not enough to bring a laugh from me. He moved them to my stomach and up slowly between my breasts, over the top of them, and up to my shoulders where he gently applied pressure. Enough that I stepped back again and again until I bumped into the bed. I sat, my breath shaking just as my hands were. Cody used one hand to thread through my hair at the back of my head and tug. I lifted my chin, and my gaze caught his desire-filled one.

Cody dipped down to take my mouth in a demanding kiss. One that had me rubbing my thighs together and reaching out to the top of Cody's jeans. With bravery, because this was Cody, this was *my* man, I undid the button on his jeans and then unzipped them.

Cody groaned against my lips when I pushed his jeans down over his hips. I broke the kiss to catch his gorgeous cock spring free from his jeans and boxers. I licked my lips. I'd never wanted to taste a cock before, but I did Cody's. I wrapped my hand around his long and thick erection. Cody's hissed-out breath encouraged me to run my hand up and down a couple of times before leaning in to lick the tip where pre-cum formed. I used my other hand to cup his balls and gently roll them while I sucked him into my mouth. I slid my tongue around while running my lips up and down his hardness.

"Jesus, Channa." His rough, dark tone told me I was doing a good job. My lower belly clenched, pleased he liked what I was doing.

Only, before I could really get started, Cody jerked back. His dick fell from my mouth and grip. I glanced up, biting my bottom lip, concerned I'd done something, but when I saw his eyes burning, I realized it was the opposite.

He took my hands, pulled me up, and dropped to yank my shorts from my body. I gasped and panted out my breaths as he ran his hands up the sides of my legs and thighs—thanking God that I'd shaved.

My body tingled when his hands rubbed, then slapped each globe of my arse cheeks. I kissed and nipped at his chest. His hands tightened for a second but then moved to my hips where he pushed back. With a shy smile, I moved to lie on the bed, watching Cody as he kicked off his jeans and stood at the end with his cock in hand, gazing at me all over.

I grazed a hand over my breasts and down my

stomach before spreading my legs to run a finger over my clit.

I paused when Cody shook his head. "Nuh-uh, angel." He climbed onto the bed, moving between my legs and took my wrist, removing my hand from myself. "That's mine now, Channa. Mine to touch, mine to pleasure, and mine to make come."

I whimpered when he lowered himself down and hooked my legs over his shoulders. My body shuddered at the first touch of his tongue over my wet folds. He groaned. "Fuck, babe, you taste like damn heaven."

A cry slipped from me when he dove back in and licked from the bottom of my slit to the top and circled my clit.

"Cody," I whispered, blindly reaching down to touch him, to hold him. His hair, his shoulder.

He hummed, and I dug my heels into his back before I realized it could hurt him and stopped. He shook his head, and I glanced down, blushing when his gaze hit mine from between my legs. "Give it all to me, angel."

Dear God. I had never enjoyed myself and felt so free, so me, in bed before. It was as if Cody was made for me. Just me.

I nodded and earned a kiss to my mound above my clit. "Cody, please come up here."

He slowly licked at my clit before he asked huskily, "You need me?"

"Yes." *God yes.*

"Where you want me, angel?"

"Inside me, Cody. Please." I needed to be filled with him.

"Told you I'd give you anythin', you just gotta ask." He lifted himself up, his arm muscles moving, flexing along with his body as he climbed up over me. He looked down between us, gripping his cock and running it up and down my soaked pussy, and paused at the opening.

"You ready for me, angel?"

"Yes." *Very much so.*

He brought his hand up and gently pinched my chin, lifting my gaze to his. "You know you're mine."

I nodded. My body hummed at the claim, the pleasure at knowing I was his and he was mine.

Reaching up, I cupped his neck and tugged him down, but when I did, he slid slowly inside, drawing out a moan. I wrapped my arms around his neck, and he dug his elbows into the bed beside my head when he took me in a scorching kiss while he thrust in and out of my slickness, and I rocked up and down with him.

"You're perfect," I panted into his ear, where I then kissed.

"Angel," he groaned, rolling us so I was on top. I planted my hands on his chest and kept his gaze when I didn't stop grinding up and down on him.

I licked my lips and whispered, "Never felt like this."

His hands on my hips tightened. "Good."

"You were made for me," I told him, riding him faster.

"Fuck me," he breathed out on a growl.

"I am, baby," I teased.

With an abrupt chuckle, he hooked an arm around my shoulder and dragged me down so he could claim my mouth with his. He thrust his hips up and down, meeting my rhythm. My belly warmed and tingled, a sure sign of how close I was.

Catching my breathing, I rested my forehead against his and whispered, "Cody."

"Christ, me too, angel. Me too."

I gripped his shoulder as he cupped my cheek, sliding his thumb into my mouth where I sucked on it. Cody groaned low, and I lost it. I dropped back down, biting his shoulder and moaning as my walls squeezed his cock. His arms tightened around my waist as he drilled in and out of me. "Fuck, Channa, comin'." He grunted before the sound turned into a long, drawn-out groan as he emptied his cum inside me.

When both of us relaxed, and I rested on top of Cody more, he said, "You got it wrong, babe."

"What?"

"You're the perfect one. You're the one made for me. But either way, I'm fuckin' damn happy I got you in my life."

Elation swept through my chest, expanding it. Lifting my head enough to reach him, I kissed his shoulder and then squirmed down on top of him into a tight hug—one that I didn't want to end. In fact, I didn't want to sleep. I wanted this moment to go on and on forever.

"So am I, honey," I whispered. "So am I."

CHAPTER EIGHTEEN

COYOTE

*A*s I rode down the road to the compound with Channa sitting on the back of my bike, I had that strange damn feeling that someone was watching me, or us, again. For the last week, it'd grown more and more. I hadn't mentioned anything to Channa, not wanting to spook her if it was nothing. Which it probably was.

It was then I noticed a man, an older one with tattered clothes and a dirty appearance, standing opposite the compound on the phone. But as I pulled up to the gates, he'd already started to walk away, still talking. Christ, maybe it was my imagination running away with me when I'd thought I was being watched. It could just be my subconscious wanting to protect Channa over something that I thought was there but wasn't. Maybe my mind liked to mess with me.

Whatever it was, it wouldn't put me in a foul mood. Not on a night like tonight, where I got to spend time with my woman and my brothers.

It was family night at the compound, and I'd been looking forward to it more this time around because it meant I got to show Channa more of me. The brothers had better not scare her off in any way, or I'd kick their arse. She was already a bundle of nerves, worse than when she'd gone to dinner with my family.

I pulled through the gates when they opened, seeing it was me. The gates were something we'd added in the last few years since Dad was sick of people showing to the compound instead of the business. The only opening to the public we had was the mechanic shop entrance, which had parking out the front. The compound was completely blocked off from outsiders unless they were invited.

After parking, I waited for Channa to climb off. Her legs shook a bit, being her first ride, but it'd be some-thing she'd get used to. From her shining smile, she looked like she'd enjoyed the ride over.

"That was epic. Scary, but amazing," she exclaimed, bouncing up and down after taking off her helmet. I climbed off, removed my open-face lid, and placed it on the tank as Channa put hers on the seat.

Curling an arm around her shoulders, I tugged her close, kissing the top of her head. "Glad you enjoyed it, angel."

We walked towards the doors, pulling to a stop when they opened and Ruin stepped out. He'd been frowning until he saw us.

"Brother and bakery girl," he yelled, coming at us. We embraced, and when he angled back, he smirked down at Channa. Yeah, we'd been texting and calling while he'd been away; he knew what was happening. Didn't mean he wouldn't give us shit for it. "So," he drew out. "He finally manned up and grew some balls to claim you."

"S-Sorry?" Channa asked.

"Yeah, my brother here was pining over you—"

"All right, enough. Babe, don't listen to him. Whatever he says is a lie."

"He's right. Like the fact he's the best rider in the club. See, all lies." With a smooth move, he reached out, grabbed Channa's wrist, and spun her so he could place his arm around her shoulders and walk her inside.

"That's my damn woman," I snarled, and I clipped him in the back of the head.

"Jesus, brother. I was just being nice and showin' her in."

"Bullshit." I shook my head and wound my arm around Channa's waist. She seemed highly amused by our actions, so at least I wouldn't have to hurt Ruin too much.

Ruin swept a hand out and bowed. "Lead the way with your wonderful woman." I didn't miss the way his smile dimmed when we walked by. My brother had shit on his mind. I'd have to catch some one-on-one time with him later.

"Thought you were headin' out?" I asked since he had been walking out of the compound.

Glancing over my shoulder, I caught him rubbing at the back of his neck. "Yeah, was just gonna head out for a minute, but it's all good now."

"Right," I drew out. Channa glanced up, nibbling on her bottom lip. She knew something was up with Ruin as well. He'd seemed fine when we'd contacted each other. I mean, I knew it wouldn't have been bliss on the trip, not under the circumstances, but there was something else putting him on edge, and I'd be sure to get to the damn bottom of it.

Just as we entered into the common room, where soft music played and people sat or stood around chilling, I leaned in, kissed Channa's temple, and whispered, "I'll have a chat with him later."

She nodded, smiling softly up at me. Fuck me, she was gorgeous. It was easy to get lost in her eyes, and with her smile and her sexy as fuck body, I couldn't get enough of her. I wanted to spend every damn moment with her. When I did see her, it was like waking up in the best damn mood anyone could ever be in.

Hell, I was a goner.

"Channa, you're here," Maya said, rushing up to us. She'd popped over when Channa happened to be at my place for dinner, and they'd met and hit it off. It meant I'd lost my time with Channa because they'd talked like they were long-lost friends. "Sorry, bro, gotta take her to meet the others."

I tightened my hold when Maya tried to pull my woman away with a hand on her wrist. "How about I introduce *my* woman to the others?"

Maya quirked a brow. "Really? You want to come hang with the women where we'll talk about our periods, pregnancy, and childbirth?"

I kissed Channa quickly and said, "I'll come save you soon."

They both laughed at me and left. Ruin cackled beside me. "Brother, you gave in too easy."

"Like to see you put up a fight when women talk about that shit."

He snorted. "I doubt they would be." We shared a look. "Then again, you never know with women and their brains."

"Exactly," I said. I nodded towards the bar. "Come get a drink with me."

With a slap to the back, he said, "Sure, I could use one."

We made our way over, greeting others along the way, which was how it took us near half an hour until we stood at the bar with a drink in hand.

Leaning back against the counter, I searched the room for Channa and smiled when I spotted her. She stood across the room laughing with Mum, Maya, Hellmouth, Swan, Chatter, Nary, and Mally. She was obviously enjoying herself, and it was good to see because this was family for me.

"Shit, brother, you're totally in love," Ruin teased.

I smirked and took a sip of beer. "Never really known what love is. Nothing like this, at least. So, all I'm gonna say is that I think it's damn close."

"Or it could already be there, and you ain't willin' to admit it to a brother before you shared it with your old lady."

Well, there was that.

What I did know was that it would be easy to love Channa. She was amazing. I knew it wouldn't all be fucking great; we had our differences and were both stubborn in our own ways. But I had a feeling we'd work through whatever we'd argue about as what we had was worth fighting for.

Ruin whispered, "You didn't even flinch when I called her your old lady." He shook his head, chuckling. "I see weddin' bells in the future."

Turning to him, I asked, "How's bein' back?"

I caught him stilling for a moment before he shrugged and faced the bar to lean his elbows on while he played with his beer bottle.

"Brother" was all I said.

Ruin sighed. "Fuck, brother."

"Talk to me," I said with a kick to his boot.

"The whole situation was intense. Fucked-up. But…." He shook his head.

"You gonna fill me in?"

He straightened and chugged back the rest of his beer, placing the empty on the bar before slapping me on the arm. "Another time. Go enjoy your night with your woman."

"Ruin—"

He grinned, but it wasn't a Ruin grin. It was clouded. "Nah, brother. It can wait. Seriously."

"Fuckin' bullshit." I dropped my bottle to the bar and clasped him on the back of the neck to give him a shake. "Channa's cool. She won't care if I disappear, but you gotta talk, and we're doin' it. Let's go to my room."

Ruin snorted. "Bossy bastard, aren't ya."

I grinned. "Yep." As we made our way across the room to the hall where the rooms were, I caught my woman's gaze. She smiled and gave me two thumbs up, which had me grinning.

Goddamn, I was lucky our worlds collided. It sucked with how it happened, but it all came together in the end, and if it meant I'd have Channa in my life for-fucking-ever, I wouldn't change a thing about it.

Channa

I GLANCED at the hallway where Cody and Ruin had disappeared a while ago. I hoped they were okay. Even though Ruin and I had only been around each other a handful of times, I could tell he seemed sad on the inside. It was in his eyes. Though he tried not to show it by being jovial, I didn't like seeing the dimness in him. I could tell Cody felt the same, especially since they were close friends. When I'd first seen them walk away together, I caught Nary watching them as well. She leaned into me and whispered, "I hope Coyote can find out what's wrong."

I took her hand and squeezed it. "So do I."

When Deanna clapped, drawing our attention her way, she asked, "So, you two done it yet?"

My face heated like I'd eaten ten chili peppers.

"Deanna," Zara scolded and screwed her nose up. "I do not want to know. That's my son we're talking about."

"Yeah, but he's not your son in blood, just claimed."

"I forgot you were Cody's stepmum," I commented, more to myself than anyone.

"And Talon's my stepdad, but we all treat each other as if we weren't 'step' anything," Maya said.

"Honestly, I wouldn't even have thought any of you were step-something. Your family is amazing." I smiled, which Zara and Maya returned. Though, I did wonder what happened to Cody's real mother.

"Anyway," Deanna drew out. "You didn't answer my question."

"And she doesn't have to," Mally replied for me, which was good because I wasn't going to say anything.

Deanna groaned. "Boring."

"Let me ask you, Deanna, when Nick is older, do you want to know if he's had sex?" Nary asked with a smirk.

I took a sip of my vodka and tonic, a drink Maya got

me, to hide my smile. When Deanna gagged and shook her head with wide eyes, we all laughed.

"Okay, I get it now," she said with a shudder. Zara patted her on the back.

I jumped when hands slid around my waist. Glancing up over my shoulder, I found Cody smiling down at me. "Can I steal my woman?"

Deanna waved a hand at us. "Go."

Cody's brows drew down in confusion. Shifting, Cody dropped an arm from my waist so I could curl one around his. "You don't want to know," I told him.

He flicked his gaze around and nodded. "I believe you."

"Don't steal her for too long. The food's coming out soon," Maya said.

Cody rolled his eyes. "Not sure you meeting my family is a good thing since now I have to share your time with them."

God, I loved that. I really did. I pressed my face into his shoulder, smiling like a maniac.

"We'll be back," he said and steered us towards the hall he'd just come from. I waved back at the women. My friends.

"Is Ruin okay?" I asked in the quiet hallway.

His arm around me tightened. "He will be. He's just gotta sort some shit out in his head." He kissed my temple. "Thanks for the time with him."

I slid my free hand across his stomach. "Cody, no need to thank me. He's your friend, your brother, and family. He needed you, and you wanted to be there for him. I can understand that."

Cody stopped just outside a door and turned me to face him. He stared down at me intently. Reaching up, I cupped his cheek. "Are you okay?" Every time I touched him freely because he was mine, surprise flittered through me. I wasn't sure I'd ever get used to him being my man. My boyfriend.

His smile warmed my insides. "Yeah, angel. I'm fuckin' amazin' because I got you."

Wow. I wanted to spout poetry, sing a love song, and tell him how much he meant to me, but instead, I buried my face into his chest and hugged him tightly to me.

I never thought I could ever be genuinely happy again after Mum died. Yet, here I was stupidly, crazy happy.

His chest moved up and down with a quiet chuckle. I heard him open the door behind him, and he pulled me into the room. I had a feeling he knew I was all gushy for him and didn't know what to say or how to say it without stuffing things up.

With a kiss to his chest, I moved from his arms and had a look around the room. It was simple, with a bed, some drawers with a television on top, and a connecting en suite, but it was nice, and it smelled like Cody.

"This your room?"

"Yeah, for whenever I wanna crash here." He rubbed

at the back of his neck. "Just wanted some quiet time with you for a moment."

Maybe whatever Ruin told him had got to him in some way. I wouldn't push him on it and hound for information. He'd share when he wanted to.

After walking back to him, I circled my arms around his neck and got to my tippytoes to press my lips against his. "I'm all for quiet time whenever you want it," I told him.

He crushed his mouth to mine, drawing a moan from within me when our mouths opened and our tongues danced a wicked and delightful tango.

The kiss broke, and we rested our foreheads together, both breathing hard. His hands ran up and down my waist while I gently scratched through his short hair at the back.

"Come sit on the bed with me for a bit?" he asked.

I took his hand and nodded. At the bed, Cody sat with his back against the headboard and spread his legs, patting the spot between them. Happy to oblige, I climbed onto the bed and over his leg, resting my back against his chest, and when his arms wrapped around my waist, I held onto them.

"Were you havin' fun with the women?"

"Yes, they're great."

"Julian calls them the muffkateers." Laughter bubbled up and out of me; Cody joined in.

"Of course he would. Too bad he couldn't make it tonight, and I'm yet to meet your uncle Mattie and their daughter."

He tucked some hair behind my ear and kissed the bridge of it. "Don't worry. There'll be a heap of time for that."

Just hearing him say that we had time had me mushy on the inside.

"How about you? Do you have any aunts or uncles?"

I tensed a little but made myself relax. "No. Both my parents were only children, and my grandparents have passed on. My mum's when I was young, and my dad's… well, I heard it was a few years ago."

"You don't talk to them?"

"They moved away, but no, I never really spoke to them even when they lived here. What about your birth mum?"

His arms tightened for a second. "Can't stand the bitch. She's a money-hungry whore, and that's putting it mildly. Dad and Mum got me outta her house the night she and her new fella decided to have an orgy with me in the house. I was thirteen or fourteen. Somethin' like that."

"Oh my God," I breathed. She sounded disgusting. "I'm sorry you had to see that, but I'm glad Talon and Zara got you out."

"Same, babe." His arms loosened so he could run his hands up and down my arms.

We fell silent for a while, until I said softly, "Mum and I ran from my father the weekend after that situation happened at high school. He used to beat us."

His arms tightened around me. "Fuck, angel. Sorry that happened to you both."

"So am I. But, in a way, I wouldn't be where I am in life otherwise. I loved the time I got to have with Mum, just her and me. How we found the passion for baking because we wouldn't have opened the bakery otherwise. She was the strong one to make the move in the first place. I made sure I would stay strong for her in life as well."

"That why you learned to fight?"

"Yes. I never wanted another person to take a hand to me or my mum again."

"Is he still around?"

I paused. I had a feeling I knew where this would go, and that would be a beaten-up father from my man. "He is, but I haven't seen him since, and I don't want to. I'd like to keep it all behind me and not rehash things, which means I would prefer if you left him alone to live his miserable life."

"Is he miserable?"

"The last time I spoke with an old friend, which was a long time ago, she told me he was a drunk and a bum. So yes, he is."

"Don't like that he took a hand to you and your mum and he didn't get any payback for it."

"He did. We left him, and it would have been a huge blow to his ego." I quickly got to my knees and spun around to face him. Cody smirked, hands to my waist as I straddled his hips. "Anyway, I can think of better things to think about and do."

He quirked a brow. "Yeah?"

"Oh yes." I leaned in and whispered into his ear, "I'm

talking about me, my mouth, and your penis. Are you up for it?"

Cody chuckled. "Like your distracting techniques, angel. I won't complain if that's what you *really* want to do."

I grinned. "I sure do."

Because even when I'd started it as a distraction, I still wanted to have Cody in my mouth. My pussy throbbed just from the thought.

I would never get enough of him.

"Just know, I'll have to return the favour," Cody said just as I kissed his neck.

I trailed kisses down over his tee-covered chest and pulled back, shrugged, and said, "I mean, it wouldn't be the worst thing in the world."

Cody chuckled again and leaned forward to kiss me on the nose. "Get at it then, woman, 'cause I got a taste, and I'm wantin' it *now*."

Of course, I quickly got down to business.

CHAPTER NINETEEN

CHANNA

"She's smiling again," Denise commented.

"Didn't know she'd be this sickly if she got herself a man," Stanley said.

"Shut it, you two," I told them as I pulled a tray of pies from the walk-in refrigerator.

"I think it's cute. God knows I need some action."

"Fucking hell, this is what I get for working with two women. Denise, I don't need to know. It's bad enough I know Channa's all happy because of her man."

I dropped the tray to the counter and asked, "Denise, was that the door opening?"

"Nope." She grinned. "Does Coyote have any friends that are single?"

I paused and looked over at her leaning against the counter. "You want me to ask Cody to set you up with a brother?"

"Oooh, look at you getting the lingo down," she teased. "Yes, if there's a nice one like Coyote."

Laughing, I shrugged. "I'll see if Cody knows of one."

"It doesn't even have to be for a relationship. Just one night and I'd be—"

"Get out the front, Denise," Stanley ordered with a glare.

Denise threw her head back and laughed loudly, but she did walk back out the front. It sounded like it was just in time, as I heard the door open definitely this time.

"You know she loves stirring you." I smiled. Stanley grunted. I didn't miss his lips twitching though. Glancing to the clock, I added, "Cody's family should be in soon. I just have to finish mixing the dough together and help you—"

"Channa, relax. They'll love your place. You do the dough and I'll get the cookies done. It's not like I've never done them."

"I know, but I hate leaving all the work to you."

He snorted and rolled his eyes. "Yeah, you slack off too much. You should do more work." He shot me a scowl. "Do what you have to and then get out the front. I've had enough of you."

Smiling, I said, "Yes, Stanley."

He grumbled something under his breath, and then I caught, "She needs some damn time off before she works herself into a grave."

God, I loved this man like a father. He was rough, gruff, but he was mine. We bickered as we continued to work, and it was something I wouldn't ever give up. I also hoped the new employee would work alongside us just as well. Susan was starting her trial run next week. She seemed nice when she came in for her interview. We didn't run out of things to say, and she knew everything I'd wanted in a baker. From her résumé, I discovered she was in her thirties, had worked in France for many years after her apprenticeship, and had only moved back to town a couple of months ago when she ran into Clary.

I had everything crossed things would work out because it meant I would get the chance to spend more time with Cody. It was the thought of more time with the man I was coming to like a lot that shot tingles of excitement to my belly.

Having had things change between Cody and me, that our relationship had shifted from friendship to more, still blew my mind. It almost seemed as if it was meant to be. I'd never felt more comfortable in my life around another man. Okay, so I'd only had two other boyfriends, but I'd never felt as… as giddy with them as I did with Cody Marcus.

When I'd gone to climb out of bed that morning at three, and like the other two mornings he'd stayed over, he'd curled his arm around me and dragged me back onto the bed. He'd hovered over me before kissing me without a care in the world over my morning breath.

"Always kiss me goodbye, angel," he'd whispered into my ear that first time. Of course, I liked to test him to see if I could sneak out of bed, but I couldn't, and his actions brought a big smile to my face every single time.

Just thinking of him had my heart racing in anticipation of seeing him again. Of kissing him, being with him.

God, I sounded lovesick, and maybe, just maybe, I was.

"Channa," Denise called.

I grinned at Stanley. He simply smirked and rolled his eyes. "Go woo his family."

With a salute, I said, "I will."

I made my way out through the doors to hear Drake ask, "And she makes all this stuff?"

"That she does," Denise told him.

"Wicked."

"Hi," I called out. Zara, Drake, Ruby, and Dillon looked up and over at me.

"This place is the shit," Drake declared.

"Drake," Zara snapped.

"Sorry, Mum, but it was called for. I want to try everything in here. Everything!"

Laughing, I said, "How about we start with two things and see how you go?"

He winked. "You got it. I'll have a jelly slice and a chocolate éclair."

Nodding, I glanced at the others. "Ruby and Dillon?"

Dillon looked to Ruby and waited for her to answer; she shot him a sweet smile and said, "I'll have a caramel slice, please."

"Can I have a custard tart?" Dillon asked.

"Of course. What about you, Zara?"

"A lamington. I haven't tried one of those yet."

"Got it. Grab a table, and I'll help Denise get the treats, then join you."

I got a chorus of "Thank you." Zara stayed back to try and slip me money, but I firmly told her not to. They were Cody's, and Cody was mine, which meant in a roundabout way, they were mine too.

"Can you find out drink orders for me?" I asked Zara.

She nodded. "You got it, and thank you again for this. The kids have been so excited, even though they've tried their best not to show it. Apparently, it's uncool to show excitement."

Smiling, I shrugged. "It's just a bakery."

She shook her head. "Yes, it is, but you have to have talent to be able to bake like you do." With that, she turned and went to the table.

It wasn't Zara who dropped back with the order though; it was Drake. He leaned his elbows onto the counter and smirked at me. After he told what everyone wanted, he drew out, "So…" I was sure I knew what was coming. He liked to tease and also annoy his brother.

"No, Drake, I won't leave Cody for you. Besides the fact you're too young, I do have these warm and fuzzy feelings for your brother."

He screwed up his nose. "Seriously? Warm and fuzzy?"

"Yes." I nodded.

He sighed. "Fine. I guess I'll live with you being my sister-in-law instead of my woman."

I pulled my hands up in front of me and waved them. "Whoa, hold up there. You're jumping a bit too far ahead."

Drake chuckled. "Yeah, right. Wait until I tell Coyote you've got warm and fuzzies for him."

"Drake," I growled. "If you say one word to him, you'll never eat anything I bake again."

His eyes widened. "You're kidding, right?"

Crossing my arms over my chest, I shook my head. "Nope."

He lifted his fingers to his lips and zipped across them. "Won't say a word."

I grinned. "Good. Can you take that tray over, and I'll help Denise with the drinks?"

"You got it."

It was after the teens had eaten their first round of cakes, and they were back up at the counter picking another, when Zara turned to me and took my hand.

Concern had my belly dipping. "Are you okay?" I asked.

Her smile was soft. "I'm fine." She patted my hand before picking up her mug of coffee. "I just wanted to touch on something."

"Anything," I told her.

"I never thought I would be where I am. Married to a biker. In fact, I dodged Talon for two years before he'd had enough and pushed into my life. I was scared of many things, but most of all, what it meant being with a man whose life is with the club. It's different, but if you stick with them, they love with everything they have. They would give you the world if they could. There'll be hard times. God knows Talon drives me crazy, but I wouldn't change it for anything." She smiled. "All I'm saying is that sometimes it might be overwhelming, but it's worth it."

Placing my hand on her arm, I nodded. "I know it will be." I shook my head. "I know Cody will be worth staying strong with."

Tears filled her eyes. "You'll be good for him."

My own welled. "He's good for me."

"Are you two gonna start crying and huggin'? 'Cause if you are, I'll take my cake to go," Drake said, sitting down with a vanilla slice.

Our tears turned into humour as we both laughed.

I honestly felt very lucky.

Cody's family stayed for another half an hour. I enjoyed the moments they were there, as it showed me how rich Cody's life was with them all in it. Not exactly Dillon, but he was proving himself, and I hoped he did stick around for the long haul because I saw great things with Ruby and Dillon. He'd gained a lot of respect when he stuck up for Ruby when Drake talked smack. But, of course, he was still going to get taunted by the older Marcus men. Still, he was a sweetheart. He pulled out her chair, opened the door for them all, and I could tell even when they ran out of things to whisper to each other about, they were relaxed in each other's company.

Drake made me laugh many times, and I knew, even with all the hell he gave to his sister, he did it out of love.

When I turned from the front door, I caught Denise's smile and returned it with my own.

"They're amazing," she commented. "Though Drake's going to be a ladies' man when he's older."

I snorted. "He already is. I honestly can't believe how great Cody's family is. He's very lucky."

She poked me in the stomach as I passed. "So are you, because anyone can tell they think the world of you."

My smile wouldn't leave. "You think so?" I asked, even though I was pretty sure she was right.

"I do."

"I agree," Stanley said from out back.

I couldn't help but clap my glee. "We're going to need to refill what Drake and Dillon ate."

Denise nodded. "I'm glad I had a daughter. I didn't know boys ate so much." She waved me off. "You get what you need from out the back, and I'll start the sandwiches for the lunch rush."

"On it." I walked through the doors and caught Stanley looking towards the back door. "What's wrong?"

He shook his head. "I was sure I heard scratching, but it could be just me hearing thi— There," he stated.

I'd heard it as well and moved to the back door. When I opened it, my blood turned cold. "Coco, Harley," I whispered. They rubbed against me, both whimpering, and I knew right away something was wrong.

"Why would they be here?" Stanley asked from just behind me, causing me to jump. "And why the back door?"

"I-I don't know… and, um, I always unlock from the back, so they could have come to where my scent was strong." Fear twisted my insides. "Stanley, I left Cody at home."

"Right, don't start to panic," Stanley ordered.

It was too late though.

"Channa, fuck, you're panicking. Close the door and sit the dogs at the back door," he said, but I was too busy running through things in my head. Why would Cody have let the dogs out? Had something happened to him? What? I thought our troubles were over.

Stanley moved me aside to close the back door. "Sit and stay," he told the dogs, and with his hands on my shoulders, he steered me to the counter.

"We'll call him," he suggested.

I nodded and licked my dry lips. "Maybe it was an accident?"

Stanley clicked his fingers and pointed at me with his right hand as he picked up the phone with the other. "Exactly."

"But they listen to him. They like him."

"They could have got out," Stanley suggested.

I dragged my top teeth over my bottom lip and shrugged. "They never have before."

And they hadn't.

All I could think was something terrible had happened.

Stanley cursed, and I jumped when the phone in his hand rang. He held it out to me. I took it and saw my hand shook. "H-Hello?"

"Think you're so fucking good, don't you?" The voice was harsh and rough. "With your pretty little bakery, cute house, and a man you obviously care about."

"What are you talking about? Who are you?" I demanded and was proud my voice didn't tremble.

The man chuckled. "You ruined my life, girly."

Girly.

No. It couldn't be.

"Dad?" I asked hesitantly. Had I jinxed myself from talking about him last night?

"Got it in one."

"What's this about?" It didn't make sense. I hadn't seen him since we left. I never wanted to…. God, maybe I did jinx it.

"What's it about?" he yelled. "What do you think it's about, you stupid little bitch? I'll tell you, you dumb cunt. *You* ruined my life. *She* always protected you, always put you first. *You* made her leave. *You* made her die, and now it's time you pay because I won't have you living in your happy little bubble you created when she isn't. I'm about to pop it."

"I don't understand. What are you talking about? I didn't kill Mum."

"You did. You wore her down like you grated on my nerves. It was why I took to drinking, why I hit you for not shutting up and her, because she always took your side."

"You have got to be kidding me. Why now? What have you done?"

"Why now? Because I never knew you were in town until someone told me. I never knew my wife, my beautiful wife, had died until someone told me. And as to what I've done… well, you'll have to come to your house and find out. But come alone, bitch, or I'll kill him."

Ice formed through my veins as my body chilled over.

Slowly, I pulled the phone away and stared at it as if I'd just imagined the call… but I hadn't because the ice-cold dread clawing through me was too real to be anything but legit.

A couple of hours earlier.

· · ·

COYOTE

I SCRUBBED a hand over my face as I walked down the hallway from Channa's bedroom. It seemed my woman wanted to take care of me by switching off the alarm and letting me sleep in instead of getting to work. Smiling, I walked into the kitchen, opened the refrigerator, and grabbed out the carton of milk. After unscrewing the lid, I drank from it, knowing that if Channa was here, she'd try and kick my arse for backwashing. Even when I told her since we were swapping spit, it shouldn't really matter to her, she'd huffed and puffed and told me it was still gross before storming out into the backyard to play with Coco and Harley. I'd gone out to her, wrapped my arms around her, and knew all was forgiven when she rested back against me.

It was moments like that, and many others, where I just knew.

She was it.

She was my something special.

Christ, I looked forward to each and every damn day we spent together. Yeah, it'd be better if we weren't so busy, but I wouldn't give us up because of our schedule. She was worth working my hours around her sleep.

I dropped the carton back in the refrigerator and closed the door when it occurred to me the dogs weren't under my feet. Usually they were in the room when I woke. I should have realized sooner. I whistled and called, "Harley, Coco?"

Silence.

That wasn't right

Worry seeped into me. I made my way to the back door. "Coco, Harley," I tried again as I unlocked and opened the door.

Stepping out, I stilled when a gun was shoved under my chin. "Move, scream, or do anything, and I'll shoot your head off."

Out of the corner of my eye, I caught sight of the old man I'd seen standing opposite the compound the previous day. "Who are you?' I clipped.

He ignored me, shoving the gun up under my chin more. "Inside, now."

"No."

He stepped closer, and I got a whiff of him, regretting the action immediately. Not only did he look homeless, but he smelled like it too. The fucker laughed. "You think you got a choice?"

"What did you do to the dogs?"

"Got rid of them. Enough questions. Get the fuck back inside."

"Why?"

"Jesus Christ, are you stupid? What's she see in you?"

Fury burned to life. "So, this is about Channa?"

He shoved the gun deeper. "Shut up."

But I wouldn't when he wanted something from Channa. From my woman.

I hit out quickly, jabbing my fist into his gut. He moaned and cursed. I grabbed for the gun and managed to punch him in the face before something hard smacked me in the back of the head.

Stumbling, I blinked rapidly and turned, only to trip and fall on my arse.

Through a haze, I looked up to the person who'd hit me. "Got to be fuckin' kiddin' me," I mumbled before passing out.

CHAPTER TWENTY

CHANNA

I was mildly aware of Stanley stomping to the doors and barking, "Shop's shutting. Something's come up."

"Stanley?" Denise questioned.

"Close it down, Denise. Now."

My heart thumped hard, my stomach lurched, and I wanted to throw up, but I fought the bile down by swallowing over and over. I'd never thought I would have to see the man again, but if it meant Cody would be safe, I'd walk through fire for him.

Hands landed on my shoulders. I jolted and looked up through tears to see Stanley. "Lucky Coyote's mum left, but you've got to call Talon."

"I can't. *He* said no one was to come or he'd kill Cody."

"Channa, you can't go in there on your own. Not for you and not for your guy."

Blinking rapidly, my bottom lip wobbled as I stared down at my babies. I had to go by myself because I wouldn't risk Cody's life for my own. Even with the nerves, the fear, I wasn't walking into a situation I didn't think I could handle. From what I got, there was only one man there. One old man. I'd dealt with worse recently. I could do this. I'd push the terror aside and ride the adrenaline when the time came.

Denise slapped through the doors, causing me to jump. The dogs growled, but as soon as I touched them, they quieted. Denise took us in, her hand shooting to her throat. "What's happened?"

"Channa's sperm donor has Coyote captured at her house. Wants her to come home on her own or he'll kill Coyote."

"What?" she whispered, the alarm clear in her voice, just like it rolled through my body.

I straightened and swallowed thickly. I started to erect a wall around my panic of running into a situation I knew nothing about. Not that it mattered. I would still head into the unknown for Cody's sake. "I'm going," I said, looking to Stanley.

His jaw clenched. "Not alone—"

"Stanley, I have to. I'm not risking Cody's life. I don't.... It doesn't make sense, *his* hostility. Yes, we left him, but he beat us. How was he wronged?" I shook my head. "Maybe I can talk him down." I had to talk him down. I wouldn't let anything happen to Cody.

I wouldn't.

It was a promise to Cody, but also myself. I'd harden my heart and barge into the scene to protect Cody and deal with *him* for the last time.

He wasn't going to wreck my life again.

He wasn't going to win.

I might have been running to him, but I would surely win. I'd make sure of it because I'd do *anything* to see him gone from my life once and for all.

All I had to do was remember I had a beautiful, loving future with Cody Marcus, and I'd protect it to make sure that future stayed true.

"I have to go," I said, my voice shaking, and I cursed at myself silently for it. Obviously my wall wasn't all the way erected around my nerves or my fear. Still, I started for the door.

"Channa," Denise called. "Please don't go on your own. What will it matter if another person is there hiding? Stanley's right. Call Talon."

I shook my head. "I can't. I won't risk it. I can do this. He's nothing compared to what I've already been through. But if I'm not there soon, something *can* happen. I won't let it. I'm going." I backed up towards the door, seeing the terror in their eyes. For me. But all I could care about was Cody.

"Let me come then—"

"No!" I shook my head. "Stanley, please, no. I'll be

too distracted and worried about you. I need my head. Please."

"I don't like this, Channa," he said.

I took another step back. "Neither do I." Yet, I would still do it.

"Take the dogs at least," Denise said. Tears streamed down over her cheeks.

I glanced behind me. Both of my babies twitched on their butts where they sat. "Okay," I said softly to appease them or I wouldn't get out of there and to Cody. "I'll be back soon," I offered.

"You'd better be," Stanley clipped.

Denise managed a nod, her bottom lip trembling. I was right there with her on the inside. I wanted to crack, to break down and sob, but I couldn't.

At the door, I lifted my hand in a small wave before I turned and walked out with my dogs following me. "Stay close," I ordered, and together we raced down the alleyway beside the shop, down the path, and I took the corner to my house, opening the side gate.

Bile threatened, and my heart wanted to explode, but I slowed as I approached the back door. With each step I took, my soul frosted over, turning me cold to deal with whatever I was about to do.

The dogs growled. I jumped when the door opened abruptly. "Heel," I commanded, my hands on each of their heads.

The man I used to know stood in the doorway. Only this man looked more weathered. He had less hair, red eyes, and tattered clothes. This man was very different from the one I remembered, yet he was still recognizable.

This man I could take on.

My babies wouldn't stop snarling low at the intruder. His hand lifted, a gun pointed my way. My walls cracked a little seeing the gun, but I patched them and reassured myself I could do this. I'd been in a situation like this.

"Leave them outside and come in."

I tipped my chin up and glared. "Where's Cody?"

"You'll see when you get in here."

I ground my teeth together. "If you've harmed him—"

"Get the fuck in here to see, you stupid bitch."

Glancing down at Coco and Harley, I ordered, "Stay." They whimpered, and Harley inched forward when I took a step. I shot a hand out and snapped, "No. Stay."

My knees may have wobbled when I made my way up the stairs, but I was determined to switch the scene my way. My dad— No, I couldn't, *wouldn't* call him that. He didn't deserve it. Percy moved back into the house, and I stepped through. He shoved me to the side, slamming the door shut and locking it. My babies howled outside, and my heart clenched.

"Where's Cody?" I asked, clasping my hands together to keep myself from punching him before I knew what was going on. I would see Cody safe before I acted and took him on.

I stilled when the cold tip of the gun pressed against

my temple. "It'd be so easy to just kill you now. Kill you like you did your mum."

"I didn't kill her," I stated clearly.

"You did. You wore her down enough to get sick. Found out all about it. Found out you stupidly moved back to town and opened that damn bakery like nothing happened." He pressed the gun in harder. "You took her from me."

Fury had me blurting, "*You* made her leave by raising a hand to us."

"No!" he bellowed, knocking the gun into my head. "You. It was all you. You annoyed me, and she wouldn't listen when it came to you. I wanted to send you off so we could be together. She wouldn't listen. You took her from me. You!" he screamed, and then in the next second, he was laughing. "But you were stupid enough to move back to town. I would have let you go if I hadn't been told you were here living your life in a happy fucking bubble after you killed your mum."

He'd wanted to get rid of me.

He'd wanted to send me off and Mum refused.

Mum protected me and got his rage for it.

"We weren't far," I told him, to rile him, to show him how blind, how selfish, how pathetic he was.

"What?" he barked.

I smirked. "If you'd looked, you would have found her. We'd only moved out a little. We were still close."

"Bullshit," he bit out, hitting me again with the gun.

"I'm not. But you didn't look. You sunk lower and

fell into your pity party." I laughed without humour. "Who's the stupid one now?"

"Shut up," he screeched and grabbed my upper arm to haul me through the kitchen and in the living room.

"No," I uttered, pressing my hands to my stomach, but nothing would settle it. Cody, my Cody, was tied to a chair, unconscious. Blood seeped from cuts on his chest, and a woman I didn't know stood behind him, holding a knife to his throat, smiling sadistically.

Two to one.

I could still take them both on, but I didn't like the thought of this bitch being so close to Cody with a weapon. I had to get her away first.

"Finally. I thought you two would dribble on and on forever," she complained in a shrill voice. She ran her free hand up and down over Cody's chest. I wanted to rip it off. I wanted to punch her, kick her, and make her pay for touching him.

My upper lip rose. "What's this?" I asked. "Who are you?"

She cackled. "I'm his." She patted Cody's chest.

I shook my head. "What?"

She rolled her eyes. "Can we get on with this?"

"Right." Percy nodded.

The woman squealed, walked around Cody, and tapped his face. "Wakey, wakey, baby." Cody made a noise but didn't open his eyes as his head dropped back. I took a step forward but stopped when she grabbed his hair on the top of his head and straightened him. "Come on, baby. I didn't hit you that hard with the pan. Wake up for me." She tapped his cheek again and again.

"Stop," I demanded and tried to shake Percy's hold off, but the dickhead's fingers bit into my arm tighter.

Percy knocked me in the back of the head with the gun. "You move and I'll kill you," he stated before dropping his hold and stalking over to the woman and Cody.

I inched forward a little until Percy stepped up behind Cody and pushed the gun to the back of his head. Dread seeped in, but I forced it away. I needed them my way. I had to get them away from Cody. Get the gun and force them to surrender. If they didn't... I would do what I had to, even if that thought put a foul taste in my mouth.

"Hey," the woman complained. "Put it on her, not my man. He's mine after all this."

Who was this woman?

Percy grunted and held the gun over Cody's head at me while he used his other hand to shake Cody. "Wake the hell up. I want this done."

Cody groaned. His eyes fluttered. "What the fuck?" he uttered.

"Hi, baby," the woman cooed, running her hand over his head. "Don't you worry about a thing, I'm here for you."

"Fuck off, Genny," Cody snarled. He groaned. "You hit me on the fuckin' head."

"Oh, baby, I had to, or you would have ruined everything. But now it's all good and we can be together."

Cody laughed, but it was a harsh bark that held no humour. "You stupid cunt. I have a woman."

Genny stomped her foot and shrilled, "No, no, no."

Dear God, this woman was unhinged, and she really had to back the fuck off from *my* man.

"You're mine. You'll always be mine."

"Enough of this," Percy bellowed. Cody looked up, blinked, and then shifted his gaze to where Percy pointed the gun, but he couldn't see around Genny. "Move aside so he can see her."

She giggled and danced to the side of Cody, resting her hand on his shoulder.

He tensed. "Channa," he whispered, and then his eyes widened when he realized where the gun was trained.

When I saw the horror evident in his eyes, my tears welled, my bottom lip trembled, and my heart cracked.

"Let her go," he said softly. His jaw clenched. "Let her the fuck go," he demanded harshly.

I shook my head. "No." I smiled sadly. This was my fault. It wouldn't be me who was going. "Let Cody go."

Percy scoffed. "Isn't that sweet."

"No, it's not," Genny snapped. She pointed at me. "You don't call him Cody. He's mine. He will always be mine, and I'll make sure of it." She laughed and shifted from one foot to another before she bent over and rubbed her cheek against the top of Cody's head. "After all, it was why I told your daddy where you were. You were getting too close to my man. I took it upon myself to protect him. I knew you weren't any good for him. So, I looked into you. Asked people about you. Eventually I got to the bottom of it. How you and your mummy ran from him…. That's just not right. Taking his wife away like that. Of course, when I learned how angry Percy was, I had to help him get to you."

"And, in turn, you get to keep Cody?" I asked. Genny's screws had definitely come loose in her head. How did she think she had a chance to keep Cody when all this was done? He wouldn't want anything to do with her.

"Why the fuck do you want me? We had one night. You sucked me off and that was it. Why me?" Cody demanded. Hearing what they had done nearly had me gagging, but I pushed it back since it was obvious this woman was crazy.

She'd soon see.

She'd soon find out just who Cody's woman was when I beat the hell out of her and knocked some sense into her.

She giggled, kissing him on the cheek. I'd never wanted to rip hair out from the roots before, but there it was. She patted his head. "Oh, baby, I heard you talking one night to Ruin. How you wanted what your daddy has. Someone special who you'd treat like your queen. I knew I was that for you. I just have to get you to see."

"What's the fuckin' plan here? What's the goal?" Cody asked.

"It's simple," Genny said. "You get to come with me

and… well, he'll do whatever he wants with her." She waved her hand my way.

"And how do you think I'll come willingly with you?" Cody questioned, and after it, he mouthed to me, "Run."

I gave a small shake of my head. He glared at me and tried again. "Run." I narrowed my own gaze. He was a fool if he thought I would leave him to them.

"It's simple. If you don't, Percy will kill her."

I snorted. "He's going to kill me anyway. You won't get Cody."

"Smart girl," Percy sneered. He moved out from behind Cody and started for me. "I would have done it when you were younger. When she started taking your side. But I didn't get the chance because she loved you, and it would have broken her." He shook his head. "I'm not losing my chance again."

Cody rocked and shifted on the chair. "Don't fuckin' touch her. Channa, run. Angel, run, please." I wanted to tell him I had the situation under control. I wanted to say we would be safe. I'd make sure of it, but I couldn't because I had yet to make it happen, and all Cody could see were bad things.

"Wait, you promised," Genny yelled.

I didn't move. I waited. I needed Percy closer and away from Cody. My body shook, the adrenaline riding me. My heart thumped, and my belly twisted, but I stayed still until he stood before me with the gun pressed to my forehead.

"Angel, no," Cody called, panic evident in his voice. I

hated he was feeling that. I hated this whole thing. Tears streamed down my face. "Fuck no. Hurt her and you die," Cody snarled, still fighting. My beautiful man was trying to get to me, to help.

"Percy, stop. You said you would follow my plan. I want Coyote," Genny complained. "This isn't how we worked it out."

Percy snorted, shaking his head. He didn't look away from me when he said to her, "You're just as stupid as this one." My head moved back when he pressed the gun harder against me.

"Stop," Genny screamed. At least I knew she wouldn't harm what she thought was hers. I had a chance to take control here, and I would use it.

I had to.

Percy smiled. The alcohol in his breath washed over me. "I won't."

Cody roared.

It was now or never.

Flashing my arm up and to the side, I knocked Percy's arm away. The front window exploded, and I faltered at the loud noise and rush of movement. Glass flew everywhere. Genny screamed and ducked behind Cody as someone rolled into the room. Percy turned and aimed. Talon stood before his son, gun in hand.

"Drop your gun," Talon barked.

A shot fired.

Blood.

It coated Talon's stomach.

I screamed and tackled Percy to the ground with my

hand around his over the gun. A weapon I didn't know how to use but would try to if it came down to it. "No, no, no," I chanted, over and over.

Out the corner of my eye, I watched as Talon stumbled to the side. The gun in his hand shook and dropped to the floor. His hands went over the wound… and it was then I saw behind him.

I saw it.

More red.

More blood.

On Cody.

His chest.

I bellowed in Percy's face, my throat stinging from the volume. We fought for control of the gun. It wasn't time for emotions. I steeled my walls more as I elbowed him in the face, his grip loosening.

I took the gun, aimed, and said, "We could have sorted through this. We could have—"

"Just shoot, girly. Shoot, or I'm going to keep coming for you and your people."

No. I couldn't let that happen. Rage spread through me. The need to protect strengthened my hold on the gun as I stared down at the man who'd made many years of my life hell.

He wouldn't do it again.

I wouldn't allow it.

I fired.

The fight in Percy fell away.

His eyes stared up with no life left in them. I gagged

but shook my head. I'd had to do it. I had to. He'd hurt Cody and Talon. There was no other way.

A high-pitched cry sounded. I turned to see Genny behind Cody with a knife raised.

"Channa go, get help," Cody begged, his anguished eyes on his still father.

Genny shook her head. "No one will have him."

But she wouldn't because he was mine and no one would take him away from me. No one would wreck my life again. I had control, and I would use it.

I aimed. I didn't think. I shot. Her mouth gaped, her eyes widened before she blinked and glanced down to the blood coating her chest. She stumbled back but tried to reach out for Cody. Her fingers grazed his shoulder before she dropped to the floor behind him.

I dropped my arm to my side. My head felt heavy, along with my heart. My chest rose and fell rapidly. I'd shot two people. One I knew for certain was dead. The other…. I whimpered, but then sucked in a deep breath and forced my walls to harden once more because I had things to do. I still had to be strong.

For Cody and Talon.

CHAPTER TWENTY-ONE

COYOTE

"Channa, angel, come untie me," I said, and my fierce woman raced over to me. I heard her sharp intake of breath when she saw Genny's body sprawled on the floor behind me. Channa made a noise in the back of her throat. She needed a moment, needed time to adjust to what she'd done, but I couldn't give it to her yet.

Not when Dad was lying on the floor, struggling with each breath.

He was pale, too pale.

Claws dug into my heart through my chest.

Stanley entered the room. He dropped the machete and scrubbed both hands over his head. "Ah, fuck, shit, fuck. I shouldn't have let you come in alone." His eyes flicked to Channa and me as he moved to my dad's side and dropped to the floor, pressing his hands to the wound. Muttering curse after curse as he shook his head.

Once free, I stood and drew Channa into my arms, ignoring the aches over my body. Her nails dug into me where she gripped, but she probably didn't even realise it, and I didn't care. I'd give her anything she needed. I cupped the back of her head, pressing it against my shoulder, and said urgently, "Angel, I promise soon you can take what you need, you can grieve, scream, anything, and I'll help you through it. I'll hold you, but now, I need to go to my dad."

She pushed me back, nodding. "Go." We moved to Dad, and I dropped to my knees opposite Stanley.

Dad's arm shook when he tried to lift it.

Fuck me. Fuck.

I ground my teeth together to stop the emotions rushing forward and took his hand in both of mine.

"Dad, you're gonna be fine."

His gaze lifted to Channa then back to me. "Y-You got a good woman...." His breath shuddered. More claws scraped at my heart. They dug deep and opened me wide. Dad sucked in a breath. "Proud of you, Cody."

I shook my head, damn tears filled my eyes. "Tell me when you're healed."

He slightly shook his head. "Proud," he whispered before his eyes closed.

Channa whimpered behind me, her hand on my

shoulder. Dread smashed into me, and I shook my head. "Dad… fuck, Dad."

"He's passed out," Stanley managed to say before people rushed into the room. "Call an ambulance."

"What the fuck happened?" Griz demanded. He fell to his knees by Dad's head, his face pinched in worry. Stanley filled him in on what he knew, but I couldn't say anything. I couldn't do anything but hold Dad's hand. I closed my eyes and dropped my chin.

Please, fucking please, if anyone's listening, don't take him from me. Don't take him from the family. We won't be the same without him. We won't.

Time went by, brothers spoke and walked around us. I thought I heard my aunt Violet, which had me relaxing a little because I knew she'd take care of anything when it came to the police, with her being a private investigator and working with them regularly.

"Cody," Channa whispered into my ear. I jolted a little, blinking through the haze of pain and fear. "Move back, honey. They need to work on him."

Nodding, I stood and stepped back a few paces, watching the paramedics frantically moving around my dad. My pulse raced when they quickly patched him up enough to get him into the ambulance.

It told me how bad things were, and Christ, that fucking gutted me.

Griz stepped in front of me. "Go with your woman to the hospital. I'm with Talon. I'll see you there."

I nodded. Griz would make sure they did what they

had to for Dad. I wanted to have Channa at my side and in my sight.

Griz turned and left, and I noticed Stanley had been bent saying something to Channa about going back to the bakery to sit with Denise.

Outside, the ambulance roared to life and sped off. It felt like a knife opened me from heart to gut. Channa had me though. She led me towards a car. Fuck, I didn't even know whose it was. But then another paramedic stepped in front of us.

"I need to see to your wound."

"No," I clipped and tried to shift around them.

They moved with me. "You're bleeding, I need to see what's going on."

"Get the fuck out of the way."

"It looks like a bullet is sticking out of your shoulder."

Reaching up, I ripped the shirt enough to stick two fingers in the wound and pull the bullet free. I dropped it to the ground. "Now it's not. If you don't move and let me get to my dad, I'll fuckin' move you myself."

"Goddamn," the paramedic cursed. He bent, grabbed out a bandage, and handed it to Channa. "Get him patched enough for the nurses to deal with at the hospital."

Channa nodded, took the bandage, and said, "I will." She tugged me to the car. I got in the passenger side, knowing I wasn't in any state to drive.

Channa leaned in and pulled my tee up. I winced as she applied the patch to my wound. She pressed her lips to my temple. Then she shifted back a little and said, "Together we'll get through this."

Not long after, we pulled into a parking spot out front of the hospital, got out, and started, hand in hand, towards the doors that read Emergency. A nurse stood by the automatic doors waiting. They must have been warned I was coming, and he stepped close, saying, "You have to be seen."

"No," I stated.

Christ, my breath caught when we stepped through the doors. There were at least a dozen brothers standing around with their arms crossed.

"Sir, please, you have to be seen," the nurse tried again.

Griz stepped forward. "He'll be seen when he knows more about his father."

The nurse took a step back, suddenly pale. He nodded. "I'll go find out."

"You do that," I bit out. When he was gone, I said, "Griz?"

"Blue's gettin' your mum and siblin's. Killer's called Gamer. He's bringin' in Nancy and pickin' up Maya on the way. She was out. They'll all be here soon."

I shook his head. "That's not what I wanna hear."

"Kid, you gotta be strong for your mum. She's gonna lose it."

My jaw clenched when I ground down hard on my teeth. "Griz."

Griz ran a hand over his face and sighed. "He stopped breathin' on the way here. They got him goin' again, but it…. Fuck, brother, it really doesn't look good."

Channa circled her hand around my elbow and moved her other to around my waist. Giving me her strength. My throat clogged, and I swallowed over and over.

I nodded as tears filled my eyes, but I quickly blinked them away. "I'll sit and wait for Mum to get here."

"Coyote," Vicious called as he stepped up. "The cops are here, but Vi's out the front with Warden dealin' with it."

Good. Violet would be able to deal with all the shit so we wouldn't have to.

Once more, I nodded, and Vicious's eyes dropped to Channa. "Don't worry about them, yeah?"

"Um, okay." She shrugged, obviously unsure what Vi could do.

"The women will be here soon to rally," he added.

I clasped him on the shoulder before I moved over to a row of seats and sat. The brothers gathered around us, facing away from us, giving me and Channa a moment and protecting us from prying eyes. If I didn't feel gutted on the inside—hollow—I would have appreciated it more than I did.

Instead, I sat there with Channa, staring down at her hand in mine, all the while praying my dad would pull through.

Fuck, please, God, make it happen.

Zara

A KNOCK SOUNDED on the front door. We hadn't been home long from seeing Channa at work. A smile formed on my lips thinking how thrilled I was to see Cody so happy. Channa was perfect for him. She reminded me a little of myself, but I would never say that to him.

Opening the door, my smile grew. "Hi, Blue—" It dropped away when I took in Blue's pained face. Alarms blasted straight to my heart. I gripped at my chest when I asked, "What's happened?"

"Darlin', it's Talon and Cody." His tone was too soft, too careful.

I stepped back, shook my head again and again. I blinked at the wetness filling my eyes. "No," I uttered. "No."

Blue reached out for me, but I backed up. "Zara, they were shot. Coyote's good, but.... They're at the hospital. We need to get you there."

I shook my head. "Blue—"

"Zara, we have to go."

"Mum, what's going on?" I spun around to find Drake standing in the hallway from the kitchen. He saw something in my expression and raced forward. "Ruby," he bellowed. My son, my beautiful boy, hugged me to him. "Blue, what the fuck happened?"

"Fuck, kid, your dad and brother are in hospital. They were shot. Coyote'll need you guys there. Your dad… he's bein' worked on. Get your sister. We need to go."

I was supposed to be the strong one. I was supposed to take care of my family.

But all I could think was that my world was about to end. All I could picture was my man, my *husband*, and my child being shot.

Drake tensed, but then he turned his head and yelled for his sister again. "Blue, Ruby has Dillon here."

"Get him to come. He'll be there for her."

"Drake?" Ruby called, and I lifted my head to see my baby girl running into the room with Dillon right behind her. She took in Blue, Drake, and then me in Drake's arms. I should have let go of my son, stood tall, and gone to her, but I couldn't. All I could do was hold onto my son.

She covered her mouth with a shaking hand. "Mum?"

"Dillon, run and get Ruby's things. We've got to go," Drake demanded.

"Where?" Ruby asked. Dillon rested his hands on her shoulders, sensing and probably seeing it was something bad, and even before she knew anything, her eyes were filling with tears.

"Dillon, do it," Drake ordered.

Dillon rushed back down the hall, and I got myself

together enough to open an arm to my girl. She raced forward, slamming into Drake and me.

"What's going on?" she whispered with a strained voice.

"Baby—" I slammed my lips closed. I couldn't get the words out. Instead, more tears poured down my face.

"It's Dad and Cody. They're in the hospital. We're goin' to them," Drake explained.

Guilt stabbed at my stomach. It should have been me holding it together, taking charge. Ruby whined, buried her face forward, and cried.

Sucking in a breath, I straightened. I could do this.

I could.

For them.

Things would be fine.

If only my heart knew it and didn't feel like it was being torn from my chest.

"Mum," Drake said. I met his pain-filled gaze. "It's okay. I've got you."

My bottom lip trembled. The tears wouldn't stop flowing. "B-But I should have *you*."

He shook his head. "No, Mum. I get it. I do. Dad's your everythin'."

Oh God.

I broke. Letting the agony take me.

He was right. Talon was my everything, and I couldn't cope. I couldn't without knowing he was okay.

"Ruby, sweetheart. Come here so we can go," Dillon said.

"Let's go, Blue," Drake said.

"Kid, let me—"

"No. I've got her." Drake shifted me around and led me towards the door, taking my bag along the way. "I've got you, Mum. Dad will be fine. He's strong. He'll fight."

All I could do was nod and pray. *Pray* he was right because I didn't want to imagine my life without Talon Marcus in it.

COYOTE

Fuck.

Fuck me.

The waiting was killing me, slicing me open wide, and my thoughts were running a mile a minute. All I wanted to do was roar, break things, and scream through the fury, the anguish burning inside me.

Yet, I sat there like a damn statue staring down at Channa's hand resting on my arm. I couldn't look away, too terrified I was going to lose her. Like I nearly did. Lose the woman who was made for me before I even had the chance to have a life with her.

Then there was a chance, a big motherfucking chance, I could lose my dad.

My dad.

I'd prefer someone to torture me, flay my skin open, burn me, shoot me again… anything, I wanted anything other than sitting there waiting, wondering if Dad would be okay.

He'd been so pale, so still in the end… I couldn't get the picture out of my head. It was riding shotgun with the image of Channa with the gun to her head.

I wanted someone to hurt. I wanted to hurt someone, and I wished those fuckers were alive so I could kill them. I could take their lives slowly.

"Cody," Channa whispered.

I lifted my gaze to her watery one. I didn't realize my jaw was aching from how hard I clenched it, but it was another thing I pushed down. Everything could wait until I had news.

"It's going to be okay," Channa tried.

I nodded. I didn't like seeing her worry, her concern; she'd been through enough, and I should have been helping her through it, but I couldn't do anything. I was lost until I heard something about Dad. I hated what she went through and that I couldn't hide the pain in my eyes. She saw it, and she still sat beside me because she was taking me on. Taking me as her man. We would get through this together.

"Coyote, your mum's here," Stoke said. He was close by with his woman under his arm. Other old ladies had arrived, but I didn't speak to anyone but Channa. I couldn't or I would shatter.

Channa stood, bent, and took my hand, gently pulling me up with her. The brothers parted, and I saw them.

I saw them and splintered.

Maya and Drake supported Mum. Nancy and Dillon supported Ruby.

Mum saw me first. She took in the blood and cried out. She ran for me. I braced but knew it would hurt. I rocked back a step until Channa was there holding on to me. Mum cried, wailed, and clung tightly.

More splintered away.

I cupped the back of her head. "He'll be fine, Mum. He will."

"He's strong, Zara," Channa added. "Just like Cody."

I blinked the fucking tears away and clenched my jaw. Maya and Drake hugged each other, both with tears in their eyes. Ruby had buried her face into Dillon. Nancy, our nanna, rubbed her back, but I could clearly see Nancy was also crying. Her man was there being her rock, though.

So many people.

So much family.

And all of us were there for my dad.

Another splinter cracked through me.

"Family for Talon Marcus?" was called, and we all turned towards the doctor.

Everyone stilled and held their breath. The room quieted to nothing.

"He's going to pull through."

Cheers erupted, and I fucking let the tears fall as I hugged Mum and Channa close. I didn't care. I could let it go because I knew our world would have a tear in it from the loss of Talon Marcus. And there was no way the world or any of us were ready for that.

EPILOGUE

CHANNA

After parking, I got out of Stanley's car and went to the trunk. I pressed the button to open it and pulled out the three long boxes full of treats. With a smile, I made my way into the garage.

"Channa, let me take that off your hands," Blue said, but I quickly dodged him.

"Not on your life, Blue. The last time you did, I heard you hid the boxes for yourself."

"Hey, can't help a guy when it comes to cakes."

I grinned. "I can. Where is he?"

"No doubt on his way out here now he knows you've arrived."

"How?"

Blue pointed out a couple of cameras. Oh shit…. "Do you mean…? No one saw…?"

"You slipping and falling on your arse only to jump up like a jack-in-the-box and limp to the car? Yep, caught it. Also saw the time you had gum on the bottom of your shoe and nearly fell when you were trying to get it off. Or there was—"

"Blue," I deadpanned.

"Yeah, honey?"

"Speak no more of it, and spread the word to whoever else saw it, or else I'm telling your women you all want a makeover on the garage."

He sighed. "Fine. Let me take the boxes anyway. You can follow me to the breakroom."

"Deal." I smiled, handing them over. I went to follow him, but then I heard a rumble of a Harley and looked to the street to see it pull into the parking area.

I knew that Harley, and I knew the rider upon it. My belly gave of an excited flutter.

"Darlin'" was called from behind me, and I faced Talon as he made his way to me. Like usual, guilt filled me, and I bit my bottom lip so I didn't frown because Talon hated when I did that. "You gotta stop bringin' food here, Channa. You spoil us too much."

I waved it off. "I like it."

He stopped beside me. "Darlin'," he said and stared. I held strong. I wasn't going to give in, and I didn't. Talon sighed, wrapping his arms around me in a hug. "You gotta stop stressin' over it and feelin' guilty, 'cause there ain't anythin' to feel guilty for." He stepped back and dropped his hands to my shoulders. "You still talkin' to your doc about it?"

"Yes."

"Good. She'll help you through this."

"It's been a while, Talon." I quickly bit my bottom lip so he wouldn't see it tremble.

"Darlin', there ain't no time limit on gettin' past this. It'll take however long it will."

"I'm sorry—"

"I swear to Christ if you tell me sorry one more time for not callin' me, I'm gonna throttle you. I get it, Channa. I do. Fuck, you know 'cause I've told you. I would have done the same if my woman was in danger and they demanded I'd come alone. You just gotta remember I'm alive. Your man is as well, and so are you." He smiled.

He'd told me that a lot of the times I'd visited the hospital. One day, I might be able to live with the choice I made, but the biggest one I had to get over was the thought that I was supposed to be in prison for what I'd done.

I killed two people. I shot them. It was in self-defence, and if it wasn't for Violet and Liam, who was a lawyer who helped them out, I would be behind bars. Maybe the guilt had a lot to do with how I thought the world was better without them in it.

I just couldn't help how I thought.

Still, I knew with the help of the amazing people I surrounded myself with, that one day I would heal. I would be able to go about my day without thinking about it.

"Dad, get your hands off my woman," Cody called. I glanced over my shoulder, and there went my belly again, the butterflies fluttering to life as my man approached us. He was another reason why I knew I would get past my troubled thoughts because he'd been my rock. My help. My everything. As soon as we knew Talon had pulled through, Cody had taken me to his house. We'd showered, we'd talked, and I'd cried. I broke down right in his arms, and he held me like he'd promised.

Talon grinned, but his hands did fall away after squeezing gently. "Take your woman and get outta here before the brothers con Channa into more fuckin' cakes we don't need."

"You good to get Stanley's car back to him?" Cody asked.

"Huh?" I said, glancing from one man to another.

"Griz is on it. Have a good ride."

My eyes widened, and I clasped my hands in front of me. "We're going for a ride?"

Both men chuckled. Cody nodded. "Yeah, angel."

"But the bakery—"

"Has Susan there now, so you don't need to stress as much. I've already spoken to her. She's also taking the morning shift."

"It wasn't her turn."

"She doesn't mind. That's what she's there for. Now, you gonna come with me?" He held his hand out.

I took it. "Always." He slid his hand in my jeans pocket and took out the keys, throwing them to his dad, who caught them easily. We started for his bike. "Bye, Talon."

"Later, darlin'. See ya, kid."

"Catch ya, Dad."

At the bike, Cody helped me into my helmet with a small smile on his lips. Lips I wanted to kiss. My gaze shifted down to his chest. He'd healed. Both Talon and he had, but it still played on my mind. Seeing them both coated in blood.

"Hey," Cody called, and I lifted my gaze. "You ready?"

"Always ready for a ride with you."

Riding while holding on to Cody was just what I needed. We hadn't done it since the… situation, and I hadn't realized how much I'd missed it. I couldn't get over the way it made me feel centred, how it put a smile on my face and cleared my mind. It also had a lot to do with the man in front of me.

"Cody," I moaned, grinding back on his cock.

His hands gripped my hips before he dropped them and leaned over me, pressing his hands to the bed where he'd bent me over. "Fuck, angel, you feel so good."

I turned my head, enough to have his mouth on

mine. He went deep and filled me deliciously, only to pull back and do it over and over.

God, I loved this. I loved him. So much.

"Cody," I whispered, my lower belly tightening, tingling. My pussy throbbed.

"Come for me, angel. Come," he growled. The words had my orgasm shooting forth.

I yelled his name as he thickened inside me, and he groaned out his own release.

His breath fanned over the back of my neck, where he kissed. "We gotta take more days off."

Laughing, I nodded, my forehead pressed into the bed, trying to catch my breath. "I agree." I shuddered when he slid out of me.

His hand cupped me between my legs, and his lips pressed onto a cheek of my butt. My heart hammered in my chest at the gesture. With moves like that, it was no wonder I wanted the man. He straightened enough to slide his free palm up my back as his hand dropped away from between my legs. He gripped my hair and tugged me back. I went willingly, straightening to rest my back against his chest. He curled an arm around my waist and licked at my neck, then bit. "Fuckin' mine, and I'm so damn grateful."

"Cody," I whispered. Resting my hands over his arm that was around my waist, I held on to this man, *my* man. It brought all my emotions up to a point where I knew it was the right moment to tell him. "I love you, honey."

He dropped his head to my shoulder and sucked in a

shaky breath. "Angel." He turned me in his arms and cupped my cheeks. "We've been through a lot, and I know I say this all the time, angel, but I promise things will settle in here over what happened." He touched a couple of fingers to my temple and slowly drifted them back down to my cheek. "No matter how long it takes, I'll be here. I'll be at your side because you're my future. I love you with everything I am."

Tears brimmed, and a silly smile took over my face. I never pictured my future would hold my knight in shining armour walking back into my life, and even when I tried to fight my feelings for him, I should have known it was inevitable because Cody "Coyote" Marcus was meant for me, and no matter what was to come, we would face it together.

ACKNOWLEDGMENTS

To everyone who has taken a chance on *Coyote*, thank you so much! Moving into the next generation had always been a scary concept for me as I wanted to do it right since they're *the* Hawks MC…. I love the way Coyote and Channa have led me through their world and I hope you do also.

A massive thank you to my awesome, kickarse editor Becky and her fab team at Hot Tree Editing—Liv and Donna.

Another big, ginormous thanks to all the bloggers, readers, authors who have helped me promote *Coyote*. The help you've given will always be appreciated.

Even as I write this my nerves over this book are present and if it wasn't for the encouragement from Lindsey, Amanda, and Rachel, I would have given up. Thank you, ladies!!

My rocking beta team—Miranda, Darlene, Nikki, Casey, and Annissia—thanks heaps for all your help.

Finally, my family, my world— I love you all so much, your support means everything!

READ ON FOR A LOOK
INSIDE RUIN

PROLOGUE

RUIN

"Enter," Talon called. I opened the door and stepped through with Coyote, my closest brother in the club, at my back. Already in the office were Griz, Blue, Vicious, Killer, Stoke, and Cowboy. Cowboy was a younger member, just twenty-one—a good guy who helped Coyote out at his Harley store.

"You should be restin'," Talon told Coyote. The guy had not long been in a car wreck with his bakery girl after some thugs tried to take them out. It was lucky I'd arrived when I had, with the brothers not far behind. Coyote stared the prez—his dad—down, earning a snort from Talon. "Yeah, I'd be the fuckin' same." We all knew what he meant. He'd still keep going to deal with the fuckers we'd caught.

"Heard from their leader?" Coyote asked.

Talon answered, "We're expectin' a call any second, since Killer used one of the guys' phones and sent a video of one of the captives gettin' worked over."

"They tell you anythin'?" I asked.

Griz snorted. "Sang like cockatoos."

"You mean canaries," Cowboy said.

Griz glared. "What?"

"The sayin' is sang like canaries." When Griz just stared Cowboy down, he added, "But it doesn't matter what kind of bird it is."

Blue snickered while my dad, Stoke, flat-out laughed.

"What did they say?" Coyote asked, wincing when he moved the wrong way.

"Sit before you fall down, Coyote." Talon eyed his son, nodding to the chair in front of his desk.

"Apparently the main guy, whose name's Cub, was goin' after Channa on his own. He roped those guys into helpin' because he wanted payback on her since she made him look like a little pussy," Dad explained.

"Did they say what they think we stole off them?" I asked, since I got the feeling they only attacked after the bakery girl made a fool of them in the first scuffle outside her place.

"All he said was that we'd have to take it up with their leader. But if that fucker doesn't tell us what it is, we'll do some more work on the guys we have. I want this finished by the time night falls." Talon rapped his knuckles on the worn oak desk.

"Agreed," Coyote stated coldly, alongside a few of the other brothers.

The phone rang, pausing the conversation. We shared a look before Talon put it on speaker. "Speak," he ordered.

"This is Wolf. I'm the leader of the Takahashi family and see you have some of my men."

"I'm not sure what you're talkin' about." Talon's voice was guarded. In case the phone call was compromised, he couldn't say too much. "But how about we meet and sort a few things out?"

There was silence for a few beats. "I'm out the front of the compound." The call ended, and shock rocked through us all.

Blue's eyebrows shot high. "He's got some damn big balls."

"He does. Let's go see what he has to say." Talon stood, and we followed him outside. Other members tried to join, but Talon told them to stay back. When we neared the locked gate, a lone man stood on the other side.

This Wolf guy, who had an Asian background, didn't look like he belonged to a thug gang. A mobster one, yeah, with his crisp white suit, black shirt, and long jacket. His long dark hair was neatly tied at the back of his neck. His eyes told a whole other story. Confidence mixed with something a little crazy bled through their depths.

"Talon, I presume?" He even didn't sound like a damn gang member. Each word was clear and correct.

"Yeah, and you're Wolf." Talon stopped just on the other side of the gate and crossed his arms over his chest. "You've come alone."

He nodded. "In good faith."

Blue snorted. "Good faith? After one of yours caused not one, but fuckin' two crashes *and* near-deaths of some of ours?"

Wolf's jaw clenched. "Cub acted alone. He's… let's say… unruly. I never wanted anyone hurt. I only ordered him to ask questions, but he has something against your club that isn't a part of my gang. I reside in Melbourne and have a few members who travel from here to the city. Cub was one of them. It was lucky I was in town checking on them when the situation happened."

"You sayin' he went out on his own for all this shit?" Talon asked.

"Yes."

Talon's silence told us he wasn't sure whether to believe this guy. Still, Talon put his hands on his waist. "He has to pay for what he's done. Two brothers are injured, and so is a woman who's under the club's protection. He was going to *kill* them all if he had his damn way."

"I wouldn't think he'd kill—"

"He had a gun to a brother's head. A gun to the woman's, and everyone who was there could see the intent in his fuckin' eyes. He was gonna kill them. If you don't believe that, I can give you the reports on the damn injuries. *No one* gets away with hurtin' anyone in Hawks."

Wolf's nostrils flared, and the hands at his sides fisted. "Fucking fool," he snarled to the ground. He looked up and met Talon's hard gaze. "He's yours."

"What?" Talon's brows shot up in surprise. I wouldn't have seen it if I wasn't standing beside him.

"Do with him what you will. He acted alone, thinking he could climb the ladder by doing something foolish without consequences. He was wrong. Punish him however you choose. I don't want problems with the Hawks MC, just an answer."

Talon ignored the last part and asked, "The others that were with him?"

"Three, I believe?"

Talon nodded.

"They were stupid to follow Cub in the first place. Put fear in them, and then if they haven't done anything to anyone in your club, release them."

"You want us to teach them a lesson?" Griz asked.

Who the fuck was this guy?

"If you believe they need it, yes."

"Who the fuck are you?" Talon barked. "And what do you think we stole off you?"

He smiled. It was only slight but still there. "As I said, I am Wolf. I control a large part of Melbourne, the women, drugs, and weaponry. I have seen what the Hawks MC can do. I want you to know we don't have an issue with one another unless you get involved in my business."

"Stay out of our territory, and we won't," Talon warned.

He nodded once. "I have heard this and will abide by it."

Talon snorted. "Jesus, you've got some damn balls comin' here without anyone with you. Tell us what you think we stole and then this shit will be done."

"Mimi Takahashi."

"Mimi?" I said, and everyone looked at me. Mimi was a club girl. She and I had had a night together, but no more. "She's a club girl." Meaning he wouldn't get his hands on her.

Wolf snarled. "So she is here?"

"What do you want with her?" Talon asked.

"She's my sister."

"And?" Blue pressed.

A tick started at Wolf's temple. He breathed deeply through his nose, which seemed to help him compose himself. "Mimi disappeared. I have been looking for her. She needs to come home."

"When a woman becomes a part of the club, they're protected."

His upper lip rose. "She shouldn't have left in the first place."

"Why did she leave?" Griz asked. We wouldn't even bring her into this if she'd been treated badly in the first place.

"It is not what you're thinking," he said roughly.

"Then tell us, and we'll see if we bring Mimi out he—" Talon's words were cut off.

"Taro?" I tensed at the word sounding from behind me, ready to step in front of Mimi, but Talon held up his hand, halting me.

Wolf's whole body became taut at seeing his sister, his gaze shifting behind us. "Mimi." The single word was barely a whisper.

"What are you doing here?" Mimi stepped between Talon and Blue, her hands positioned protectively around herself.

"Finding you."

"I'm not coming back." Defiance lifted her words.

"Mimi—"

"No, Taro. I told them I refuse. I know it brings shame to the family, but I won't do it."

Wolf glanced around at us, obviously hesitant to speak in front of us, and I couldn't blame the guy. Obviously, it was a family issue.

"I have control over the family now, Mimi."

A small gasp escaped her as she cupped her throat. "Father?"

The clenching of Wolf's jaw was the only tell he gave, letting us know he didn't want to be discussing anything right now. "I would rather speak with you in private."

Mimi inhaled, the sound ragged, and she nodded.

"Come with me then." Wolf's gaze and tone softened.

"Ruin, you go with them," Talon ordered.

With pleasure. I'd have her back, even if she was pissed at me for not taking up her offer for another hook-up.

Wolf's gaze hardened when he speared Talon with it. "She is family. She does not need a guard dog with her when with me."

"She's also been Hawks for six months. She's family to us, and she left your family for a reason. I won't have her goin' on her own."

"Mimi." Wolf's single word was clipped.

Mimi turned to Talon. "It's okay, Mr Marcus. I'm sorry I brought this trouble to your doorstep, but I will be safe with my brother." It did sound like she trusted her brother, but there was still a situation with her family.

Talon shook his head. "Mimi, girl, you've been here for a while. You know how this works. You walked into this compound and became a part of Hawks. No matter where you're goin' or what type of situation it is, we'll have your back. Take Ruin. He can stand away while you talk. But I'd feel better with a brother there."

Before Mimi could say anything, Wolf did. "Thank you for protecting her. Ruin is allowed to accompany us."

"Ruin?" Talon called.

"I'll follow behind," I said.

"Keep us posted." Talon hit me with a solid look, making his expectations clear.

"You got it, Prez," I replied and patted Coyote on the back before I moved off to my ride.

CHAPTER ONE

RUIN

The situation was fucked.

I'd do anything for Mimi because she was a sweet woman. The problem was she just wasn't mine, and it made me feel like a heartless jackass since she'd made it clear she wanted me for more than just the one-night stand.

While we had our personal shit to deal with, I hoped it didn't mess with her other crap we were heading into. I followed Mimi and her brother as they drove to a nearby diner that was always open in the early hours. Once parked, I slipped off my ride and went inside after them.

Sitting a couple of booths away from them, I rested back and waited for the server to come and take my order. I needed a damn strong coffee to keep me going, and the day was just getting started. I hoped, with being far enough away but still in earshot, it would give Wolf a sense of comfort that I wasn't listening in, which I totally was.

"As I was saying in the car, Mimi, Father is on his deathbed. He wishes to see you, and you're telling me you do not want to come home?"

She winced and shook her head. "No, Taro."

"Mimi, I would not have come if I didn't believe I could take care of you."

"I know, brother, but you know what our uncles are like."

"They are not in charge. I am. They will listen to whatever I say. I will make sure of it."

"Taro, I trust you, I do. Leaving you has been the hardest decision in my life, but I knew you were strong, not like me. Women in our family aren't respected. We're ordered."

"I will change this."

She gave him a sad smile. "I hope you can, but it has been this way for decades."

The waitress approached them, and they asked for coffee. When she stopped at my table, I ordered two extra hot, double-strength coffees.

"Under my ruling, it will. Please, Mimi, come home with me this final time. I know you will regret this if you don't see him one last time."

"Taro...."

"Please. I will protect you. You could even bring him along for extra security." He thumbed over his shoulder my way.

Her nose screwed up as she shook her head. Mimi drew in a deep breath. "Are you certain the uncles can't force this marriage on me?"

What the fuck?

"They won't. I will not allow it."

"My intended was fifty, Taro. *Fifty* to my nineteen years. Father was going to give me away to an old man for an alliance. Why would I want to see him?"

That was so messed up, I didn't even know what to think about it. Her father, the man who was supposed to take care of her, wanted her to marry an old fucker. I had a shit dad who beat my mum, but then Declan Stoke came into our lives, became my dad, and he was a man who loved with every fibre of his body. I goddamn looked up to him in many ways. He wouldn't stand for this shit if it was happening to anyone he knew. I wasn't going to either.

If Mimi was heading home, I'd go along for the ride and make sure no one screwed her over, since I didn't completely trust her brother. I'd feel better for having her back.

"Do it for you," Wolf said. "Tell Father exactly what you think. Be there for Mother. She will need you."

"She is the one who told me to run in the first place. If Father found out, he would have killed her."

"I wouldn't have allowed it. I have control over the

family, the faction. I have my own people within the gang, ones who will only follow me, ones who I trust with my life and the lives of those I love. It will never be that way again. You and Mother will be taken care of. Things have changed. Trust me, Mimi, everything is better."

It had better be.

I gave a smile to the waitress when she dropped off my drinks before I pulled my phone out, placing it on the booth.

"Thank you," Mimi said to the waitress before she left and then looked back to her brother. "All right, Taro. I'll come back, but I will not stay long."

"I understand."

I shot a quick text to my club president, Talon.

Me: **Mimi's heading back to Melbourne. Her dad's on his deathbed. But shit at home don't look good. She ran because the dick dad tried to marry her off to a fifty-year-old dude for an alliance.**

Talon: **Fucking hell. You going with?**

Me: **Was thinking it. For added security. She still seems worried about her uncles trying to control her.**

Talon: **Yeah, go. Since the shit here has calmed, you'll have the time on your hands. If you run into any shit, have the brothers in Caroline Springs back you.**

Me: **You got it, boss.**

Talon: **Get back here and pack.**

Me: **On it.**

When I finished my second coffee, and they looked like they'd had enough chit-chat for one night, I stood and went to the counter to pay for all the coffees. They were just getting out of the booth when I turned and waited for them at the front door.

I tipped my chin up and said, "Talon has me on her security, so I'll be coming with you—"

"No!" Mimi snapped and glared up at me. She was cute when fiery. It was a damn shame I didn't see her as my one. I wished to Christ I did. She was stunning. I hated that I'd hurt her when I was an arsehole by telling her I didn't see us going further than that one night. I couldn't lie to her though. I couldn't have her thinking there was more between us.

I wanted what Stoke had with my mum.

What the prez had with his woman.

What Cody, my closest mate in the Hawks MC brotherhood, would soon have with bakery girl if he got his shit together.

I knew Mimi was pissed at me for the way I treated her, even though I'd been nice in the way I let her down. I wasn't going to walk away from helping her when she needed it.

Eventually she'd get over whatever she felt for me. *If* she still did feel something more than hatred for me.

I mean… I was a catch, but I knew, no, I *felt*, I honestly wasn't for Mimi. She had someone else waiting for her in the future.

Damn, I sound like a clairvoyant.

Raising my gaze to her brother, I lifted a brow,

waiting to see if he had any objections. He nodded once. "I will allow this, for the club's sake, since you all have taken care of Mimi for so long."

"Thanks."

"No, I won't allow it. Ruin is…. He's annoying and… a pig."

"Harsh, babe, but true. I ain't the cleanest person when it comes to bedrooms." I grinned down at Mimi, who was still scowling, but I could feel Wolf's gaze burning into me. What was this guy thinking?

"Mimi, if this is what Talon wants, then allow him to come for his sake. We do not need the motorcycle club worrying." He knew I would have followed no matter because Talon had given me the go-ahead. It was good he knew not to mess with our club. Showed he was smart.

Mimi bit her bottom lip. She looked back to me. "Can't it be anyone but you? I'd even take Griz, and he scares me."

"Has he hurt you?" Wolf demanded.

When Mimi didn't answer right away, Wolf took it as a yes. He went to grab for me, but I dodged to the left, only I didn't see how fucking fast he was as he brought his leg up in a kick to the arm. I stumbled back into the wall, and his hand wrapped around my neck. I punched him in the gut. A noise escaped through his lips, but he didn't drop his hold. I went for the kidney. He blocked it with his knee and punched me in the fucking side.

"Stop," Mimi called. She pressed into her brother's

side, holding his arm where his hand was still wrapped around my neck. Only it wasn't too tight, more holding me in place. "We…. Look, it was between Ruin and me, but it's fine." She stepped back with a small smile on her face. "Besides, I'm sure you've taught him a lesson."

"Have I?" Wolf asked darkly as he leaned into me.

"Sure." I smirked. If we weren't in a diner, I would have given him shit back and kept this going to see who would come out on top.

He moved away, dropping his hand, then walked out the front door. Mimi grinned at me as she swept by, following her brother.

She enjoyed seeing me get roughed up by her brother, even though I gave my own back, but honestly, I didn't give a shit. I deserved the beatdown for being a dickhead to her in the first place. Though, her brother had better not get an idea he could do it again. I'd have him on his back in seconds.

Jesus, I have to watch what I think, because that sounded sexual. I snorted internally at my choice of words. I supposed he was a good-looking guy, but fuck that, dudes just didn't do it for me.

Stepping out the door, I met them at the car. "We'll head back to the compound. Mimi and I can grab some shit, then we'll hit the road. That is, if you're not too tired, Wolf? Do you need a nap? That scuffle made you look ruffled. You need some beauty sleep?"

"It's nice of you to think I'm beautiful, but I'll be fine to drive."

I jerked my head back. "I did not call you beautiful," I insisted, incredulous.

"I think you did," Mimi added, looking to be having far too much fun.

"I so fuckin' didn't." Both smirked at me. "Christ, whatever. Let's just get there and on the damn road."

The sun was rising as I stalked off to my ride. Annoyance hissed through me, no doubt because of lack of sleep. At least the coffees I'd had would give me a nice buzz for a few hours, until I could get more in me.

I didn't have a clue what would happen in Melbourne. I just had to make sure I'd be alert. Already, I didn't like the sound of Mimi's family. The brother *seemed* okay, since he tried to kick my arse for his sister's honour, but I wasn't trusting him yet.

Even though I was heading into shit on my own, I had brothers, close friends in the Caroline Springs charter. I'd have help in a matter of moments should I need it.

Just sucked Coyote couldn't make the trip with me. But he had a store to run and a woman to claim. Other brothers would easily cover my shifts at the job site. I'd been working in construction since I turned eighteen and loved the hard work. Though, it'd be good to have some time off, since it'd been a while. But with no idea what my time off would involve, I couldn't wait to see exactly what I was up against.

ALSO BY LILA ROSE

Hawks MC: Ballarat Charter

Holding Out (Free)

Outplayed (standalone related to the Hawks MC)

Climbing Out

Finding Out (novella)

Black Out

No Way Out

Coming Out (m/m novella)

Out to Find Freedom (standalone related to the Hawks MC)

Hawks MC: Caroline Springs Charter

The Secret's Out

Hiding Out

Down and Out

Living Without

Walkout (novella)

Hear Me Out (m/m)

Break Out (novella)

Fallout

Hawks MC: next generation

Coyote

Ruin (m/m)

Texas

Standalones related to the Hawks MC

Out of the Blue

Out Gamed (novella)

Romantic Comedies

Making Changes

Making Sense

Fumbled Love

Bumbled Love

Polished P & P series (m/m romance)

Wreck Me Forever

Never a Saint

Working Out West

Titles under L. Rose

**The Hidden Kingdom Trilogy
(reverse harem romance)**

A Torn Paige

A Lost Paige

A Final Paige

Standalones

Infinite Bond (m/m/m/m)

www.ingramcontent.com/pod-product-compliance
Lightning Source LLC
Chambersburg PA
CBHW070536120726
47909CB00007B/2152